MORE THAN SOMEWHAT

E. C. BENTLEY

SELECTED THESE STORIES BY

DAMON RUNYON

AND WROTE THE INTRODUCTION

NICOLAS BENTLEY

DREW THE PICTURES

British Library Cataloguing-in-Publication Data
A catalogue record for this book is available from the
British Library

CONTENTS

Damon Runyon

Alfred Damon Runyon was born in Kansas, USA in 1880. He spent most of his youth in Colorado, where he worked under his father in the newspaper trade. Runyon served in the U.S. Army during the Spanish-American War, before moving to New York City in 1910. He was a successful baseball reporter for many years (in 1967, he was inducted into the Baseball Hall of Fame), before turning to fiction-writing in the twenties. Best-known for his short stories celebrating Brooklyn during the Prohibition era, and featuring gamblers, hustlers and gangsters, in his day Runyon was a popular author. More than ten of his tales were adapted for the stage and screen. Runyan died aged 66.

INTRODUCTION

Before Damon Runyon began writing his stories of the bandits of Broadway, he had made himself a national reputation in America as a newspaper-man; a descriptive reporter who could deal with any event in the day's doings, from a horserace at Miami to an electrocution at Ossining, in a manner that put him in a class by himself. In particular, he wrote of sporting matters with a style and a fund of expert knowledge that were enjoyed from ocean to ocean. But this was not, by its nature, the sort of work that endures. He broke into literature, quite suddenly, with a hilarious short story of the gangsters and crooks infesting a certain section of Broadway, the main artery of New York's life—the Hardened Artery, as Walter Winchell has called it. He followed it up with many others of the same sort; all of them, in fact, told by the same imaginary narrator, and told in a tone and a language that make up one of the richest contributions to comic literature in our time.

So, at least, I think; and I have not yet met any critical reader of Runyon's tales who does not think so too.

I have made this selection of Damon Runyon's stories with the idea of showing as many aspects as possible of his narrative genius, ranging as they do from the most uproarious farce to such sadness as goes to the depths of the heart. The note of pathos is not often touched, it is true: when it is, it gains force from the contrast with its setting of quaint, unemotional, unconscious cynicism. If, after reading *The Lily of St. Pierre* in this book you do not agree with that judgment, then—as Runyon's narrator would say—you must be such a guy as will never be moved by anything short of an earthquake.

In the little world inhabited by Runyon's people every male human being is a guy, every female a doll. There are in that world other names for dolls, it is true, such as broads, or pancakes, or tomatoes; but the narrator prefers not to use such terms, which he claims are not respectful. Do not ask me if there really is such a world. I only know that it is a world, and a very lively world, at that. But it is certainly founded on fact, if you like things founded on fact. We have been hearing of guys like Dave the Dude, and Benny South Street, and Germany Schwartz, and Franky Ferocious (whose square monicker is Ferroccio), and Milk Ear Willie, and Izzy Cheesecake, for many years past; ever since gangsters and racketeers began to be news: also of dolls like Rosa Midnight, and Miss Cleghorn, the Arabian Acrobatic dancer, and Miss Muriel O'Neill, who works in the Half Moon night club, and the doll named Silk, who associates so much more with guys than she does with other dolls that she finally gets so she thinks like a guy, and has a guy's slant on things in general.

We have heard of them all before; but Damon Runyon puts life into them as no other writer has done yet, and I do not expect any other in the future to make crime, and violence, and dissipation, and predatory worthlessness, together with occasional off-hand decency where you would least expect it, as keenly interesting and as frantically funny as Damon Runyon does.

You cannot help liking his guys and dolls. I do not mean that they—the guys, anyway—would be nice to know, or even safe. In fact, if it is left to me, I will as soon go in bathing with a school of sharks, or maybe sooner. (I am sorry, but I find it impossible not to drift into Runyonese when writing of the creatures of his brain.) I do not mean that they are unselfish, good-hearted, high-minded guys and dolls. I do not mean that you will shed tears when Angie the Ox gets cooled off by Lance McGowan, or when Joey Perhaps gets what is coming to him from Ollie Ortega, which is a short knife in the throat, or when The Brain gets carved up quite some, and finally hauls off and dies. I merely mean that they have a reckless, courageous vitality that makes you like hearing about them; that is, if you are an ordinary human being, such as has always liked hearing about desperados. As a certain newspaper guy in one of the Runyon stories puts it, many legitimate guys are much interested in the doings of tough guys, and consider them very romantic. I do not see anything against this, so long as you also consider them very indefensible, and are strongly in favour of discouraging them in a severely practical manner.

But what you will probably like without reserve is the endless comedy that Damon Runyon extracts from their dangerous and disreputable way of life, and the wonderful style in which he gives it expression.

Just as I, an Englishman, cannot say how far the New York underworld he shows you corresponds to the real thing, so I do not know if the talk of these guys and dolls is the sort of conversation you will actually hear in the section between Times Square and Columbus Circle. But those who ought to know give both them and their speech a high character for trueness to life. Heywood Broun, for instance, who lives quite near at hand, declares that he recognizes Runyon's characters as actual people, and that their talk is put down almost literally.

That "almost" is, no doubt, quite necessary. Damon Runyon, an artist in words, must have worked up his raw material with loving care; and in all likelihood he has made some contribution of his own. For Runyon, be it said, has long been among the recognized personal influences in the development of current American slang. In the days when he was known mainly as a sports-writer with a vast public, he was included in a short list of such influences by W. J.

Funk, the New York publisher; and so high an authority as Henry Mencken, in his work on *The American Language*, has approved of that inclusion. It is doubtful if the ineffable felicity of so many passages in these stories could have been achieved by any merely phonographic method.

Nevertheless, the style of them is exclusively a conversational style. They are all talk; the talk of the guy who is telling them, or of other guys as reported by him. For English readers, I suppose, the most curious thing about that guy's talk will be his resolute avoidance of the past tense; the remarkable things he does with the historic present. The same thing is known in our own vulgar tongue, of course; but it is incidental, and apt to take a debased form—for example, "So I says to him, 'Did you hear what I said?' " In Runyonese this would be, "So I say to him, 'Do you hear what I say?' " Runyon's guy will say, "About three weeks ago, Big Nig is down taking the waters in Hot Springs, and anything else there may be to take in Hot Springs." He will not say, "When I heard Bugs Lonigan say this, I wished I had never been born" he will say, "When I hear Bugs Lonigan say this, I wish I am never born." There is a sort of ungrammatical purity about it, an almost religious exactitude, that to me, at least, has the strongest appeal. In all the Runyon stories, as published in America, I have found only one single instance of a verb in the past tense. It occurs in one of those included in this book; and you may try to find it, if—as Runyon's guy

6

might say—you figure there is any percentage in doing so. And, as that same guy might go on to say, I will lay plenty of 6 to 5 that it is nothing but a misprint; but I do not think it is the proper caper for me to improve on Runyon's prose, so I leave it.

I do not know what the history of this dread of the past tense may be. Possibly it is quite a long history. From the literature of the cattle industry in the West—I mean serious literature—it is to be seen that the cowboy of half a century ago, when West was West indeed, had a dialect all his own, in which the past tense did not figure. For instance, Alfred Henry Lewis's old cattleman, calling on his memories of long ago, says:

The most ornery party I ever knows is Curly Ben. This yere Ben is killed, final, by old Captain Moon, when Curly is playin' kyards. He's jest dealin', when Moon comes Injunin' up from the far, an' drills Curly through the head with a 45 Colt's. Which the queer part is this: Curly, as I states—an' he never knows what hits him, an' is as dead as Santa Anna in a moment—is dealin' the kyards. He's got the deck in his hands. An' yet, when the public picks Curly off the floor, he's pulled his two guns, an' has got one cocked.

A psychological curiosity which would have fitted very nicely into Runyon's account of the cooling off of various guys.

Very interesting, to my mind, is the personality of the guy who tells these stories. He does not give himself a name at any time, but it will do no harm to call him X. In some ways X is a strange guy to be mobbed up with such characters as he tells about. He is a nervous guy, for one thing; and even more remarkable, in the circumstances, than his nervousness, is his passion for respectability. He is "greatly opposed to guys who violate the law," as he insists again and again; and he can think of a million things he will rather do than be seen in the company of such guys. But as he is, on his own showing, practically never in any other kind of society, he must spend a harassing time. The truth is, X is very far from being one of the high shots, but is simply known to one and all as a guy who is just around. In fact, they figure him as harmless as a bag of marsh-mallows. Just the same, X is well known to every wrong gee on Broadway; and if one of them sees him and gives him a huge hello, what can X do? It would be very unsafe indeed if X tried playing the chill for such a guy. There are the professional assassins, like Ropes McGonnigle. There are the casual and temperamental killers, like Rusty Charley, the genial but uncertain-tempered guy in whose presence even such citizens as Nick the Greek or Joey Uptown become silent and nervous. There are the dangerous criminals, like Big Jule, who is wanted for robbery and burglary in a dozen different States, and who claims that he will catch cold if he goes out of doors without the holsters under Ins arms. There are various guys who are known to have cooled other guys off from time to time, and who are regarded consequently as rather suspicious characters. There are the git-em-up guys like Dancing Dan; and the guys who open safes for a living, like Big Butch; and the guys who are on the snatch (which it is very illiterate to call kidnapping), like Spanish John; and the guys who ride the tubs—that is to say, who live by cheating at cards on the Atlantic liners—like Little Manuel; and the guys who specialize in telling the tale, like the Lemon Drop Kid. There is also Pussy McGuire, who does very well at stealing valuable dogs and cats.

Besides these, there are of course the influential citizens who are interested in wet merchandise; for the Runyon stories reach back into the days of Prohibition, and if they "date" at all, I suppose it will be because of that—though I am never sure that the importing dodge is so very dead, at that, considering what the taxation is on legal liquor. Naturally, guys who are interested in wet merchandise do not count seriously as illegal characters; but then many of them are also interested in artichokes, and extortion, and gambling joints, and other hot propositions. All such guys as these know X well, and seem to have a liking for his company; and X will often make himself useful to such guys by taking a message, for instance, to some citizen that it would be a good idea if he left town, and stayed away, instead of bringing beer into another guy's territory. In fact, if you come right down to it, the chances are that the nearest X ever comes to having a job of any kind is being more or less on the pay-roll of guys like Dave the Dude; which is not such a bum connection, at that, as Dave the Dude handles nothing but genuine champagne and Scotch, wishing no part of that trade in cut goods which brings in plenty of scratch to other importers who are not so particular.

The one and only guy in X's circle of acquaintance who is strictly legit is Judge Henry G. Blake. Of course, Judge Blake is not a judge, and never has been a judge, but he is called Judge because he looks like a judge, and talks slow, and puts in many long words. Judge Blake is very good at poker; and at pool he is just naturally a curly wolf; so he makes a living by building up suckers into playing against him for real money at these games.

Much as X is opposed to law-breaking, he is not bigoted about it. When he happens to hear of a promising job of burglary, with a little blackmail as a chaser, he remembers Harry the Horse, and throws it his way; for he knows that Harry the Horse is feeling the economic depression keenly, because if nobody is making any money, there is nobody for him to rob. Furthermore, Harry the Horse is never a bargain at any time, and is such a guy as you would much rather stand good with than have sored up at you for any reason.

Another curious feature of X's passion for legality is that it does not make him at all fond of policemen. In fact, the way X figures it, there are far too many coppers in this world. He believes, naturally, in being courteous to them at all times, but he does not care for them, even when they are fairly good guys, such as the copper who has the tears come into his eyes when he tells about the poor people who have all their lifetime savings in Israel Ib's busted jug.

Another way in which X seems to be a somewhat inconsistent guy is in his attitude towards liquor. To hear him tell it, he is by no means a rumpot, and indeed very seldom indulges in fermented beverages in any form. Yet from the derogatory things X says about the liquor in Good Time Charley's little speak, and in various other deadfalls, it is clear that he knows more than somewhat about the subject. Furthermore, at least two of X's adventures happen when he certainly has his pots on, rye whisky being the raw material in both cases; and he knows what it is like to have such a noggin the morning after that he does not feel much more than a hop ahead of the undertaker. So if X's putting himself away as an abstemious guy is not a lie, it will do until a he comes along; and the chances are he is not the only guy in the same position, at that.

Whatever the truth may be about X as regards wine, his

reactions to woman and song are fairly clear. X is a good, even an exacting, judge of dolls, and many of his remarks on the subject are well worth bearing in mind. He is by no means blind to the possibilities of romance as between young guys and dolls; he knows that the right conditions, such as the moon shining on the river, and what not, may be a dead cold set-up for love. But X is not such a guy as will get a high blood pressure over any doll; he has never been in love, and barring a bad break, never expects to be in love, to say nothing of being married. Most of the guys in his circle are bachelors, and the rest wish they were, but at the same time many of them take a great practical interest in dolls, including The Brain, who maintains four separate establishments, and guesses that love costs him about as much dough as any guy that ever lives. But The Brain can easily afford this, being the biggest guy in gambling operations in the East.

On the other hand, X is an enthusiast about song. If there is one thing he loves to do more than anything else, it is to sing in quartet, taking the baritone part. He likes to sing in quartet in Good Time Charley's little joint, because Good Time Charley sings a nice bass, and there are seldom any customers there until after the other places are closed; so that it is fairly quiet in there until about 5 a.m. Though you can never be quite sure, at that, because things may happen such as when Jack O'Hearts looks in unexpectedly, and outs with the old equalizer and shoots the right ear off Louie the Lug, who is singing a very fair tenor in the quartet, and then chases Louie out the back door and gets another crack at him which finishes him. Of course this breaks up the quartet, and nobody is happy, not even Jack O'Hearts, who complains that the light in Charley's dump is no good, as he ought to get Louie the first shot, and it is very sloppy work.

Another taste which X has strongly developed is horserace betting; a taste which he shares with practically every guy mentioned in these stories. In fact, the only guys I can think of at the moment who do not back horses are two guys who happen to be bookmakers. Some of X's friends, like Hot Horse Herbie, are such guys as never think of anything else in this world but betting on horses; but those who are mainly interested in crime, and so cannot be considered as serious horse-players, mostly devote a good deal of the proceeds to this form of amusement. Playing the horses is a necessary part of X's life. He despises football, and he cannot imagine why anybody takes an interest in such a thing as lawn tennis; baseball means nothing to him, and as for pugilism, X will not give you a bad two-bit piece to see a fight anywhere, because half the time the result is arranged beforehand, and X does not believe in encouraging dishonesty. His thoughts, and the thoughts of most of his acquaintance, are apt to express themselves in terms of betting; as for instance when the monkey steals the baby and carries it off to the roof of a house, and seems disposed to heave the baby into the street, and Big Nig, the crap shooter, is around among the hysterical crowd offering to lay 7 to 5 against the baby, which, X observes, is not a bad price, at that.

The most renowned short-story-teller of New York life in the past was O. Henry, whose work has long been the delight of a multitude of readers in this country. The question of a comparison between O. Henry and Damon Runyon is therefore bound to arise; and it can be easily answered. The two have hardly anything in common, apart from the faculty of invention. To begin with, O. Henry wrote of the New York life of thirty to forty years ago, which is a long time in the history of that metropolis. Also, while he knew its rich and its poor, its clerks and its shopgirls, its politicians and its sportsmen and its loafers, there is no sign—despite one or two romantic efforts of the Jimmy Valentine sort—that he had much acquaintance with the habitual criminal class. Again, if he had known it as it was in his day, he would have known a class very different from the one to which most of Runyon's characters belong, children as they are of a new age of crime, equipped with all the technical resources of the twentieth century; freed at the same time, by the advance of a brutish materialism, from the last rags of scruple and compassion; and to a great extent financed as crime never was financed before, first, by the enormous profits of a generally tolerated, not to say welcomed, smuggling trade, and then by the even easier money from organized extortion on a grand scale. O. Henry did not live to see national Prohibition, and never heard of racketeering.

His style and method, too, were wholly different from Damon Runyon's. All of the Runyon stories, as I have said, are told with the mouth and in the distinctive speech of one of the characters, who is a very real person indeed. O. Henry seldom resorted to this way of story-telling; and when he did—as in *The Gentle Grafter*—both the imaginary narrator and his talk were obviously not intended to be like life; they were meant merely for the producing of burlesque effect.

One English reader of these stories made the remark—so I am told—that a glossary would help you to understand them. I do not suppose he really meant this: if he did, I cannot imagine a more abject confession of dullness. Let us take it that he was paying an indirect compliment to the freshness and pungency of this variety of American speech. The truth is, X is particularly easy to understand. It is the greatest of the many merits of his style. Even if a term or a phrase is unfamiliar, the context tells you instantly what it means. It may be news to you that to cool a guy off means to kill him; or that a doll taking a run-out powder on her husband means her deserting him; or that playing the duck for a guy means trying to avoid him: but if when you read these things in a Runyon story you do not understand what they mean, then you must be such a guy as will never understand much of anything in this world.

I can recall several cases of glossaries attached to English editions of American stories; and they always struck me as fussy and even, in a vague way, offensive, implying that the kind of slang in question was an unintelligible lingo of barbarians. One of the most famous of modern American novels was gravely introduced to English readers with a glossary, from which one could learn, with surprise, that a getaway meant an escape, or that junk meant rubbish. I have no idea of insulting readers by providing them with a glossary to help them to tear out the hidden significance of the statement, for example, that Israel lb has a large snozzle and is as homely as a mud fence, but is well known to be a coming guy in the banking dodge. The only terms I can think of that are not self-explanatory refer to sums of money: it is, from time to time, important to remember that a thousand dollars are a grand, or a G; a hundred dollars, a yard, or a C; ten dollars, a sawbuck; five dollars, a finnif, a fin, or a pound note; two dollars, a deuce; one dollar, a buck, or a bob.

Speaking generally, all this affectation about American speech being an alien thing is tiresome and many years out of date. Every office-boy uses the terms he has picked up from the Hollywood films; and our more sophisticated slang-users of both sexes have a much larger vocabulary drawn from American books. In fact, we produce little slang of our own to-day: what we have that is English is of old standing. Our borrowing in this way is, I suppose, one of the results of the enormous impression made on us (whether we like it or not) by the vigour, the vivacity, the originality, the self-sufficiency, the drama and melodrama of American life. And it is because we are under that impression that I believe English readers will welcome and enjoy these stories by Damon Runyon.

The only jarring note is Spanish John sitting beside the bed looking at me.

1

BREACH OF PROMISE

One day a certain party by the name of Judge Goldfobber, who is a lawyer by trade, sends word to me that he wishes me to call on him at his office in lower Broadway, and while ordinarily I do not care for any part of lawyers, it happens that Judge Goldfobber is a friend of mine, so I go to see him.

Of course Judge Goldfobber is not a judge, and never is a judge, and he is 100 to 1 in my line against ever being a judge, but he is called Judge because it pleases him, and everybody always wishes to please Judge Goldfobber, as he is one of the surest-footed lawyers in this town, and beats more tough beefs for different citizens than seems possible. He is a wonderful hand for keeping citizens from getting into the sneezer, and better than Houdini when it comes to getting them out of the sneezer after they are in.

Personally, I never have any use for the professional services of Judge Goldfobber, as I am a law-abiding citizen at all times, and am greatly opposed to guys who violate the law, but I know the Judge from around and about for many years. I know him from around and about the night clubs, and other deadfalls, for Judge Goldfobber is such a guy as loves to mingle with the public in these spots, as he picks up much law business there, and sometimes a nice doll.

Well, when I call on Judge Goldfobber, he takes me into his private office and wishes to know if I can think of a couple of deserving guys who are out of employment, and who will like a job of work, and if so, Judge Goldfobber says, he can offer them a first-class position.

"Of course," Judge Goldfobber says, "it is not steady employment, and in fact it is nothing but piece-work, but the parties must be extremely reliable parties, who can be depended on in a pinch. This is out-of-town work that requires tact, and," he says, "some nerve."

Well, I am about to tell Judge Goldfobber that I am no employment agent, and go on about my business, because I can tell from the way he says the parties must be parties who can be depended on in a pinch, that a pinch is apt to come up on the job any minute, and I do not care to steer any friends of mine against a pinch.

But as I get up to go, I look out of Judge Goldfobber's window, and I can see Brooklyn in the distance beyond the river, and seeing Brooklyn I get to thinking of certain parties over there that I figure must be suffering terribly from the unemployment situation. I get to thinking of Harry the Horse, and Spanish John and Little Isadore, and the reason I figure they must be suffering from the unemployment situation is because if nobody is working and making any money, there is nobody for them to rob, and if there is nobody for them to rob, Harry the Horse and Spanish John and Little Isadore are just naturally bound to be feeling the depression keenly.

Anyway, I finally mention the names of these parties to Judge Goldfobber, and furthermore I speak well of their reliability in a pinch, and of their nerve, although I cannot conscientiously recommend their tact, and Judge Goldfobber is greatly delighted, as he often hears of Harry the Horse, and Spanish John and Little Isadore.

He asks me for their addresses, but of course nobody knows exactly where Harry the Horse and Spanish John and Little Isadore live, because they do not live anywhere in particular. However, I tell him about a certain spot in Clinton Street where he may be able to get track of them, and then I leave Judge Goldfobber for fear he may wish me to take word to these parties, and if there is anybody in this whole world I will not care to take word to, or to have any truck with in any manner, shape, or form, it is Harry the Horse, and Spanish John and Little Isadore.

Well, I do not hear anything more of the matter for several

weeks, but one evening when I am in Mindy's restaurant on Broadway enjoying a little cold borscht, which is a most refreshing matter in hot weather such as is going on at the time, who bobs up but Harry the Horse, and Spanish John and Little Isadore, and I am so surprised to see them that some of my cold borscht goes down the wrong way, and I almost choke to death.

However, they seem quite friendly, and in fact Harry the Horse pounds me on the back to keep me from choking, and while he pounds so hard that he almost caves in my spine, I consider it a most courteous action, and when I am able to talk again, I say to him as follows:

"Well, Harry," I say, "it is a privilege and a pleasure to see you again, and I hope and trust you will all join me in some cold borscht, which you will find very nice, indeed."

"No," Harry says, "we do not care for any cold borscht. We are looking for Judge Goldfobber. Do you see Judge Goldfobber round and about lately?"

Well, the idea of Harry the Horse and Spanish John and Little Isadore looking for Judge Goldfobber sounds somewhat alarming to me, and I figure maybe the job Judge Goldfobber gives them turns out bad and they wish to take Judge Goldfobber apart, but the next minute Harry says to me like this:

"By the way," he says, "we wish to thank you for the job of

work you throw our way. Maybe some day we will be able to do as much for you. It is a most interesting job," Harry says, "and while you are snuffing your cold borscht I will give you the details, so you will understand why we wish to see Judge Goldfobber."

It turns out [Harry the Horse says] that the job is not for Judge Goldfobber personally, but for a client of his, and who is this client but Mr. Jabez Tuesday, the rich millionaire, who owns the Tuesday string of one-arm joints where many citizens go for food and wait on themselves. Judge Goldfobber comes to see us in Brooklyn in person, and sends me to see Mr. Jabez Tuesday with a letter of introduction, so Mr. Jabez Tuesday can explain what he wishes me to do, because Judge Goldfobber is too smart a guy to be explaining such matters to me himself.

In fact, for all I know maybe Judge Goldfobber is not aware of what Mr. Jabez Tuesday wishes me to do, although I am willing to lay a little 6 to 5 that Judge Goldfobber does not think Mr. Jabez Tuesday wishes to hire me as a cashier in any of his one-arm joints.

Anyway, I go to see Mr. Tuesday at a Fifth Avenue hotel where he makes his home, and where he has a very swell layout of rooms, and I am by no means impressed with Mr. Tuesday, as he hems and haws quite a bit before he tells me the nature of the employment he has in mind for me. He is a little guy, somewhat dried out, with a bald head, and a small mouser on his upper lip, and he wears specs, and seems somewhat nervous.

Well, it takes him some time to get down to cases, and tell me what is eating him, and what he wishes to do, and then it all sounds very simple, indeed, and in fact it sounds so simple that I think Mr. Jabez Tuesday is a little daffy when he tells me he will give me ten G's for the job.

What Mr. Tuesday wishes me to do is to get some letters that he personally writes to a doll by the name of Miss Amelia Bodkin, who lives in a house just outside Tarrytown, because it seems that Mr. Tuesday makes certain cracks in these letters that he is now sorry for, such as speaking of love and marriage and one thing and another to Miss Amelia Bodkin, and he is afraid she is going to sue him for breach of promise.

"Such an idea will be very embarrassing to me," Mr. Jabez Tuesday says, "as I am about to marry a party who is a member of one of the most high-toned families in this country. It is true," Mr. Tuesday says, "that the Scarwater family does not have as much money now as formerly, but there is no doubt about its being very, very high-toned, and my fiancée, Miss Valerie Scarwater, is one of the high-tonedest of them all. In fact," he says, "she is so high-toned that the chances are she will be very huffy about anybody suing me for breach of promise, and cancel everything."

Well, I ask Mr. Tuesday what a breach of promise is, and he explains to me that it is when somebody promises to do something and fails to do this something, although of course we have a different name for a proposition of this nature in Brooklyn, and deal with it accordingly.

"This is a very easy job for a person of your standing," Mr. Tuesday says. "Miss Amelia Bodkin lives all alone in her house the other side of Tarrytown, except for a couple of servants, and they are old and harmless. Now the idea is," he says, "you are not to go to her house as if you are looking for the letters, but as if you are after something else, such as her silverware, which is quite antique, and very valuable.

"She keeps the letters in a big inlaid box in her room," Mr. Tuesday says, "and if you just pick up this box and carry it away along with the silverware, no one will ever suspect that you are after the letters, but that you take the box thinking it contains valuables. You bring the letters to me and get your ten G's," Mr. Tuesday says, "and," he says, "you can keep the silverware, too. Be sure you get a Paul Revere teapot with the silverware," he says. "It is worth plenty."

"Well," I say to Mr. Tuesday, "every guy knows his own business best, and I do not wish to knock myself out of a nice soft job, but," I say, "it seems to me the simplest way of carrying on this transaction is to buy the letters off this doll, and be done with it. Personally," I say, "I do not believe there is a doll in the world who is not willing to sell a whole post-office full of letters for ten G's, especially in these times, and throw in a set of Shakespeare with them."

"No, no," Mr. Tuesday says. "Such a course will not do with Miss Amelia Bodkin at all. You see," he says, "Miss Bodkin, and I are very, very friendly for a matter of maybe fifteen or sixteen years. In fact, we are very friendly, indeed. She does not have any idea at this time that I wish to break off this friendship with her. Now," he says, "if I try to buy the letters from her, she may become suspicious. The idea," Mr. Tuesday says, "is for me to get the letters first, and then explain to her about breaking off the friendship, and make suitable arrangements with her afterwards.

"Do not get Miss Amelia Bodkin wrong," Mr. Tuesday says. "She is an excellent person, but," he says, "you know the saying, 'Hell hath no fury like a woman scorned.' And maybe Miss Amelia Bodkin may figure I am scorning her if she finds out I am going to marry Miss Valerie Scarwater, and furthermore," he says, "if she still has the letters she may fall into the hands of unscrupulous lawyers, and demand a very large sum, indeed. But," Mr. Tuesday says, "this does not worry me half as much as the idea that Miss Valerie Scarwater may learn about the letters and get a wrong impression of my friendship with Miss Amelia Bodkin."

Well, I round up Spanish John and Little Isadore the next afternoon, and I find Little Isadore playing klob with a guy by the name of Educated Edmund, who is called Educated Edmund because he once goes to Erasmus High School and is considered a very fine scholar, indeed, so I invite Educated Edmund to go along with us. The idea is, I know Educated Edmund makes a fair living playing klob with Little Isadore, and I figure as long as I am depriving Educated Edmund of a living for awhile, it is only courteous to toss something else his way. Furthermore, I figure as long as letters are involved in this proposition it may be a good thing to have Educated Edmund handy in case any reading becomes necessary, because Spanish John and Little Isadore do not read at all, and I read only large print.

We borrow a car off a friend of mine in Clinton Street, and with me driving we start for Tarrytown, which is a spot up the Hudson River, and it is a very enjoyable ride for one and all on account of the scenery. It is the first time Educated Edmund and Spanish John and Little Isadore ever see the scenery along the Hudson although they all reside on the banks of this beautiful river for several years at Ossining. Personally, I am never in Ossining, although once I make Auburn, and once Comstock, but the scenery in these localities is nothing to speak of.

We hit Tarrytown about dark, and follow the main drag

through this burg, as Mr. Tuesday tells me, until finally we come to the spot I am looking for, which is a little white cottage on a slope of ground above the river, not far off the highway. This little white cottage has quite a piece of ground around it, and a low stone wall, with a driveway from the highway to the house, and when I spot the gate to the driveway I make a quick turn, and what happens but I run the car slap-dab into a stone gatepost, and the car folds up like an accordion.

You see, the idea is we are figuring to make this a fast stick-up job without any foolishness about it, maybe leaving any parties we come across tied up good and tight while we make a getaway, as I am greatly opposed to house-breaking, or sneak jobs, as I do not consider them dignified. Furthermore, they take too much time, so I am going to run the car right up to the front door when this stone post gets in my way.

The next thing I know, I open my eyes to find myself in a strange bed, and also in a strange bedroom, and while I wake up in many a strange bed in my time, I never wake up in such a strange bedroom as this. It is all very soft and dainty, and the only jarring note in my surroundings is Spanish John sitting beside the bed looking at me.

Naturally I wish to know what is what, and Spanish John says I am knocked snoring in the collision with the gatepost, although none of the others are hurt, and that while I am stretched in the driveway with the blood running out of a bad gash in my noggin, who pops out of the house but a doll and an old guy who seems to be a butler, or some such, and the doll insists on them lugging me into the house, and placing me in this bedroom.

Then she washes the blood off of me, Spanish John says, and wraps my head up and personally goes to Tarrytown to get a croaker to see if my wounds are fatal, or what, while Educated Edmund and Little Isadore are trying to patch up the car. So, Spanish John says, he is sitting there to watch me until she comes back, although of course I know what he is really sitting there for is to get first search at me in case I do not recover.

Well, while I am thinking all this over, and wondering what is to be done, in pops a doll of maybe forty odd, who is built from the ground up, but who has a nice, kind-looking pan, with a large smile, and behind her is a guy I can see at once is a croaker, especially as he is packing a little black bag, and has a grey goatee. I never see a nicer-looking doll if you care for middling-old dolls, although personally I like them young, and when she sees me with my eyes open, she speaks as follows:

"Oh," she says, "I am glad you are not dead, you poor chap. But," she says, "here is Doctor Diffing-well, and he will see how badly you are injured. My name is Miss Amelia Bodkin, and this is my house, and this is my own bedroom, and I am very, very sorry you are hurt."

Well, naturally I consider this a most embarrassing situation, because here I am out to clip Miss Amelia Bodkin of her letters and her silverware, including her Paul Revere teapot, and there she is taking care of me in first-class style, and saying she is sorry for me.

But there seems to be nothing for me to say at this time, so I hold still while the croaker looks me over, and after he peeks at my noggin, and gives me a good feel up and down, he states as follows:

"This is a very bad cut," he says. "I will have to stitch it up, and then he must be very quiet for a few days, otherwise," he says, "complications may set in. It is best to move him to a hospital at once."

But Miss Amelia Bodkin will not listen to such an idea as moving me to a hospital. Miss Amelia Bodkin says I must rest right where I am, and she will take care of me, because she says I am injured on her premises by her gatepost, and it is only fair that she does something for me. In fact, from the way Miss Amelia Bodkin takes on about me being moved, I figure maybe it is the old sex appeal, although afterwards I find out it is only because she is lonesome, and nursing me will give her something to do.

Well, naturally I am not opposing her idea, because the way I look at it, I will be able to handle the situation about the letters, and also the silverware, very nicely as an inside job, so I try to act even worse off than I am, although of course anybody who knows about the time I carry eight slugs in my body from Broadway and Fiftieth Street to Brooklyn will laugh very heartily at the idea of a cut on the noggin keeping me in bed.

After the croaker gets through sewing me up, and goes away, I tell Spanish John to take Educated Edmund and Little Isadore and go on back to New York, but to keep in touch with me by telephone, so I can tell them when to come back, and then I go to sleep, because I seem to be very tired. When I wake up later in the night, I seem to have a fever, and am really somewhat sick, and Miss Amelia Bodkin is sitting beside my bed swabbing my noggin with a cool cloth, which feels very pleasant, indeed.

I am better in the morning, and am able to knock over a little breakfast which she brings to me on a tray, and I am commencing to see where being an invalid is not so bad, at that, especially when there are no coppers at your bedside every time you open your eyes asking who does it to you.

I can see Miss Amelia Bodkin gets quite a bang out of having somebody to take care of, although of course if she knows who she is taking care of at this time, the chances are

31

she will be running up the road calling for the gendarmes. It is not until after breakfast that I can get her to go and grab herself a little sleep, arid while she is away sleeping the old guy who seems to be the butler is in and out of my room every now and then to see how I am getting along.

He is a gabby old guy, and pretty soon he is telling me all about Miss Amelia Bodkin, and what he tells me is that she is the old-time sweetheart of a guy in New York who is at the head of a big business, and very rich, and of course I know this guy is Mr. Jabez Tuesday, although the old guy who seems to be the butler never mentions his name.

"They are together many years," he says to me. "He is very poor when they meet, and she has a little money, and establishes him in business, and by her management of this business, and of him, she makes it a very large business, indeed. I know, because I am with them almost from the start," the old guy says. "She is very smart in business, and also very kind, and nice, if anybody asks you.

"Now," the old guy says, "I am never able to figure out why they do not get married, because there is no doubt she loves him, and he loves her, but Miss Amelia Bodkin once tells me that it is because they are too poor at the start, and too busy later on to think of such things as getting married, and so they drift along the way they are, until all of a sudden he is rich. Then," the old guy says, "I can see he is getting away from her, although she never sees it herself, and I am not surprised when a few years ago he convinces her it is best for her to retire from active work, and move out to this spot.

"He comes out here fairly often at first," the old guy says, "but gradually he stretches the time between his visits, and now we do not see him once in a coon's age. Well," the old guy says, "it is just such a case as often comes up in life. In fact, I personally know of some others. But Miss Amelia Bodkin still thinks he loves her, and that only business keeps him away so much, so you can see she either is not as smart as she looks, or is kidding herself. Well," the old guy says, "I will now bring you a little orange-juice, although I do not mind saying you do not look to me like a guy who drinks orange-juice as a steady proposition."

Now I am taking many a gander around the bedroom to see if I can case the box of letters that Mr. Jabez Tuesday speaks of, but there is no box such as he describes in sight. Then in the evening, when Miss Amelia Bodkin is in the room, and I seem to be dozing, she pulls out a drawer in the bureau, and hauls out a big inlaid box, and sits down at a table under a reading-lamp, and opens this box and begins reading some old letters. And as she sits there reading those letters, with me watching her through my eyelashes, sometimes she smiles, but once I see little tears rolling down her cheeks.

All of a sudden she looks at me, and catches me with my eyes wide open, and I can see her face turn red, and then she laughs, and speaks to me, as follows:

"Old love letters," she says, tapping the box. "From my old sweetheart," she says. "I read some of them every night of my life. Am I not foolish and sentimental to do such a thing?"

Well, I tell Miss Amelia Bodkin she is sentimental all right, but I do not tell her just how foolish she is to be letting me in on where she plants these letters, although of course I am greatly pleased to have this information. I tell Miss Amelia Bodkin that personally I never write a love letter, and never get a love letter, and in fact, while I hear of these propositions, I never even see a love letter before, and this is all as true as you are a foot high. Then Miss Amelia Bodkin laughs a little, and says to me as follows:

"Why," she says, "you are a very unusual chap, indeed, not to know what a love letter is like. Why," she says, "I think I will read you a few of the most wonderful love letters in this world. It will do no harm," she says, "because you do not know the writer, and you must lie there and think of me, not old and ugly, as you see me now, but as young, and maybe a little bit pretty."

So Miss Amelia Bodkin opens a letter and reads it to me,

and her voice is soft and low as she reads, but she scarcely ever looks at the letter as she is reading, so I can see she knows it pretty much by heart. Furthermore, I can see that she thinks this letter is quite a masterpiece, but while I am no judge of love letters, because this is the first one I ever hear, I wish to say I consider it nothing but great nonsense.

"Sweetheart mine," this love letter says, "I am still thinking of you as I see you yesterday standing in front of the house with the sunlight turning your dark brown hair to wonderful bronze. Darling," it says, "I love the colour of your hair. I am so glad you are not a blonde. I hate blondes, they are so emptyheaded, and mean, and deceitful. Also they are bad-tempered," the letter says. "I will never trust a blonde any farther than I can throw a bull by the tail. I never see a blonde in my life who is not a plumb washout," it says. "Most of them are nothing but peroxide, anyway. Business is improving," it says. "Sausage is going up. I love you now and always, my baby doll."

Well, there are others worse than this, and all of them speak of her as sweetheart, or baby, or darlingest one, and also as loveykins, and precious, and angel, and I do not know what all else, and several of them speak of how things will be after they marry, and as I judge these are Mr. Jabez Tuesday's letters, all right, I can see where they are full of dynamite for a guy who is figuring on taking a run-out powder on a doll.

In fact, I say something to this general effect to Miss Amelia Bodkin, just for something to say.

"Why," she says, "what do you mean?"

"Well," I say, "documents such as these are known to bring large prices under certain conditions."

Now Miss Amelia Bodkin looks at me a moment, as if wondering what is in my mind, and then she shakes her head as if she gives it up, and laughs and speaks as follows:

"Well," she says, "one thing is certain, my letters will never bring a price, no matter how large, under any conditions, even if anybody ever wants them. Why," she says, "these are my greatest treasure. They are my memories of my happiest days. Why," she says, "I will not part with these letters for a million dollars."

Naturally I can see from this remark that Mr. Jabez Tuesday makes a very economical deal with me at ten G's for the letters, but of course I do not mention this to Miss Amelia Bodkin as I watch her put her love letters back in the inlaid box, and put the box back in the drawer of the bureau. I thank her for letting me hear the letters, and then I tell her good-night, and I go to sleep, and the next day I telephone to a certain number in Clinton Street and leave word for Educated Edmund and Spanish John and Little Isadore to come and get me, as I am tired of being an invalid.

Now the next day is Saturday, and the day that comes

after is bound to be Sunday, and they come to see me on Saturday, and promise to come back for me Sunday, as the car is now unravelled and running all right, although my friend in Clinton Street is beefing no little about the way his fenders are bent. But before they arrive Sunday morning, who is there ahead of them bright and early but Mr. Jabez Tuesday in a big town car.

Furthermore, as he walks into the house, all dressed up in a cutaway coat, and a high hat, he grabs Miss Amelia Bodkin in his arms, and kisses her ker-plump right on the smush, which information I afterwards receive from the old guy who seems to be the butler. From upstairs I can personally hear Miss Amelia Bodkin crying more than somewhat, and then I hear Mr. Jabez Tuesday speak in a loud, hearty voice as follows:

"Now, now, now, 'Mely," Mr. Tuesday says. "Do not be crying, especially on my new white vest. Cheer up," Mr. Tuesday says, "and listen to the arrangements I make for our wedding to-morrow, and our honeymoon in Montreal. Yes, indeed, 'Mely," Mr. Tuesday says, "you are the only one for me, because you understand me from A to Izzard. Give me another big kiss, 'Mely, and let us sit down and talk things over."

Well, I judge from the sound that he gets his kiss, and it is a very large kiss, indeed, with the cut-out open, and then

I hear them chewing the rag at great length in the living-room downstairs. Finally I hear Mr. Jabez Tuesday speak as follows:

"You know, 'Mely," he says, "you and I are just plain ordinary folks without any lugs, and," he says, "this is why we fit each other so well. I am sick and tired of people who pretend to be high-toned and mighty, when they do not have a white quarter to their name. They have no manners whatever. Why, only last night," Mr. Jabez Tuesday says, "I am calling on a high-toned family in New York by the name of Scarwater, and out of a clear sky I am grossly insulted by the daughter of the house, and practically turned out in the street. I never receive such treatment in my life," he says. "'Mely," he says, "give me another kiss, and see if you feel a bump here on my head."

Of course, Mr. Jabez Tuesday is somewhat surprised to see me present later on, but he never lets on he knows me, and naturally I do not give Mr. Jabez any tumble whatever at the moment, and by and by Educated Edmund and Spanish John and Little Isadore come for me in the car, and I thank Miss Amelia Bodkin for her kindness to me, and leave her standing on the lawn with Mr. Jabez Tuesday waving us good-bye.

And Miss Amelia Bodkin looks so happy as she snuggles up close to Mr. Jabez Tuesday that I am glad I take the chance, which is always better than an even-money chance these days, that Miss Valerie Scarwater is a blonde, and send Educated Edmund to her to read her Mr. Tuesday's letter in which he speaks of blondes. But of course I am sorry that this and other letters that I tell Educated Edmund to read to her heats her up so far as to make her forget she is a lady and causes her to slug Mr. Jabez Tuesday on the bean with an 18-carat vanity case, as she tells him to get out of her life.

So [Harry the Horse says] there is nothing more to the story, except we are now looking for Judge Goldfobber to get him to take up a legal matter for us with Mr. Jabez Tuesday. It is true Mr. Tuesday pays us the ten G's, but he never lets us take the silverware he speaks of, not even the Paul Revere teapot, which he says is so valuable, and in fact when we drop around to Miss Amelia Bodkin's house to pick up these articles one night not long ago, the old guy who seems to be the butler lets off a double-barrelled shotgun at us, and acts very nasty in general.

So [Harry says] we are going to see if we can get Judge Goldfobber to sue Mr. Jabez Tuesday for breach of promise.

"I am going to get you arrested as sure as my name is Lola sapola, you simple-looking tramp!"

2

ROMANCE IN THE ROARING FORTIES

Only a rank sucker will think of taking two peeks at Dave the Dude's doll, because while Dave may stand for the first peek, figuring it is a mistake, it is a sure thing he will get sored up at the second peek, and Dave the Dude is certainly not a man to have sored up at you.

But this Waldo Winchester is one hundred per cent sucker, which is why he takes quite a number of peeks at Dave's doll. And what is more, she takes quite a number of peeks right back at him. And there you are. When a guy and a doll get to taking peeks back and forth at each other, why, there you are indeed.

This Waldo Winchester is a nice-looking young guy who writes pieces about Broadway for the *Morning Item*. He writes about the goings-on in night clubs, such as fights, and one thing and another, and also about who is running around with who, including guys and dolls.

Sometimes this is very embarrassing to people who may be married and are running around with people who are not married, but of course Waldo Winchester cannot be expected to ask one and all for their marriage certificates before he writes his pieces for the paper.

The chances are if Waldo Winchester knows Miss Billy Perry is Dave the Dude's doll, he will never take more than his first peek at her, but nobody tips him off until his second or third peek, and by this time Miss Billy Perry is taking her peeks back at him and Waldo Winchester is hooked.

In fact, he is plumb gone, and being a sucker, like I tell you, he does not care whose doll she is. Personally, I do not blame him much, for Miss Billy Perry is worth a few peeks, especially when she is out on the floor of Miss Missouri Martin's Sixteen Hundred Club doing her tap dance. Still, I do not think the best tap-dancer that ever lives can make me take two peeks at her if I know she is Dave the Dude's doll, for Dave somehow thinks more than somewhat of his dolls.

He especially thinks plenty of Miss Billy Perry, and sends her fur coats, and diamond rings, and one thing and another, which she sends back to him at once, because it seems she does not take presents from guys. This is considered most surprising all along Broadway, but people figure the chances are she has some other angle.

Anyway, this does not keep Dave the Dude from liking her just the same, and so she is considered his doll by one and all, and is respected accordingly until this Waldo Winchester comes along.

It happens that he comes along while Dave the Dude is off in the Modoc on a little run down to the Bahamas to get some goods for his business, such as Scotch and champagne, and by the time Dave gets back Miss Billy Perry and Waldo Winchester are at the stage where they sit in corners between her numbers and hold hands.

Of course nobody tells Dave the Dude about this, because they do not wish to get him excited. Not even Miss Missouri Martin tells him, which is most unusual because Miss Missouri Martin, who is sometimes called "Mizzoo" for short, tells everything she knows as soon as she knows it, which is very often before it happens.

You see, the idea is when Dave the Dude is excited he may blow somebody's brains out, and the chances are it will be nobody's brains but Waldo Winchester's, although some claim that Waldo Winchester has no brains or he will not be hanging around Dave the Dude's doll.

I know Dave is very, very fond of Miss Billy Perry, because I hear him talk to her several times, and he is most polite to her and never gets out of line in her company by using cuss words, or anything like this. Furthermore, one night when One-eyed Solly Abrahams is a little stewed up he refers to Miss Billy Perry as a broad, meaning no harm whatever, for this is the way many of the boys speak of the dolls.

But right away Dave the Dude reaches across the table and bops One-eyed Solly right in the mouth, so everybody knows from then on that Dave thinks well of Miss Billy Perry. Of course Dave is always thinking fairly well of some doll as far as this goes, but it is seldom he gets to bopping guys in the mouth over them.

Well, one night what happens but Dave the Dude walks into the Sixteen Hundred Club, and there in the entrance, what does he see but this Waldo Winchester and Miss Billy Perry kissing each other back and forth friendly. Right away Dave reaches for the old equalizer to shoot Waldo Winchester, but it seems Dave does not happen to have the old equalizer with him, not expecting to have to shoot anybody this particular evening.

So Dave the Dude walks over and, as Waldo Winchester hears him coming and lets go his strangle-hold on Miss Billy Perry, Dave nails him with a big right hand on the chin. I will say for Dave the Dude that he is a fair puncher with his right hand, though his left is not so good, and he knocks Waldo Winchester bow-legged. In fact, Waldo folds right up on the floor.

Well, Miss Billy Perry lets out a screech you can hear clear to the Battery and runs over to where Waldo Winchester lights, and falls on top of him squalling very loud. All anybody can make out of what she says is that Dave the

Dude is a big bum, although Dave is not so big, at that, and that she loves Waldo Winchester.

Dave walks over and starts to give Waldo Winchester the leather, which is considered customary in such cases, but he seems to change his mind, and instead of booting Waldo around, Dave turns and walks out of the joint looking very black and mad, and the next anybody hears of him he is over in the Chicken Club doing plenty of drinking.

This is regarded as a very bad sign indeed, because while everybody goes to the Chicken Club now and then to give Tony Bertazzola, the owner, a friendly play, very few people care to do any drinking there, because Tony's liquor is not meant for anybody to drink except the customers.

Well, Miss Billy Perry gets Waldo Winchester on his pegs again, and wipes his chin off with her handkerchief, and by and by he is all okay except for a big lump on his chin. And all the time she is telling Waldo Winchester what a big bum Dave the Dude is, although afterwards Miss Missouri Martin gets hold of Miss Billy Perry and puts the blast on her plenty for chasing a two-handed spender such as Dave the Dude out of the joint.

"You are nothing but a little sap," Miss Missouri Martin tells Miss Billy Perry. "You cannot get the right time off this newspaper guy, while everybody knows Dave the Dude is a very fast man with a dollar."

"But I love Mr. Winchester," says Miss Billy Perry. "He is so romantic. He is not a bootlegger and a gunman like Dave the Dude. He puts lovely pieces in the paper about me, and he is a gentleman at all times."

Now of course Miss Missouri Martin is not in a position to argue about gentlemen, because she meets very few in the Sixteen Hundred Club and anyway, she does not wish to make Waldo Winchester mad as he is apt to turn around and put pieces in his paper that will be a knock to the joint, so she lets the matter drop.

Miss Billy Perry and Waldo Winchester go on holding hands between her numbers, and maybe kissing each other now and then, as young people are liable to do, and Dave the Dude plays the chill for the Sixteen Hundred Club and everything seems to be all right. Naturally we are all very glad there is no more trouble over the proposition, because the best Dave can get is the worst of it in a jam with a newspaper guy.

Personally, I figure Dave will soon find himself another doll and forget all about Miss Billy Perry, because now that I take another peek at her, I can see where she is just about the same as any other tap-dancer, except that she is red-headed. Tap-dancers are generally blackheads, but I do not know why.

Moosh, the doorman at the Sixteen Hundred Club, tells

me Miss Missouri Martin keeps plugging for Dave the Dude
with Miss Billy Perry in a quiet way, because he says he hears
Miss Missouri Martin make the following crack one night
to her: "Well, I do not see any Simple Simon on your lean
and linger."

This is Miss Missouri Martin's way of saying she sees no
diamond on Miss Billy Perry's finger, for Miss Missouri
Martin is an old experienced doll, who figures if a guy loves
a doll he will prove it with diamonds. Miss Missouri Martin
has many diamonds herself, though how any guy can ever
get himself heated up enough about Miss Missouri Martin
to give her diamonds is more than I can see.

I am not a guy who goes around much, so I do not see
Dave the Dude for a couple of weeks, but late one Sunday
afternoon little Johnny McGowan, who is one of Dave's
men, comes and says to me like this: "What do you think?
Dave grabs the scribe a little while ago and is taking him out
for an airing!"

Well, Johnny is so excited it is some time before I can
get him cooled out enough to explain. It seems that Dave
the Dude gets his biggest car out of the garage and sends
his driver, Wop Joe, over to the *Item* office where Waldo
Winchester works, with a message that Miss Billy Perry
wishes to see Waldo right away at Miss Missouri Martin's
apartment on Fifty-ninth Street.

Of course this message is nothing but the phonus bolonus, but Waldo drops in for it and gets in the car. Then Wop Joe drives him up to Miss Missouri Martin's apartment, and who gets in the car there but Dave the Dude. And away they go.

Now this is very bad news indeed, because when Dave the Dude takes a guy out for an airing the guy very often does not come back. What happens to him I never ask, because the best a guy can get by asking questions in this man's town is a bust in the nose.

But I am much worried over this proposition, because I like Dave the Dude, and I know that taking a newspaper guy like Waldo Winchester out for an airing is apt to cause talk, especially if he does not come back. The other guys that Dave the Dude takes out for airings do not mean much in particular, but here is a guy who may produce trouble, even if he is a sucker, on account of being connected with a newspaper.

I know enough about newspapers to know that by and by the editor or somebody will be around wishing to know where Waldo Winchester's pieces about Broadway are, and if there are no pieces from Waldo Winchester, the editor will wish to know why. Finally it will get around to where other people will wish to know, and after a while many people will be running around saying: "Where is Waldo Winchester?"

And if enough people in this town get to running around

saying where is So-and-so, it becomes a great mystery and the newspapers hop on the cops and the cops hop on everybody, and by and by there is so much heat in town that it is no place for a guy to be.

But what is to be done about this situation I do not know. Personally, it strikes me as very bad indeed, and while Johnny goes away to do a little telephoning, I am trying to think up some place to go where people will see me, and remember afterwards that I am there in case it is necessary for them to remember.

Finally Johnny comes back, very excited, and says: "Hey, the Dude is up at the Woodcock Inn on the Pelham Parkway, and he is sending out the word for one and all to come at once. Good Time Charley Bernstein just gets the wire and tells me. Something is doing. The rest of the mob are on their way, so let us be moving."

But here is an invitation which does not strike me as a good thing at all. The way I look at it, Dave the Dude is no company for a guy like me at this time. The chances are he either does something to Waldo Winchester already, or is getting ready to do something to him which I wish no part of.

Personally, I have nothing against newspaper guys, not even the ones who write pieces about Broadway. If Dave the Dude wishes to do something to Waldo Winchester, all right, but what is the sense of bringing outsiders into it? But the next thing I know, I am in Johnny McGowan's roadster, and he is zipping along very fast indeed, paying practically no attention to traffic lights or anything else.

As we go busting out the Concourse, I get to thinking the situation over, and I figure that Dave the Dude probably keeps thinking about Miss Billy Perry, and drinking liquor such as they sell in the Chicken Club, until finally he blows his topper. The way I look at it, only a guy who is off his nut will think of taking a newspaper guy out for an airing over a doll, when dolls are a dime a dozen in this man's town.

Still, I remember reading in the papers about a lot of different guys who are considered very sensible until they get tangled up with a doll, and maybe loving her, and the first thing anybody knows they hop out of windows, or shoot themselves, or somebody else, and I can see where even a guy like Dave the Dude may go daffy over a doll.

I can see that little Johnny McGowan is worried, too, but he does not say much, and we pull up in front of the Woodcock Inn in no time whatever, to find a lot of other cars there ahead of us, some of which I recognize as belonging to different parties.

The Woodcock Inn is what is called a road house, and is run by Big Nig Skolsky, a very nice man indeed, and a friend of everybody's. It stands back a piece off the Pelham Parkway and is a very pleasant place to go to, what with Nig having a good band and a floor show with a lot of fair-looking dolls, and everything else a man can wish for a good time. It gets a nice play from nice people, although Nig's liquor is nothing extra.

Personally, I never go there much, because I do not care for road houses, but it is a great spot for Dave the Dude when he is pitching parties, or even when he is only drinking single-handed. There is a lot of racket in the joint as we drive up, and who comes out to meet us but Dave the Dude himself with a big hello. His face is very red, and he seems heated up no little, but he does not look like a guy who is meaning any harm to anybody, especially a newspaper guy.

"Come in, guys!" Dave the Dude yells. "Come right in!"

So we go in, and the place is full of people sitting at tables, or out on the floor dancing, and I see Miss Missouri Martin with all her diamonds hanging from her in different places, and Good Time Charley Bernstein, and Feet Samuels, and Tony Bertazzola, and Skeets Boliver, and Nick the Greek, and Rochester Red, and a lot of other guys and dolls from around and about.

In fact, it looks as if everybody from all the joints on Broadway are present, including Miss Billy Perry, who is all dressed up in white and is lugging a big bundle of orchids and so forth, and who is giggling and smiling and shaking hands

51

and going on generally. And finally I see Waldo Winchester, the scribe, sitting at a ringside table all by himself, but there is nothing wrong with him as far as I can see. I mean, he seems to be all in one piece so far.

"Dave," I say to Dave the Dude, very quiet, "what is coming off here? You know a guy cannot be too careful what he does around this town, and I will hate to see you tangled up in anything right now."

"Why," Dave says, "what are you talking about? Nothing is coming off here but a wedding, and it is going to be the best wedding anybody on Broadway ever sees. We are waiting for the preacher now."

"You mean somebody is going to be married?" I ask, being now somewhat confused.

"Certainly," Dave the Dude says. "What do you think? What is the idea of a wedding, anyway?"

"Who is going to be married?" I ask.

"Nobody but Billy and the scribe," Dave says. "This is the greatest thing I ever do in my life. I run into Billy the other night and she is crying her eyes out because she loves this scribe and wishes to marry him, but it seems the scribe has nothing he can use for money. So I tell Billy to leave it to me, because you know I love her myself so much I wish to see her happy at all times, even if she has to marry to be that way.

"So I frame this wedding party, and after they are married I am going to stake them to a few G's so they can get a good running start," Dave says. "But I do not tell the scribe and I do not let Billy tell him as I wish it to be a big surprise to him. I kidnap him this afternoon and bring him out here and he is scared half to death thinking I am going to scrag him.

"In fact," Dave says, "I never see a guy so scared. He is still so scared nothing seems to cheer him up. Go over and tell him to shake himself together, because nothing but happiness for him is coming off here."

Well, I wish to say I am greatly relieved to think that Dave intends doing nothing worse to Waldo Winchester than getting him married up, so I go over to where Waldo is sitting. He certainly looks somewhat alarmed. He is all in a huddle with himself, and he has what you call a vacant stare in his eyes. I can see that he is indeed frightened, so I give him a jolly slap on the back and I say: "Congratulations, pal! Cheer up, the worst is yet to come!"

"You bet it is," Waldo Winchester says, his voice so solemn I am greatly surprised.

"You are a fine-looking bridegroom," I say. "You look as if you are at a funeral instead of a wedding. Why do you not laugh ha-ha, and maybe take a dram or two and go to cutting up some?"

"Mister," says Waldo Winchester, "my wife is not going to care for me getting married to Miss Billy Perry."

"Your wife?" I say, much astonished. "What is this you are speaking of? How can you have any wife except Miss Billy Perry? This is great foolishness."

"I know," Waldo says, very sad. "I know. But I got a wife just the same, and she is going to be very nervous when she hears about this. My wife is very strict with me. My wife does not allow me to go around marrying people. My wife is Lola Sapola, of the Rolling Sapolas, the acrobats, and I am married to her for five years. She is the strong lady who juggles the other four people in the act. My wife just gets back from a year's tour of the Interstate time, and she is at the Marx Hotel right this minute. I am upset by this proposition."

"Does Miss Billy Perry know about this wife?" I ask.

"No," he says. "No. She thinks I am single-o."

"But why do you not tell Dave the Dude you are already married when he brings you out here to marry you off to Miss Billy Perry?" I ask. "It seems to me a newspaper guy must know it is against the law for a guy to marry several different dolls unless he is a Turk, or some such."

"Well," Waldo says, "if I tell Dave the Dude I am married after taking his doll away from him, I am quite sure Dave will be very much excited, and maybe do something harmful to my health."

Now there is much in what the guy says, to be sure. I am inclined to think, myself, that Dave will be somewhat disturbed when he learns of this situation, especially when Miss Billy Perry starts in being unhappy about it. But what is to be done I do not know, except maybe to let the wedding go on, and then when Waldo is out of reach of Dave, to put in a claim that he is insane, and that the marriage does not count. It is a sure thing I do not wish to be around when Dave the Dude hears Waldo is already married.

I am thinking that maybe I better take it on the lam out of there, when there is a great row at the door and I hear Dave the Dude yelling that the preacher arrives. He is a very nice-looking preacher, at that, though he seems somewhat surprised by the goings-on, especially when Miss Missouri Martin steps up and takes charge of him. Miss Missouri Martin tells him she is fond of preachers, and is quite used to them, because she is twice married by preachers, and twice by justices of the peace, and once by a ship's captain at sea.

By this time one and all present, except maybe myself and Waldo Winchester, and the preacher and maybe Miss Billy Perry, are somewhat corned. Waldo is still sitting at his table looking very sad and saying "Yes" and "No" to Miss Billy Perry whenever she skips past him, for Miss Billy Perry is too much pleasured up with happiness to stay long in one spot.

Dave the Dude is more corned than anybody else, because he has two or three days' running start on everybody. And when Dave the Dude is corned I wish to say that he is a very unreliable guy as to temper, and he is apt to explode right in your face any minute. But he seems to be getting a great bang out of the doings.

Well, by and by Nig Skolsky has the dance floor cleared, and then he moves out on the floor a sort of arch of very beautiful flowers. The idea seems to be that Miss Billy Perry and Waldo Winchester are to be married under this arch. I can see that Dave the Dude must put in several days planning this whole proposition, and it must cost him plenty of the old do-re-mi, especially as I see him showing Miss Missouri Martin a diamond ring as big as a cough drop.

"It is for the bride," Dave the Dude says. "The poor loogan she is marrying will never have enough dough to buy her such a rock, and she always wishes a big one. I get it off a guy who brings it in from Los Angeles. I am going to give the bride away myself in person, so how do I act, Mizzoo? I want Billy to have everything according to the book."

Well, while Miss Missouri Martin is trying to remember back to one of her weddings to tell him, I take another peek at Waldo Winchester to see how he is making out. I once see two guys go to the old warm squativoo up in Sing Sing, and I wish to say both are laughing heartily compared to Waldo

Winchester at this moment.

Miss Billy Perry is sitting with him and the orchestra leader is calling his men dirty names because none of them can think of how "Oh, Promise Me" goes, when Dave the Dude yells: "Well, we are all set! Let the happy couple step forward!"

Miss Billy Perry bounces up and grabs Waldo Winchester by the arm and pulls him up out of his chair. After a peek at his face I am willing to lay 6 to 5 he does not make the arch. But he finally gets there with everybody laughing and clapping their hands, and the preacher comes forward, and Dave the Dude looks happier than I ever see him look before in his life as they all get together under the arch of flowers.

Well, all of a sudden there is a terrible racket at the front door of the Woodcock Inn, with some doll doing a lot of hollering in a deep voice that sounds like a man's, and naturally everybody turns and looks that way. The doorman, a guy by the name of Slugsy Sachs, who is a very hard man indeed, seems to be trying to keep somebody out, but pretty soon there is a heavy bump and Slugsy Sachs falls down, and in comes a doll about four feet high and five feet wide.

In fact, I never see such a wide doll. She looks all hammered down. Her face is almost as wide as her shoulders, and makes me think of a great big full moon. She comes in bounding-like, and I can see that she is all churned up about something.

As she bounces in, I hear a gurgle, and I look around to see Waldo Winchester slumping down to the floor, almost dragging Miss Billy Perry with him.

Well, the wide doll walks right up to the bunch under the arch and says in a large bass voice: "Which one is Dave the Dude;"

"I am Dave the Dude," says Dave the Dude, stepping up. "What do you mean by busting in here like a walrus and gumming up our wedding?"

"So you are the guy who kidnaps my ever-loving husband to marry him off to this little red-headed pancake here, are you?" the wide doll says, looking at Dave the Dude, but pointing at Miss Billy Perry.

Well now, calling Miss Billy Perry a pancake to Dave the Dude is a very serious proposition, and Dave the Dude gets very angry. He is usually rather polite to dolls, but you can see he does not care for the wide doll's manner whatever.

"Say, listen here," Dave the Dude says, "you better take a walk before somebody clips you. You must be drunk," he says. "Or daffy," he says. "What are you talking about, anyway?"

"You will see what I am talking about," the wide doll yells. "The guy on the floor there is my lawful husband. You probably frighten him to death, the poor dear. You kidnap him to marry this red-headed thing, and I am going to get you arrested as sure as my name is Lola Sapola, you simple-looking tramp!"

Naturally, everybody is greatly horrified at a doll using such language to Dave the Dude, because Dave is known to shoot guys for much less, but instead of doing something to the wide doll at once, Dave says: "What is this talk I hear? Who is married to who? Get out of here!" Dave says, grabbing the wide doll's arm.

Well, she makes out as if she is going to slap Dave in the face with her left hand, and Dave naturally pulls his kisser out of the way. But instead of doing anything with her left, Lola Sapola suddenly drives her right fist smack-dab into Dave the Dude's stomach, which naturally comes forward as his face goes back.

I wish to say I see many a body punch delivered in my life, but I never see a prettier one than this. What is more, Lola Sapola steps in with the punch, so there is plenty on it.

Now a guy who eats and drinks like Dave the Dude does cannot take them so good in the stomach, so Dave goes "oof," and sits down very hard on the dance floor, and as he is sitting there he is fumbling in his pants pocket for the old equalizer, so everybody around tears for cover except Lola Sapola, and Miss Billy Perry, and Waldo Winchester.

But before he can get his pistol out, Lola Sapola reaches down and grabs Dave by the collar and hoists him to his feet. She lets go her hold on him, leaving Dave standing on his pins, but teetering around somewhat, and then she drives her right hand to Dave's stomach a second time.

The punch drops Dave again, and Lola steps up to him as if she is going to give him the foot. But she only gathers up Waldo Winchester from off the floor and slings him across her shoulder like he is a sack of oats, and starts for the door. Dave the Dude sits up on the floor again and by this time he has the old equalizer in his duke.

"Only for me being a gentleman I will fill you full of slugs," he yells.

Lola Sapola never even looks back, because by this time she is petting Waldo Winchester's head and calling him loving names and saying what a shame it is for bad characters like Dave the Dude to be abusing her precious one. It all sounds to me as if Lola Sapola thinks well of Waldo Winchester.

Well, after she gets out of sight, Dave the Dude gets up off the floor and stands there looking at Miss Billy Perry, who is out to break all crying records. The rest of us come out from under cover, including the preacher, and we are wondering how mad Dave the Dude is going to be about the wedding being ruined. But Dave the Dude seems only disappointed and sad.

"Billy," he says to Miss Billy Perry, "I am mighty sorry you do not get your wedding. All I wish for is your happiness, but I do not believe you can ever be happy with this scribe if he also has to have his lion tamer around. As Cupid I am a total bust. This is the only nice thing I ever try to do in my whole life, and it is too bad it does not come off. Maybe if you wait until he can drown her, or something——"

"Dave," says Miss Billy Perry, dropping so many tears that she seems to finally wash herself right into Dave the Dude's arms, "I will never, never be happy with such a guy as Waldo Winchester. I can see now you are the only man for me."

"Well, well, well," Dave the Dude says, cheering right up. "Where is the preacher? Bring on the preacher and let us have our wedding anyway."

I see Mr. and Mrs. Dave the Dude the other day, and they seem very happy. But you never can tell about married people, so of course I am never going to let on to Dave the Dude that I am the one who telephones Lola Sapola at the Marx Hotel, because maybe I do not do Dave any too much of a favour, at that.

3

DREAM STREET ROSE

Of an early evening when there is nothing much doing anywhere else, I go around to Good Time Charley's little speak in West Forty-seventh Street that he calls the Gingham Shoppe, and play a little klob with Charley, because business is quiet in the Gingham Shoppe at such an hour, and Charley gets very lonesome.

He once has a much livelier spot in Forty-eighth Street that he calls the Crystal Room, but one night a bunch of G-guys step into the joint and bust it wide open, besides confiscating all of Charley's stock of merchandise. It seems that these G-guys are members of a squad that comes on from Washington, and being strangers in the city they do not know that Good Time Charley's joint is not supposed to be busted up, so they go ahead and bust it, just the same as if it is any other joint.

Well, this action causes great indignation in many quarters, and a lot of citizens advise Charley to see somebody about it. But Charley says no. Charley says if this is the way the government is going to treat him after the way he walks himself bow-legged over in France with the Rainbow Division, making the Germans hard to catch, why, all right. But he is not going to holler copper about it, although Charley says he has his own opinion of Mr. Hoover, at that.

Personally, I greatly admire Charley for taking the disaster so calmly, especially as it catches him with very few potatoes. Charley is a great hand for playing the horses with any dough he makes out of the Crystal Room, and this particular season the guys who play the horses are being murdered by the bookies all over the country, and are in terrible distress.

So I know if Charley is not plumb broke that he has a terrible crack across his belly, and I am not surprised that I do not see him for a couple of weeks after the government guys knock off the Crystal Room. I hear rumours that he is at home reading the newspapers very carefully every day, especially the obituary notices, for it seems that Charley figures that some of the G-guys may be tempted to take a belt or two at the merchandise they confiscate, and Charley says if they do, he is even for life.

Finally I hear that Charley is seen buying a bolt of gingham in Bloomington's one day, so I know he will be in action again very soon, for all Charley needs to go into action is a bolt of gingham and a few bottles of Golden Wedding. In fact, I know Charley to go into action without the gingham, but as a rule he likes to drape a place of business with gingham to make it seem more homelike to his customers, and I wish to say that when it comes to draping gingham, Charley can make a sucker of Joseph Urban, or anybody else.

Well, when I arrive at the Gingham Shoppe this night I am talking about, which is around ten o'clock, I find Charley in a very indignant state of mind, because an old tomato by the name of Dream Street Rose comes in and tracks up his floor, just after Charley gets through mopping it up, for Charley does his mopping in person, not being able as yet to afford any help.

Rose is sitting at a table in a corner, paying no attention to Charley's remarks about wiping her feet on the Welcome mat at the door before she comes in, because Rose knows there is no Welcome mat at Charley's door, anyway, but I can see where Charley has a right to a few beefs, at that, as she leaves a trail of black hoofprints across the clean floor as if she is walking around in mud somewhere before she comes in, although I do not seem to remember that it is raining when I arrive.

Now this Dream Street Rose is an old doll of maybe fifty-odd, and is a very well-known character around and about, as she is wandering through the Forties for many a year, and especially through West Forty-seventh Street between Sixth and Seventh Avenues, and this block is called Dream Street. And the reason it is called Dream Street is because in this block are many characters of one kind and another who always seem to be dreaming of different matters.

In Dream Street there are many theatrical hotels, and rooming houses, and restaurants, and speaks, including Good Time Charley's Gingham Shoppe, and in the summer time the characters I mention sit on the stoops or lean against the railings along Dream Street, and the gab you hear sometimes sounds very dreamy indeed. In fact, it sometimes sounds very pipe-dreamy.

Many actors, male and female, and especially vaudeville actors, live in the hotels and rooming houses, and vaudeville actors, both male and female, are great hands for sitting around dreaming out loud about how they will practically assassinate the public in the Palace if ever they get a chance.

Furthermore, in Dream Street are always many handbookies and horse players, who sit on the church steps on the cool side of Dream Street in the summer and dream about big killings on the races, and there are also nearly always many fight managers, and sometimes fighters, hanging out in front of the restaurants, picking their teeth and dreaming about winning championships of the world, although up to this time no champion of the world has yet come out of Dream Street.

In this street you see burlesque dolls, and hoofers, and guys who write songs, and saxophone players, and newsboys, and newspaper scribes, and taxi drivers, and blind guys, and midgets, and blondes with Pomeranian pooches, or maybe French poodles, and guys with whiskers, and night-club entertainers, and I do not know what all else. And all of these characters are interesting to look at, and some of them are very interesting to talk to, although if you listen to several I know long enough, you may get the idea that they are somewhat daffy, especially the horse players.

But personally I consider all horse players more or less daffy anyway. In fact, the way I look at it, if a guy is not daffy he will not be playing the horses.

Now this Dream Street Rose is a short, thick-set, square-looking old doll, with a square pan, and square shoulders, and she has heavy iron-grey hair that she wears in a square bob, and she stands very square on her feet. In fact, Rose is the squarest-looking doll I ever see, and she is as strong and lively as Jim Londos, the wrestler. In fact, Jim Londos will never be any better than 6 to 5 in my line over Dream Street Rose, if she is in any kind of shape.

Nobody in this town wishes any truck with Rose if she has a few shots of grog in her, and especially Good Time

Charley's grog, for she can fight like the dickens when she is grogged up. In fact, Rose holds many a decision in this town, especially over coppers, because if there is one thing she hates and despises more than somewhat it is a copper, as coppers are always heaving her into the old can when they find her jerking citizens around and cutting up other didoes.

For many years Rose works in the different hotels along Dream Street as a chambermaid. She never works in any one hotel very long, because the minute she gets a few bobs together she likes to go out and enjoy a little recreation, such as visiting around the speaks, although she is about as welcome in most speaks as a G-guy with a search warrant. You see, nobody can ever tell when Rose may feel like taking the speak apart, and also the customers.

She never has any trouble getting a job back in any hotel she ever works in, for Rose is a wonderful hand for making up beds, although several times, when she is in a hurry to get off, I hear she makes up beds with guests still in them, which causes a few mild beefs to the management, but does not bother Rose. I speak of this matter only to show you that she is a very quaint character indeed, and full of zest.

Well, I sit down to play klob with Good Time Charley, but about this time several customers come into the Gingham Shoppe, so Charley has to go and take care of them, leaving me alone. And while I am sitting there alone I hear Dream Street Rose mumbling to herself over in the corner, but I pay no attention to her, although I wish to say I am by no means unfriendly with Rose.

In fact, I say hello to her at all times, and am always very courteous to her, as I do not wish to have her bawling me out in public, and maybe circulating rumours about me, as she is apt to do, if she feels I am snubbing her.

Finally I notice her motioning to me to come over to her table, and I go over at once and sit down, because I can see that Rose is well grogged up at this time, and I do not care to have her attracting my attention by chucking a cuspidor at me. She offers me a drink when I sit down, but of course I never drink anything that is sold in Good Time Charley's, as a personal favour to Charley. He says he wishes to retain my friendship.

So I just sit there saying nothing much whatever, and Rose keeps on mumbling to herself, and I am not able to make much of her mumbling, until finally she looks at me and says to me like this:

"I am now going to tell you about my friend," Rose says.

"Well, Rose," I say, "personally I do not care to hear about your friend, although," I say, "I have no doubt that what you wish to tell me about this friend is very interesting. But I am here to play a little klob with Good Time Charley, and I do not have time to hear about your friend."

"Charley is busy selling his poison to the suckers," Rose says. "I am now going to tell you about my friend. It is quite a story," she says. "You will listen."

So I listen.

It is a matter of thirty-five years ago [Dream Street Rose says] and the spot is a town in Colorado by the name of Pueblo, where there are smelters and one thing and another. My friend is at this time maybe sixteen or seventeen years old, and a first-class looker in every respect. Her papa is dead, and her mamma runs a boarding-house for the guys who work in the smelters, and who are very hearty eaters. My friend deals them off the arm for the guys in her mamma's boarding-house to save her mamma the expense of a waitress.

Now among the boarders in this boarding-house are many guys who are always doing a little pitching to my friend, and trying to make dates with her to take her places, but my friend never gives them much of a tumble, because after she gets through dealing them off the arm all day her feet generally pain her too much to go anywhere on them except to the hay.

Finally, however, along comes a tall, skinny young guy from the East by the name of Frank something, who has things to say to my friend that are much more interesting than anything that has ever been said to her by a guy before,

69

including such things as love and marriage, which are always very interesting subjects to any young doll.

This Frank is maybe twenty-five years old, and he comes from the East with the idea of making his fortune in the West, and while it is true that fortunes are being made in the West at this time, there is little chance that Frank is going to make any part of a fortune, as he does not care to work very hard. In fact, he does not care to work at all, being much more partial to playing a little poker, or shooting a few craps, or maybe hustling a sucker around Mike's pool room on Santa Fe Avenue, for Frank is an excellent pool player, especially when he is playing a sucker.

Now my friend is at this time a very innocent young doll, and a good doll in every respect, and her idea of love includes a nice little home, and children running here and there and around and about, and she never has a wrong thought in her life, and believes that everybody else in the world is like herself. And the chances are if this Frank does not happen along, my friend will marry a young guy in Pueblo by the name of Higginbottom, who is very fond of her indeed, and who is a decent young guy and afterwards makes plenty of potatoes in the grocery dodge.

But my friend goes very daffy over Frank and cannot see anybody but him, and the upshot of it all is she runs away with him one day to Denver, being dumb enough to believe that he means it when he tells her that he loves her and is going to marry her. Why Frank ever bothers with such a doll as my friend in the first place is always a great mystery to one and all, and the only way anybody can explain it is that she is young and fresh, and he is a heel at heart.

"Well, Rose," I say, "I am now commencing to see the finish of this story about your friend, and," I say, "it is such a story as anybody can hear in a speak at any time in this town, except," I say, "maybe your story is longer than somewhat. So I will now thank you, and excuse myself, and play a little klob with Good Time Charley."

"You will listen," Dream Street Rose says, looking me slap-dab in the eye.

So I listen.

Moreover, I notice now that Good Time Charley is standing behind me, bending in an ear, as it seems that his customers take the wind after a couple of slams of Good Time Charley's merchandise, a couple of slams being about all that even a very hardy customer can stand at one session.

Of course [Rose goes on] the chances are Frank never intends marrying my friend at all, and she never knows until long afterward that the reason he leads her to the parson is that the young guy from Pueblo by the name of Higginbottom catches up with them at the old Windsor Hotel where they are stopping and privately pokes a six-pistol against Frank's

71

ribs and promises faithfully to come back and blow a hole in Frank you can throw a water-melon through if Frank tries any phenagling around with my friend.

Well, in practically no time whatever, love's young dream is over as far as my friend is concerned. This Frank turns out to be a most repulsive character indeed, especially if you are figuring him as an ever-loving husband. In fact, he is no good. He mistreats my friend in every way any guy ever thought of mistreating a doll, and besides the old established ways of mistreating a doll, Frank thinks up quite a number of new ways, being really quite ingenious in this respect.

Yes, this Frank is one hundred per cent heel.

It is not so much that he gives her a thumping now and then, because, after all, a thumping wears off, and hurts heal up, even when they are such hurts as a broken nose and fractured ribs, and once an ankle cracked by a kick. It is what he does to her heart, and to her innocence. He is by no means a good husband, and does not know how to treat an ever-loving wife with any respect, especially as he winds up by taking my friend to San Francisco and hiring her out to a very loose character there by the name of Black Emanuel, who has a dance joint on the Barbary Coast, which, at the time I am talking about, is hotter than a stove. In this joint my friend has to dance with the customers, and get them to buy beer for her and one thing and another, and this occupation is most distasteful to my friend, as she never cares for beer.

It is there Frank leaves her for good after giving her an extra big thumping for a keepsake, and when my friend tries to leave Black Emanuel's to go looking for her ever-loving husband, she is somewhat surprised to hear Black Emanuel state that he pays Frank three C's for her to remain there and continue working. Furthermore, Black Emanuel resumes the thumpings where Frank leaves off, and by and by my friend is much bewildered and down-hearted and does not care what happens to her.

Well, there is nothing much of interest in my friend's life for the next thirty-odd years, except that she finally gets so she does not mind the beer so much, and, in fact, takes quite a fondness for it, and also for light wines and Bourbon whisky, and that she comes to realize that Frank does not love her after all, in spite of what he says. Furthermore, in later years, after she drifts around the country quite some, in and out of different joints, she realizes that the chances are she will never have a nice little home, with children running here and there, and she often thinks of what a disagreeable influence Frank has on her life.

In fact, this Frank is always on her mind more than somewhat. In fact, she thinks of him night and day, and says many a prayer that he will do well. She manages to keep track of him, which is not hard to do, at that, as Frank is in New York, and is becoming quite a guy in business, and is often in the newspapers. Maybe his success is due to my friend's prayers, but the chances are it is more because he connects up with some guy who has an invention for doing something very interesting to steel, and by grabbing an interest in this invention Frank gets a shove toward plenty of potatoes. Furthermore, he is married, and is raising up a family.

About ten or twelve years ago my friend comes to New York, and by this time she is getting a little faded around the edges. She is not so old, at that, but the air of the Western and Southern joints is bad on the complexion, and beer is no good for the figure. In fact, my friend is now quite a haybag, and she does not get any better-looking in the years she spends in New York as she is practically all out of the old sex appeal, and has to do a little heavy lifting to keep eating. But she never forgets to keep praying that Frank will continue to do well, and Frank certainly does this, as he is finally spoken of everywhere very respectfully as a millionaire and a high-class guy.

In all the years she is in New York my friend never runs into Frank, as Frank is by no means accustomed to visiting the spots where my friend hangs out, but my friend goes to a lot of bother to get acquainted with a doll who is a maid for some time in Frank's town house in East Seventy-fourth Street, and through this doll my friend keeps a pretty fair line on the way Frank lives. In fact, one day when Frank and his family are absent, my friend goes to Frank's house with her friend, just to see what it looks like, and after an hour there my friend has the joint pretty well cased.

So now my friend knows through her friend that on very hot nights such as to-night Frank's family is bound to be at their country place at Port Washington, but that Frank himself is spending the night at his town house, because he wishes to work on a lot of papers of some kind. My friend knows through her friend that all of Frank's servants are at Port Washington, too, except my friend's friend, who is in charge of the town house, and Frank's valet, a guy by the name of Sloggins.

Furthermore, my friend knows through her friend that both her friend and Sloggins have a date to go to a movie at 8.30 o'clock, to be gone a couple of hours, as it seems Frank is very big-hearted about giving his servants time off for such a purpose when he is at home alone; although one night he squawks no little when my friend is out with her friend drinking a little beer, and my friend's friend loses her door key and has to ring the bell to the servants' entrance, and rousts Frank out of a sound sleep.

Naturally, my friend's friend will be greatly astonished if

she ever learns that it is with this key that my friend steps into Frank's house along about nine o'clock to-night. An electric light hangs over the servants' entrance, and my friend locates the button that controls this light just inside the door and turns it off, as my friend figures that maybe Frank and his family will not care to have any of their high-class neighbours, or anyone else, see an old doll who has no better hat than she is wearing, entering or leaving their house at such an hour.

It is an old-fashioned sort of house, four or five stories high, with the library on the third floor in the rear, looking out through French windows over a nice little garden, and my friend finds Frank in the library where she expects to find him, because she is smart enough to figure that a guy who is working on papers is not apt to be doing this work in the cellar.

But Frank is not working on anything when my friend moves in on him. He is dozing in a chair by the window, and, looking at him after all these years, she finds something of a change, indeed. He is much heavier than he is thirty-five years back, and his hair is white, but he looks pretty well to my friend, at that, as she stands there for maybe five minutes watching him. Then he seems to realize somebody is in the room, as sleeping guys will do, for his regular breathing stops with a snort, and he opens his eyes, and looks into my friend's eyes, but without hardly stirring. And finally my friend speaks to Frank as follows:

"Well, Frank," she says, "do you know me?"

"Yes," he says, after a while, "I know you. At first I think maybe you are a ghost, as I once hear something about your being dead. But," he says, "I see now the report is a canard. You are too fat to be a ghost."

Well, of course, this is a most insulting crack, indeed, but my friend passes it off as she does not wish to get in any arguments with Frank at this time. She can see that he is upset more than somewhat and he keeps looking around the room as if he hopes he can see somebody else he can cut in on the conversation. In fact, he acts as if my friend is by no means a welcome visitor.

"Well, Frank," my friend says, very pleasant, "there you are, and here I am. I understand you are now a wealthy and prominent citizen of this town. I am glad to know this, Frank," she says. "You will be surprised to hear that for years and years I pray that you will do well for yourself and become a big guy in every respect, with a nice family, and everything else. I judge my prayers are answered," she says. "I see by the papers that you have two sons at Yale, and a daughter in Vassar, and that your ever-loving wife is getting to be very high mucky-mucky in society. Well, Frank," she says, "I am very glad. I pray something like all this will happen to you."

Now, at such a speech, Frank naturally figures that my friend is all right, at that, and the chances are he also figures that she still has a mighty soft spot in her heart for him, just as she has in the days when she deals them off the arm to keep him in gambling and drinking money. In fact, Frank brightens up somewhat, and he says to my friend like this:

"You pray for my success?" he says. "Why, this is very thoughtful of you, indeed. Well," he says, "I am sitting on top of the world. I have everything to live for."

"Yes," my friend says, "and this is exactly where I pray I will find you. On top of the world," she says, "and with everything to live for. It is where I am when you take my life. It is where I am when you kill me as surely as if you strangle me with your hands. I always pray you will not become a bum," my friend says, "because a bum has nothing to live for, anyway. I want to find you liking to live, so you will hate so much to die."

Naturally, this does not sound so good to Frank, and he begins all of a sudden to shake and shiver and to stutter somewhat.

"Why," he says, "what do you mean? Are you going to kill me?"

"Well," my friend says, "that remains to be seen. Personally," she says, "I will be much obliged if you will kill yourself, but it can be arranged one way or the other. However, I will explain the disadvantages of me killing you.

"The chances are," my friend says, "if I kill you I will be caught and a very great scandal will result, because," she says, "I have on my person the certificate of my marriage to you in Denver, and something tells me you never think to get a divorce. So," she says, "you are a bigamist."

"I can pay," Frank says. "I can pay plenty."

"Furthermore," my friend says, paying no attention to his remark, "I have a sworn statement from Black Emanuel about your transaction with him, for Black Emanuel gets religion before he dies from being shivved by Johnny Mizzoo, and he tries to round himself up by confessing all the sins he can think of, which are quite a lot. It is a very interesting statement," my friend says.

"Now then," she says, "if you knock yourself off you will leave an unsullied, respected name. If I kill you, all the years and effort you have devoted to building up your reputation will go for nothing. You are past sixty," my friend says, "and any way you figure it, you do not have so very far to go. If I kill you," she says, "you will go in horrible disgrace, and everybody around you will feel the disgrace, no matter how much dough you leave them. Your children will hang their heads in shame. Your ever-loving wife will not like it," my friend says.

"I wait on you a long time, Frank," my friend says. "A dozen times in the past twenty years I figure I may as well call on you and close up my case with you, but," she says, "then I always persuade myself to wait a little longer so you would rise higher and higher and life will be a bit sweeter to you. And there you are, Frank," she says, "and here I am."

Well, Frank sits there as if he is knocked plumb out, and he does not answer a word; so finally my friend outs with a large John Roscoe which she is packing in the bosom of her dress, and tosses it in his lap, and speaks as follows:

"Frank," she says, "do not think it will do you any good to pot me in the back when I turn around, because," she says, "you will be worse off than ever. I leave plenty of letters scattered around in case anything happens to me. And remember," she says, "if you do not do this job yourself, I will be back. Sooner or later, I will be back."

So [Dream Street Rose says] my friend goes out of the library and down the stairs, leaving Frank sprawled out in his chair, and when she reaches the first floor she hears what may be a shot in the upper part of the house, and then again maybe only a door slamming. My friend never knows for sure what it is, because a little later as she nears the servants' entrance she hears quite a commotion outside, and a guy cussing a blue streak, and a doll tee-heeing, and pretty soon my friend's friend, the maid, and Sloggins, the valet, come walking in.

Well, my friend just has time to scroonch herself back in a dark corner, and they go upstairs, the guy still cussing and the doll still giggling, and my friend cannot make out what it is all about except that they come home earlier than she figures. So my friend goes tippy-toe out of the servants' entrance, to grab a taxi not far from the house and get away from this neighbourhood, and now you will soon hear of the suicide of a guy who is a millionaire, and it will be all even with my friend.

"Well, Rose," I say, "it is a nice long story, and full of romance and all this and that, and," I say, "of course I will never be ungentlemanly enough to call a lady a liar, but," I say, "if it is not a lie, it will do until a lie comes along."

"All right," Rose says. "Anyway, I tell you about my friend. Now," she says, "I am going where the liquor is better, which can be any other place in town, because," she says, "there is no chance of liquor anywhere being any worse."

So she goes out, making more tracks on Good Time Charley's floor, and Charley speaks most impolitely of her after she goes, and gets out his mop to clean the floor, for one thing about Charley, he is as neat as a pin, and maybe neater.

Well, along toward one o'clock I hear a newsboy in the street outside yelling something I cannot make out, because he is yelling as if he has a mouthful of mush, as newsboys are bound to do. But I am anxious to see what goes in the first race at Belmont, on account of having a first-class tip, so I poke my noggin outside Good Time Charley's and buy a paper, and across the front page, in large letters, it states that the wealthy Mr. Frank Billingsworth McQuiggan knocks himself off by putting a slug through his own noggin.

It says Mr. McQuiggan is found in a chair in his library as dead as a door-nail with the pistol in his lap with which he knocks himself off, and the paper states that nobody can figure what causes Mr. McQuiggan to do such a thing to himself as he is in good health and has plenty of potatoes and is at the peak of his career. Then there is a lot about his history.

When Mr. McQuiggan is a young fellow returning from a visit to the Pacific Coast with about two hundred dollars in his pocket after paying his railroad fare, he meets in the train Jonas Calloway, famous inventor of the Calloway steel process. Calloway, also then young, is desperately in need of funds and he offers Mr. McQuiggan a third interest in his invention for what now seems the paltry sum of one hundred dollars. Mr. McQuiggan accepts the offer and thus paves the way to his own fortune.

I am telling all this to Good Time Charley while he is mopping away at the floor, and finally I come on a paragraph down near the finish which goes like this: "The body was discovered by Mr. McQuiggan's faithful valet, Thomas Sloggins, at eleven o'clock. Mr. McQuiggan was then apparently dead a couple of hours. Sloggins returned home shortly before ten o'clock with another servant after changing his mind about going to a movie. Instead of going to see his employer at once, as is his usual custom, Sloggins went to his own quarters and changed his clothes.

" 'The light over the servants' entrance was out when I returned home,' the valet said, 'and in the darkness I stumbled over some scaffolding and other material left near this entrance by workmen who are to regravel the roof of the house to-morrow, upsetting all over the entranceway a large bucket of tar, much of which got on my apparel when I fell, making a change necessary before going to see Mr. McQuiggan.' "

Well, Good Time Charley keeps on mopping harder than ever, though finally he stops a minute and speaks to me as follows:

"Listen," Charley says, "understand I do not say the guy does not deserve what he gets, and I am by no means hollering copper, but," Charley says, "if he knocks himself off, how does it come the rod is still in his lap where Dream Street Rose says her friend tosses it? Well, never mind," Charley says, "but can you think of something that will remove tar from a wood floor? It positively will not mop off."

He is so surprised he is practically tottering when he leaves the room.

4

THE OLD DOLL'S HOUSE

Now it seems that one cold winter night, a party of residents of Brooklyn comes across the Manhattan Bridge in an automobile wishing to pay a call on a guy by the name of Lance McGowan, who is well known to one and all along Broadway as a coming guy in the business world.

In fact, it is generally conceded that, barring accident, Lance will someday be one of the biggest guys in this country as an importer, and especially as an importer of such merchandise as fine liquors, because he is very bright, and has many good connections throughout the United States and Canada.

Furthermore, Lance McGowan is a nice-looking young guy and he has plenty of ticker, although some citizens say he does not show very sound business judgment in trying to move in on Angie the Ox over in Brooklyn, as Angie the Ox is an importer himself, besides enjoying a splendid trade in other lines, including artichokes and extortion.

Of course Lance McGowan is not interested in artichokes at all, and very little in extortion, but he does not see any reason why he shall not place his imports in a thriving territory such as Brooklyn, especially as his line of merchandise is much superior to anything handled by Angie the Ox.

Anyway, Angie is one of the residents of Brooklyn in the party that wishes to call on Lance McGowan, and besides Angie the party includes a guy by the name of Mockie Max, who is a very prominent character in Brooklyn, and another guy by the name of The Louse Kid, who is not so prominent, but who is considered a very promising young guy in many respects, although personally I think The Louse Kid has a very weak face.

He is supposed to be a wonderful hand with a burlap bag when anybody wishes to put somebody in such a bag, which is considered a great practical joke in Brooklyn, and in fact The Louse Kid has a burlap bag with him on the night in question, and they are figuring on putting Lance McGowan in the bag when they call on him, just for a laugh. Personally, I consider this a very crude form of humour, but then Angie the Ox and the other members of his party are very crude characters, anyway.

Well, it seems they have Lance McGowan pretty well cased, and they know that of an evening along toward ten o'clock he nearly always strolls through West Fifty-fourth Street on his way to a certain spot on Park Avenue that is called the Humming Bird Club, which has a very high-toned clientele, and the reason Lance goes there is because he has a piece of the joint, and furthermore he loves to show off his shape in a tuxedo to the swell dolls.

So these residents of Brooklyn drive in their automobile along this route, and as they roll past Lance McGowan, Angie the Ox and Mockie Max let fly at Lance with a couple of sawed-offs, while The Louse Kid holds the burlap bag, figuring for all I know that Lance will be startled by the sawed-offs and will hop into the bag like a rabbit.

But Lance is by no means a sucker, and when the first blast of slugs from the sawed-offs breezes past him without hitting him, what does he do but hop over a brick wall alongside him and drop into a yard on the other side. So Angie the Ox, and Mockie Max and The Louse Kid get out of their automobile and run up close to the wall themselves because they commence figuring that if Lance McGowan starts popping at them from behind this wall, they will be taking plenty the worst of it, for of course they cannot figure Lance to be strolling about without being rodded up somewhat.

But Lance is by no means rodded up, because a rod is apt to create a bump in his shape when he has his tuxedo on, so the story really begins with Lance McGowan behind the brick wall, practically defenceless, and the reason I know this story is because Lance McGowan tells most of it to me, as Lance knows that I know his real name is Lancelot, and he feels under great obligation to me because I never mention the matter publicly.

Now, the brick wall Lance hops over is a wall around a pretty fair-sized yard, and the yard belongs to an old two-story stone house, and this house is well known to one and all in this man's town as a house of great mystery, and it is pointed out as such by the drivers of sightseeing buses.

This house belongs to an old doll by the name of Miss Abigail Ardsley, and anybody who ever reads the newspapers will tell you that Miss Abigail Ardsley has so many potatoes that it is really painful to think of, especially to people who have no potatoes whatever. In fact, Miss Abigail Ardsley has practically all the potatoes in the world, except maybe a few left over for general circulation.

These potatoes are left to her by her papa, old Waldo Ardsley, who accumulates same in the early days of this town by buying corner real estate very cheap before people realize this real estate will be quite valuable later on for fruit-juice stands and cigar stores.

It seems that Waldo is a most eccentric old bloke, and is very strict with his daughter, and will never let her marry, or even as much as look as if she wishes to marry, until finally she is so old she does not care a cuss about marrying, or anything else, and becomes very eccentric herself.

In fact, Miss Abigail Ardsley becomes so eccentric that she cuts herself off from everybody, and especially from a lot of relatives who are wishing to live off of her, and any time anybody cuts themselves off from such characters they are considered very eccentric, indeed, especially by the relatives. She lives in the big house all alone, except for a couple of old servants, and it is very seldom that anybody sees her around and about, and many strange stories are told of her.

Well, no sooner is he in the yard than Lance McGowan begins looking for a way to get out, and one way he does not wish to get out is over the wall again, because he figures Angie the Ox and his sawed-offs are bound to be waiting for him in Fifty-fourth Street. So Lance looks around to see if there is some way out of the yard in another direction, but it seems there is no such way, and pretty soon he sees the snozzle of a sawed-off come poking over the wall, with the ugly kisser of Angie the Ox behind it, looking for him, and there is Lance McGowan all cornered up in the yard, and not feeling so good, at that.

Then Lance happens to try a door on one side of the house, and the door opens at once and Lance McGowan hastens in to find himself in the living-room of the house. It is a very large living-room with very nice furniture standing around and about, and oil paintings on the walls, and a big old grandfather's clock as high as the ceiling, and statuary here and there. In fact, it is such a nice, comfortable-looking room that Lance McGowan is greatly surprised, as he is expecting to find a regular mystery-house room such as you see in the movies, with cobwebs here and there, and everything all rotted up, and maybe Boris Karloff wandering about making strange noises.

But the only person in this room seems to be a little old doll all dressed in soft white, who is sitting in a low rocking-chair by an open fireplace in which a bright fire is going, doing some tatting.

Well, naturally Lance McGowan is somewhat startled by this scene, and he is figuring that the best thing he can do is to guzzle the old doll before she can commence yelling for the gendarmes, when she looks up at him and gives him a soft smile, and speaks to him in a soft voice, as follows:

"Good evening," the old doll says.

Well, Lance cannot think of any reply to make to this at once, as it is certainly not a good evening for him, and he stands there looking at the old doll, somewhat dazed, when she smiles again and tells him to sit down.

So the next thing Lance knows, he is sitting there in a chair in front of the fireplace chewing the fat with the old doll as pleasant as you please, and of course the old doll is nobody but Miss Abigail Ardsley. Furthermore, she does not seem at all alarmed, or even much surprised, at seeing Lance in her house, but then Lance is never such a looking guy as is apt to scare old dolls, or young dolls either, especially when he is all slicked up.

Of course Lance knows who Miss Abigail Ardsley is, because he often reads stories in the newspapers about her the same as everybody else, and he always figures such a character must be slightly daffy to cut herself off from everybody when she has all the potatoes in the world, and there is so much fun going on, but he is very courteous to her, because after all he is a guest in her home.

"You are young," the old doll says to Lance McGowan, looking him in the kisser. "It is many years since a young man comes through yonder door. Ah, yes," she says, "so many years."

And with this she lets out a big sigh, and looks so very sad that Lance McGowan's heart is touched.

"Forty-five years now," the old doll says in a low voice, as if she is talking to herself. "So young, so handsome, and so good."

And although Lance is in no mood to listen to reminiscences at this time, the next thing he knows he is hearing a very pathetic love story, because it seems that Miss Abigail Ardsley is once all hotted up over a young guy who is nothing but a clerk in her papa's office.

It seems from what Lance McGowan gathers that there is nothing wrong with the young guy that a million bobs will not cure, but Miss Abigail Ardsley's papa is a mean old waffle, and he will never listen to her having any truck with a poor guy, so they dast not let him know how much they love each other.

But it seems that Miss Abigail Ardsley's ever-loving young guy has plenty of moxie, and every night he comes to see her after her papa goes to the hay, and she lets him in through the same side-door Lance McGowan comes through, and they sit by the fire and hold hands, and talk in low tones, and plan what they will do when the young guy makes a scratch.

Then one night it seems Miss Abigail Ardsley's papa has the stomach ache, or some such, and cannot sleep a wink, so he comes wandering downstairs looking for the Jamaica ginger, and catches Miss Abigail Ardsley and her ever-loving guy in a clutch that will win the title for any wrestler that can ever learn it.

Well, this scene is so repulsive to Miss Abigail Ardsley's papa that he is practically speechless for a minute, and then he orders the young guy out of his life in every respect, and tells him never to darken his door again, especially the side-door.

But it seems that by this time a great storm is raging

outside, and Miss Abigail Ardsley begs and pleads with her papa to let the young guy at least remain until the storm subsides, but between being all sored up at the clutching scene he witnesses, and his stomach ache, Mr. Ardsley is very hard-hearted, indeed, and he makes the young guy take the wind.

The next morning the poor young guy is found at the side-door frozen as stiff as a board, because it seems that the storm that is raging is the blizzard of 1888, which is a very famous event in the history of New York, although up to this time Lance McGowan never hears of it before, and does not believe it until he looks the matter up afterwards. It seems from what Miss Abigail Ardsley says that as near as anyone can make out, the young guy must return to the door seeking shelter after wandering about in the storm a while, but of course by this time her papa has the door all bolted up, and nobody hears the young guy.

"And," Miss Abigail Ardsley says to Lance McGowan, after giving him all these details, "I never speak to my papa again as long as he lives, and no other man ever comes in or out of yonder door, or any other door of this house, until your appearance to-night, although," she says, "this side-door is never locked in case such a young man comes seeking shelter."

Then she looks at Lance McGowan in such a way that he

wonders if Miss Abigail Ardsley hears the sawed-offs going when Angie the Ox and Mockie Max are tossing slugs at him, but he is too polite to ask.

Well, all these old-time memories seem to make Miss Abigail Ardsley feel very tough, and by and by she starts to weep, and if there is one thing Lance McGowan cannot stand it is a doll weeping, even if she is nothing but an old doll. So he starts in to cheer Miss Abigail Ardsley up, and he pats her on the arm, and says to her like this:

"Why," Lance says, "I am greatly surprised to hear your statement about the doors around here being so little used. Why, Sweetheart," Lance says, "if I know there is a doll as good-looking as you in the neighbourhood, and a door unlocked, I will be busting in myself every night. Come, come, come," Lance says, "let us talk things over and maybe have a few laughs, because I may have to stick around here a while. Listen, Sweetheart," he says, "do you happen to have a drink in the joint?"

Well, at this Miss Abigail Ardsley dries her eyes, and smiles again, and then she pulls a sort of a rope near her, and in comes a guy who seems about ninety years old, and who seems greatly surprised to see Lance there. In fact, he is so surprised that he is practically tottering when he leaves the room after hearing Miss Abigail Ardsley tell him to bring some wine and sandwiches.

And the wine he brings is such wine that Lance McGowan has half a mind to send some of the lads around afterwards to see if there is any more of it in the joint, especially when he thinks of the unlocked side-door, because he can sell this kind of wine by the carat.

Well, Lance sits there with Miss Abigail Ardsley sipping wine and eating sandwiches, and all the time he is telling her stories of one kind and another, some of which he cleans up a little when he figures they may be a little too snappy for her, and by and by he has her laughing quite heartily indeed.

Finally he figures there is no chance of Angie and his sawed-offs being outside waiting for him, so he says he guesses he will be going, and Miss Abigail Ardsley personally sees him to the door, and this time it is the front door, and as Lance is leaving he thinks of something he once sees a guy do on the stage, and he takes Miss Abigail Ardsley's hand and raises it to his lips and gives it a large kiss, all of which is very surprising to Miss Abigail Ardsley, but more so to Lance McGowan when he gets to thinking about it afterwards.

Just as he figures, there is no one in sight when he gets out in the street, so he goes on over to the Humming Bird Club, where he learns that many citizens are greatly disturbed by his absence, and are wondering if he is in The Louse Kid's burlap bag, for by this time it is pretty well known that

95

Angie the Ox and his fellow citizens of Brooklyn are around and about.

In fact, somebody tells Lance that Angie is at the moment over in Good Time Charley's little speak in West Forty-ninth Street, buying drinks for one and all, and telling how he makes Lance McGowan hop a brick wall, which of course sounds most disparaging of Lance.

Well, while Angie is still buying these drinks, and still speaking of making Lance a brick-wall hopper, all of a sudden the door of Good Time Charley's speak opens and in comes a guy with a Betsy in his hand and this guy throws four slugs into Angie the Ox before anybody can say hello.

Furthermore, the guy throws one slug into Mockie Max, and one slug into The Louse Kid, who are still with Angie the Ox, so the next thing anybody knows there is Angie as dead as a door-nail, and there is Mockie Max even deader than Angie, and there is The Louse making a terrible fuss over a slug in his leg, and nobody can remember what the guy who plugs them looks like, except a couple of stool pigeons who state that the guy looks very much like Lance McGowan.

So what happens but early the next morning Johnny Brannigan, the plain-clothes copper, puts the arm on Lance McGowan for plugging Angie the Ox, and Mockie Max and The Louse Kid, and there is great rejoicing in copper circles generally because at this time the newspapers are weighing in the sacks on the coppers quite some, claiming there is too much lawlessness going on around and about and asking why somebody is not arrested for something.

So the collar of Lance McGowan is water on the wheel of one and all because Lance is so prominent, and anybody will tell you that it looks as if it is a sure thing that Lance will be very severely punished, and maybe sent to the electric chair, although he hires Judge Goldstein, who is one of the surest-footed lawyers in this town, to defend him. But even Judge Goldstein admits that Lance is in a tough spot, especially as the newspapers are demanding justice, and printing long stories about Lance, and pictures of him, and calling him some very uncouth names.

Finally Lance himself commences to worry about his predicament, although up to this time a little thing like being charged with murder in the first degree never bothers Lance very much. And in fact he will not be bothering very much about this particular charge if he does not find the D. A. very fussy about letting him out on bail. In fact, it is nearly two weeks before he lets Lance out on bail, and all this time Lance is in the sneezer, which is a most mortifying situation to a guy as sensitive as Lance.

Well, by the time Lance's trial comes up, you can get 3 to 1 anywhere that he will be convicted, and the price goes up to 5 when the prosecution gets through with its case, and proves by the stool pigeons that at exactly twelve o'clock on the night of January 5th, Lance McGowan steps into Good Time Charley's little speak and plugs Angie the Ox, Mockie Max and The Louse Kid.

Furthermore, several other witnesses who claim they know Lance McGowan by sight testify that they see Lance in the neighbourhood of Good Time Charley's around twelve o'clock, so by the time it comes Judge Goldstein's turn to put on the defence, many citizens are saying that if he can do no more than beat the chair for Lance he will be doing a wonderful job.

Well, it is late in the afternoon when Judge Goldstein gets up and looks all around the courtroom, and without making any opening statement to the jury for the defence, as these mouthpieces usually do, he says like this:

"Call Miss Abigail Ardsley," he says.

At first nobody quite realizes just who Judge Goldstein is calling for, although the name sounds familiar to one and all present who read the newspapers, when in comes a little old doll in a black silk dress that almost reaches the floor, and a black bonnet that makes a sort of a frame for her white hair and face.

Afterwards I read in one of the newspapers that she looks like she steps down out of an old-fashioned ivory miniature and that she is practically beautiful, but of course Miss

Abigail Ardsley has so many potatoes that no newspaper dast to say she looks like an old chromo.

Anyway, she comes into the courtroom surrounded by so many old guys you will think it must be recess at the Old Men's Home, except they are all dressed up in clawhammer coat tails, and high collars, and afterwards it turns out that they are the biggest lawyers in this town, and they all represent Miss Abigail Ardsley one way or another, and they are present to see that her interests are protected, especially from each other.

Nobody ever sees so much bowing and scraping before in a courtroom. In fact, even the judge bows, and although I am only a spectator I find myself bowing too, because the way I look at it, anybody with as many potatoes as Miss Abigail Ardsley is entitled to a general bowing. When she takes the witness-stand, her lawyers grab chairs and move up as close to her as possible, and in the street outside there is practically a riot as word goes around that Miss Abigail Ardsley is in the court, and citizens come running from every which way, hoping to get a peek at the richest old doll in the world.

Well, when all hands finally get settled down a little, Judge Goldstein speaks to Miss Abigail Ardsley as follows:

"Miss Ardsley," he says, "I am going to ask you just two or three questions. Kindly look at this defendant," Judge

Goldstein says, pointing at Lance McGowan, and giving Lance the office to stand up. "Do you recognize him?"

Well, the little old doll takes a gander at Lance, and nods her head yes, and Lance gives her a large smile, and Judge Goldstein says:

"Is he a caller in your home on the night of January fifth?" Judge Goldstein asks.

"He is," Miss Abigail Ardsley says.

"Is there a clock in the living-room in which you receive this defendant?" Judge Goldstein says.

"There is," Miss Abigail Ardsley says. "A large clock," she says. "A grandfather's clock."

"Do you happen to notice," Judge Goldstein says, "and do you now recall the hour indicated by this clock when the defendant leaves your home?"

"Yes," Miss Abigail Ardsley says, "I do happen to notice. It is just twelve o'clock by my clock," she says. "Exactly twelve o'clock," she says.

Well, this statement creates a large sensation in the courtroom, because if it is twelve o'clock when Lance McGowan leaves Miss Abigail Ardsley's house in West Fifty-fourth Street, anybody can see that there is no way he can be in Good Time Charley's little speak over five blocks away at the same minute unless he is a magician, and the judge begins peeking over his specs at the coppers in the courtroom very severe, and the cops begin scowling at the stool pigeons, and I am willing to lay plenty of 6 to 5 that the stools will wish they are never born before they hear the last of this matter from the gendarmes.

Furthermore, the guys from the D. A.'s office who are handling the prosecution are looking much embarrassed, and the jurors are muttering to each other, and right away Judge Goldstein says he moves that the case against his client be dismissed, and the judge says he is in favour of the motion, and he also says he thinks it is high time the gendarmes in this town learn to be a little careful who they are arresting for murder, and the guys from the D. A.'s office do not seem to be able to think of anything whatever to say.

So there is Lance as free as anybody, and as he starts to leave the courtroom he stops by Miss Abigail Ardsley, who is still sitting in the witness-chair surrounded by her mouthpieces, and he shakes her hand and thanks her, and while I do not hear it myself, somebody tells me afterwards that Miss Abigail Ardsley says to Lance in a low voice, like this:

"I will be expecting you again some night, young man," she says.

"Some night, Sweetheart," Lance says, "at twelve o'clock."

And then he goes on about his business, and Miss Abigail

Ardsley goes on about hers, and everybody says it is certainly a wonderful thing that a doll as rich as Miss Abigail Ardsley comes forward in the interests of justice to save a guy like Lance McGowan from a wrong rap.

But of course it is just as well for Lance that Miss Abigail Ardsley does not explain to the court that when she recovers from the shock of the finding of her ever-loving young guy frozen to death, she stops all the clocks in her house at the hour she sees him last, so for forty-five years it is always twelve o'clock in her house.

5

BLOOD PRESSURE

It is maybe eleven-thirty of a Wednesday night, and I am standing at the corner of Forty-eighth Street and Seventh Avenue, thinking about my blood pressure, which is a proposition I never before think much about.

In fact, I never hear of my blood pressure before this Wednesday afternoon when I go around to see Doc Brennan about my stomach, and he puts a gag on my arm and tells me that my blood pressure is higher than a cat's back, and the idea is for me to be careful about what I eat, and to avoid excitement, or I may pop off all of a sudden when I am least expecting it.

"A nervous man such as you with a blood pressure away up in the paint cards must live quietly," Doc Brennan says. "Ten bucks, please," he says.

Well, I am standing there thinking it is not going to be so tough to avoid excitement the way things are around this town right now, and wishing I have my ten bucks back to bet it on Sun Beau in the fourth race at Pimlico the next day, when all of a sudden I look up, and who is in front of me but Rusty Charley.

These are very tough guys indeed.

Now if I have any idea Rusty Charley is coming my way, you can go and bet all the coffee in Java I will be somewhere else at once, for Rusty Charley is not a guy I wish to have any truck with whatever. In fact, I wish no part of him. Furthermore, nobody else in this town wishes to have any part of Rusty Charley, for he is a hard guy indeed. In fact, there is no harder guy anywhere in the world. He is a big wide guy with two large hard hands and a great deal of very bad disposition, and he thinks nothing of knocking people down and stepping on their kissers if he feels like it.

In fact, this Rusty Charley is what is called a gorill, because he is known to often carry a gun in his pants pocket, and sometimes to shoot people down as dead as door-nails with it if he does not like the way they wear their hats—and Rusty Charley is very critical of hats. The chances are Rusty Charley shoots many a guy in this man's town, and those he does not shoot he sticks with his shiv—which is a knife—and the only reason he is not in jail is because he just gets out of it, and the law does not have time to think up something to put him back in again for.

Anyway, the first thing I know about Rusty Charley being in my neighbourhood is when I hear him saying: "Well, well, well, here we are!"

Then he grabs me by the collar, so it is no use of me thinking of taking it on the lam away from there, although

I greatly wish to do so.

"Hello, Rusty," I say, very pleasant. "What is the score?"

"Everything is about even," Rusty says. "I am glad to see you, because I am looking for company. I am over in Philadelphia for three days on business."

"I hope and trust that you do all right for yourself in Philly, Rusty," I say; but his news makes me very nervous, because I am a great hand for reading the papers and I have a pretty good idea what Rusty's business in Philly is. It is only the day before that I see a little item from Philly in the papers about how Gloomy Gus Smallwood, who is a very large operator in the alcohol business there, is guzzled right at his front door.

Of course, I do not know that Rusty Charley is the party who guzzles Gloomy Gus Smallwood, but Rusty Charley is in Philly when Gus is guzzled, and I can put two and two together as well as anybody. It is the same thing as if there is a bank robbery in Cleveland, Ohio, and Rusty Charley is in Cleveland, Ohio, or near there. So I am very nervous, and I figure it is a sure thing my blood pressure is going up every second.

"How much dough do you have on you?" Rusty says. "I am plumb broke."

"I do not have more than a couple of bobs, Rusty," I say. "I pay a doctor ten bucks to-day to find out my blood pressure is very bad. But of course you are welcome to what I have."

"Well, a couple of bobs is no good to high-class guys like you and me," Rusty says. "Let us go to Nathan Detroit's crap game and win some money."

Now, of course, I do not wish to go to Nathan Detroit's crap game; and if I do wish to go there I do not wish to go with Rusty Charley, because a guy is sometimes judged by the company he keeps, especially around crap games, and Rusty Charley is apt to be considered bad company. Anyway, I do not have any dough to shoot craps with, and if I do have dough to shoot craps with, I will not shoot craps with it at all, but will bet it on Sun Beau, or maybe take it home and pay off some of the overhead around my joint, such as rent.

Furthermore, I remember what Doc Brennan tells me about avoiding excitement, and I know there is apt to be excitement around Nathan Detroit's crap game if Rusty Charley goes there, and maybe run my blood pressure up and cause me to pop off very unexpected. In fact, I already feel my blood jumping more than somewhat inside me, but naturally I am not going to give Rusty Charley any argument, so we go to Nathan Detroit's crap game.

This crap game is over a garage in Fifty-second Street this particular night, though sometimes it is over a restaurant in Forty-seventh Street, or in back of a cigar store in Forty-fourth Street. In fact, Nathan Detroit's crap game is apt to be anywhere, because it moves around every night, as there is no sense in a crap game staying in one spot until the coppers find out where it is.

So Nathan Detroit moves his crap game from spot to spot, and citizens wishing to do business with him have to ask where he is every night; and of course almost everybody on Broadway knows this, as Nathan Detroit has guys walking up and down, and around and about, telling the public his address, and giving out the password for the evening.

Well, Jack the Beefer is sitting in an automobile outside the garage in Fifty-second Street when Rusty Charley and I come along, and he says "Kansas City," very low, as we pass, this being the password for the evening; but we do not have to use any password whatever when we climb the stairs over the garage, because the minute Solid John, the doorman, peeks out through his peephole when we knock, and sees Rusty Charley with me, he opens up very quick indeed, and gives us a big castor-oil smile, for nobody in this town is keeping doors shut on Rusty Charley very long.

It is a very dirty room over the garage, and full of smoke, and the crap game is on an old pool table; and around the table, and packed in so close you cannot get a knitting-needle between any two guys with a mawl, are all the high shots in town, for there is plenty of money around at this time, and many citizens are very prosperous. Furthermore, I wish to say there are some very tough guys around the table, too, including guys who will shoot you in the head, or maybe the stomach, and think nothing whatever about the matter.

In fact, when I see such guys as Harry the Horse, from Brooklyn, and Sleepout Sam Levinsky, and Lone Louie, from Harlem, I know this is a bad place for my blood pressure, for these are very tough guys indeed, and are known as such to one and all in this town.

But there they are wedged up against the table with Nick the Greek, Big Nig, Grey John, Okay Okun, and many other high shots, and they all have big coarse G notes in their hands which they are tossing around back and forth as if these G notes are nothing but pieces of waste paper.

On the outside of the mob at the table are a lot of small operators who are trying to cram their fists in between the high shots now and then to get down a bet, and there are also guys present who are called Shylocks, because they will lend you dough when you go broke at the table, on watches or rings, or maybe cuff-links, at very good interest.

Well, as I say, there is no room at the table for as many as one more very thin guy when we walk into the joint, but Rusty Charley lets out a big hello as we enter, and the guys all look around, and the next minute there is space at the table big enough not only for Rusty Charley but for me, too. It really is quite magical the way there is suddenly room for us when there is no room whatever for anybody when we come in.

"Who is the gunner?" Rusty Charley asks, looking all around.

"Why, you are, Charley," Big Nig, the stick man in the game, says very quick, handing Charley a pair of dice, although afterward I hear that his pal is right in the middle of a roll trying to make nine when we step up to the table. Everybody is very quiet, just looking at Charley. Nobody pays any attention to me, because I am known to one and all as a guy who is just around, and nobody figures me in on any part of Charley, although Harry the Horse looks at me once in a way that I know is no good for my blood pressure, or for anybody else's blood pressure as far as this goes.

Well, Charley takes the dice and turns to a little guy in a derby hat who is standing next to him scrooching back so Charley will not notice him, and Charley lifts the derby hat off the little guy's head, and rattles the dice in his hand and chucks them into the hat and goes "Hah!" like crap shooters always do when they are rolling the dice. Then Charley peeks into the hat and says "Ten," although he does not let anybody else look in the hat, not even me, so nobody knows if Charley throws a ten, or what.

But, of course, nobody around is going to up and doubt that Rusty Charley throws a ten, because Charley may figure it is the same thing as calling him a liar, and Charley is such a guy as is apt to hate being called a liar.

Now Nathan Detroit's crap game is what is called a head-and-head game, although some guys call it a fading game, because the guys bet against each other rather than against the bank, or house. It is just the same kind of game as when two guys get together and start shooting craps against each other, and Nathan Detroit does not have to bother with a regular crap table and a layout such as they have in gambling houses. In fact, about all Nathan Detroit has to do with the game is to find a spot, furnish the dice and take his percentage, which is by no means bad.

In such a game as this there is no real action until a guy is out on a point, and then the guys around commence to bet he makes this point, or that he does not make this point, and the odds in any country in the world that a guy does not make a ten with a pair of dice before he rolls seven, is 2 to 1.

Well, when Charley says he rolls ten in the derby hat nobody opens their trap, and Charley looks all around the table, and all of a sudden he sees Jew Louie at one end, although Jew Louie seems to be trying to shrink himself up when Charley's eyes light on him.

"I will take the odds for five C's," Charley says, "and Louie, you get it"—meaning he is letting Louie bet him $1000 to

$500 that he does not make his ten.

Now Jew Louie is a small operator at all times and more of a Shylock than he is a player, and the only reason he is up there against the table at all at this moment is because he moves up to lend Nick the Greek some dough; and ordinarily there is no more chance of Jew Louie betting a thousand to five hundred on any proposition whatever than there is of him giving his dough to the Salvation Army, which is no chance at all. It is a sure thing he will never think of betting a thousand to five hundred a guy will not make ten with the dice, and when Rusty Charley tells Louie he has such a bet, Louie starts trembling all over.

The others around the table do not say a word, and so Charley rattles the dice again in his duke, blows on them, and chucks them into the derby hat and says "Hah!" But, of course, nobody can see in the derby hat except Charley, and he peeks in at the dice and says "Five." He rattles the dice once more and chucks them into the derby and says "Hah!" and then after peeking into the hat at the dice he says "Eight." I am commencing to sweat for fear he may heave a seven in the hat and blow his bet, and I know Charley has no five C's to pay off with, although, of course, I also know Charley has no idea of paying off, no matter what he heaves.

On the next chuck, Charley yells "Money!"—meaning he finally makes his ten, although nobody sees it but him; and he reaches out his hand to Jew Louie, and Jew Louie hands him a big fat G note, very, very slow. In all my life I never see a sadder-looking guy than Louie when he is parting with his dough. If Louie has any idea of asking Charley to let him see the dice in the hat to make sure about the ten, he does not speak about the matter, and as Charley does not seem to wish to show the ten around, nobody else says anything either, probably figuring Rusty Charley isn't a guy who is apt to let anybody question his word, especially over such a small matter as a ten.

"Well," Charley says, putting Louie's G note in his pocket, "I think this is enough for me to-night," and he hands the derby hat back to the little guy who owns it and motions me to come on, which I am glad to do, as the silence in the joint is making my stomach go up and down inside me, and I know this is bad for my blood pressure. Nobody as much as opens his face from the time we go in until we start out, and you will be surprised how nervous it makes you to be in a big crowd with everybody dead still, especially when you figure it a spot that is liable to get hot any minute. It is only just as we get to the door that anybody speaks, and who is it but Jew Louie, who pipes up and says to Rusty Charley like this:

"Charley," he says, "do you make it the hard way?"

Well, everybody laughs, and we go on out, but I never

hear myself whether Charley makes his ten with a six and a four, or with two fives—which is the hard way to make a ten with the dice—although I often wonder about the matter afterward.

I am hoping that I can now get away from Rusty Charley and go on home, because I can see he is the last guy in the world to have around a blood pressure, and, furthermore, that people may get the wrong idea of me if I stick around with him, but when I suggest going to Charley, he seems to be hurt.

"Why," Charley says, "you are a fine guy to be talking of quitting a pal just as we are starting out. You will certainly stay with me because I like company, and we will go down to Ikey the Pig's and play stuss. Ikey is an old friend of mine, and I owe him a complimentary play."

Now, of course, I do not wish to go to Ikey the Pig's, because it is a place away downtown, and I do not wish to play stuss, because this is a game which I am never able to figure out myself, and, furthermore, I remember Doc Brennan says I ought to get a little sleep now and then; but I see no use in hurting Charley's feelings, especially as he is apt to do something drastic to me if I do not go.

So he calls a taxi, and we start downtown for Ikey the Pig's, and the jockey who is driving the short goes so fast that it makes my blood pressure go up a foot to a foot and a half from the way I feel inside, although Rusty Charley pays no attention to the speed. Finally I stick my head out the window and ask the jockey to please take it a little easy, as I wish to get where I am going all in one piece, but the guy only keeps busting along.

We are at the corner of Nineteenth and Broadway when all of a sudden Rusty Charley yells at the jockey to pull up a minute, which the guy does. Then Charley steps out of the cab and says to the jockey like this:

"When a customer asks you to take it easy, why do you not be nice and take it easy? Now see what you get."

And Rusty Charley hauls off and clips the jockey a punch on the chin that knocks the poor guy right off the seat into the street, and then Charley climbs into the seat himself and away we go with Charley driving, leaving the guy stretched out as stiff as a board. Now Rusty Charley once drives a short for a living himself, until the coppers get an idea that he is not always delivering his customers to the right address, especially such as may happen to be drunk when he gets them, and he is a pretty fair driver, but he only looks one way, which is straight ahead.

Personally, I never wish to ride with Charley in a taxicab under any circumstances, especially if he is driving, because he certainly drives very fast. He pulls up a block from Ikey the Pig's, and says we will leave the short there until somebody finds it and turns it in, but just as we are walking away from the short up steps a copper in uniform and claims we cannot park the short in this spot without a driver.

Well, Rusty Charley just naturally hates to have coppers give him any advice, so what does he do but peek up and down the street to see if anybody is looking, and then haul off and clout the copper on the chin, knocking him bow-legged. I wish to say I never see a more accurate puncher than Rusty Charley, because he always connects with that old button. As the copper tumbles, Rusty Charley grabs me by the arm and starts me running up a side street, and after we go about a block we dodge into Ikey the Pig's.

It is what is called a stuss house, and many prominent citizens of the neighbourhood are present playing stuss. Nobody seems any too glad to see Rusty Charley, although Ikey the Pig lets on he is tickled half to death. This Ikey the Pig is a short fat-necked guy who will look very natural at New Year's, undressed, and with an apple in his mouth, but it seems he and Rusty Charley are really old-time friends, and think fairly well of each other in spots.

But I can see that Ikey the Pig is not so tickled when he finds Charley is there to gamble, although Charley flashes his G note at once, and says he does not mind losing a little dough to Ikey just for old time's sake. But I judge Ikey the Pig knows he is never going to handle Charley's G note, because Charley puts it back in his pocket and it never comes out again even though Charley gets off loser playing stuss right away.

Well, at five o'clock in the morning, Charley is stuck one hundred and thirty G's, which is plenty of money even when a guy is playing on his muscle, and of course Ikey the Pig knows there is no chance of getting one hundred and thirty cents off of Rusty Charley, let alone that many thousands. Everybody else is gone by this time and Ikey wishes to close up. He is willing to take Charley's marker for a million if necessary to get Charley out, but the trouble is in stuss a guy is entitled to get back a percentage of what he loses, and Ikey figures Charley is sure to wish this percentage even if he gives a marker, and the percentage will wreck Ikey's joint.

Furthermore, Rusty Charley says he will not quit loser under such circumstances because Ikey is his friend, so what happens but Ikey finally sends out and hires a cheater by the name of Dopey Goldberg, who takes to dealing the game and in no time he has Rusty Charley even by cheating in Rusty Charley's favour.

Personally, I do not pay much attention to the play, but grab myself a few winks of sleep in a chair in a corner, and the rest seems to help my blood pressure no little. In fact, I am not noticing my blood pressure at all when Rusty Charley and I get out of Ikey the Pig's, because I figure Charley will let me go home and I can go to bed. But although it is six o'clock, and coming on broad daylight when we leave Ikey's, Charley is still full of zing, and nothing will do him but we must go to a joint that is called the Bohemian Club.

Well, this idea starts my blood pressure going again, because the Bohemian Club is nothing but a deadfall where guys and dolls go when there is positively no other place in town open, and it is run by a guy by the name of Knife O'Halloran, who comes from down around Greenwich Village and is considered a very bad character. It is well known to one and all that a guy is apt to lose his life in Knife O'Halloran's any night, even if he does nothing more than drink Knife O'Halloran's liquor.

But Rusty Charley insists on going there, so naturally I go with him; and at first everything is very quiet and peaceful, except that a lot of guys and dolls in evening clothes, who wind up there after being in the night clubs all night, are yelling in one corner of the joint. Rusty Charley and Knife O'Halloran are having a drink together out of a bottle which Knife carries in his pocket, so as not to get it mixed up with the liquor he sells his customers, and are cutting up old touches of the time when they run with the Hudson Dusters together, when all of a sudden in comes four coppers in plain clothes.

Now these coppers are off duty and are meaning no harm

to anybody, and are only wishing to have a dram or two before going home, and the chances are they will pay no attention to Rusty Charley if he minds his own business, although of course they know who he is very well indeed and will take great pleasure in putting the old sleeve on him if they only have a few charges against him, which they do not. So they do not give him a tumble. But if there is one thing Rusty Charley hates it is a copper, and he starts eyeing them from the minute they sit down at a table, and by and by I hear him say to Knife O'Halloran like this:

"Knife," Charley says, "what is the most beautiful sight in the world?"

"I do not know, Charley," Knife says. "What is the most beautiful sight in the world?"

"Four dead coppers in a row," Charley says.

Well, at this I personally ease myself over toward the door, because I never wish to have any trouble with coppers and especially with four coppers, so I do not see everything that comes off. All I see is Rusty Charley grabbing at the big foot which one of the coppers kicks at him, and then everybody seems to go into a huddle, and the guys and dolls in evening dress start squawking, and my blood pressure goes up to maybe a million.

I get outside the door, but I do not go away at once as anybody with any sense will do, but stand there listening to what is going on inside, which seems to be nothing more than a loud noise like ker-bump, ker-bump, ker-bump. I am not afraid there will be any shooting, because as far as Rusty Charley is concerned he is too smart to shoot any coppers, which is the worst thing a guy can do in this town, and the coppers are not likely to start any blasting because they will not wish it to come out that they are in a joint such as the Bohemian Club off duty. So I figure they will all just take it out in pulling and hauling.

Finally the noise inside dies down, and by and by the door opens and out comes Rusty Charley, dusting himself off here and there with his hands and looking very much pleased indeed, and through the door before it flies shut again I catch a glimpse of a lot of guys stretched out on the floor. Furthermore, I can still hear guys and dolls hollering.

"Well, well," Rusty Charley says, "I am commencing to think you take the wind on me, and am just about to get mad at you, but here you are. Let us go away from this joint, because they are making so much noise inside you cannot hear yourself think. Let us go to my joint and make my old woman cook us up some breakfast, and then we can catch some sleep. A little ham and eggs will not be bad to take right now."

Well, naturally ham and eggs are appealing to me no little at this time, but I do not care to go to Rusty Charley's joint.

As far as I am personally concerned, I have enough of Rusty Charley to do me a long, long time, and I do not care to enter into his home life to any extent whatever, although to tell the truth I am somewhat surprised to learn he has any such life. I believe I do once hear that Rusty Charley marries one of the neighbours' children, and that he lives somewhere over on Tenth Avenue in the Forties, but nobody really knows much about this, and everybody figures if it is true his wife must lead a terrible dog's life.

But while I do not wish to go to Charley's joint, I cannot very well refuse a civil invitation to eat ham and eggs, especially as Charley is looking at me in a very much surprised way because I do not seem so glad, and I can see that it is not everyone that he invites to his joint. So I thank him, and say there is nothing I will enjoy more than ham and eggs such as his old woman will cook for us, and by and by we are walking along Tenth Avenue up around Forty-fifth Street.

It is still fairly early in the morning, and business guys are opening up their joints for the day, and little children are skipping along the sidewalks going to school and laughing tee-hee, and old dolls are shaking bedclothes and one thing and another out of the windows of the tenement houses, but when they spot Rusty Charley and me everybody becomes very quiet indeed, and I can see that Charley is greatly respected in his own neighbourhood. The business guys hurry into their joints, and the little children stop skipping and tee-heeing and go tip-toeing along, and the old dolls yank in their noodles, and a great quiet comes to the street. In fact, about all you can hear is the heels of Rusty Charley and me hitting on the sidewalk.

There is an ice wagon with a couple of horses hitched to it standing in front of a store, and when he sees the horses Rusty Charley seems to get a big idea. He stops and looks the horses over very carefully, although as far as I can see they are nothing but horses, and big and fat, and sleepy-looking horses, at that. Finally Rusty Charley says to me like this:

"When I am a young guy," he says, "I am a very good puncher with my right hand, and often I hit a horse on the skull with my fist and knock it down. I wonder," he says, "if I lose my punch. The last copper I hit back there gets up twice on me."

Then he steps up to one of the ice-wagon horses and hauls off and biffs it right between the eyes with a right-hand smack that does not travel more than four inches, and down goes old Mister Horse to his knees looking very much surprised indeed. I see many a hard puncher in my day including Dempsey when he really can punch, but I never see a harder punch than Rusty Charley gives this horse.

Well, the ice-wagon driver comes busting out of the store

all heated up over what happens to his horse, but he cools out the minute he sees Rusty Charley, and goes on back into the store leaving the horse still taking a count, while Rusty Charley and I keep walking. Finally we come to the entrance of a tenement house that Rusty Charley says is where he lives, and in front of this house is a wop with a push-cart loaded with fruit and vegetables and one thing and another, which Rusty Charley tips over as we go into the house, leaving the wop yelling very loud, and maybe cussing us in wop for all I know. I am very glad, personally, we finally get somewhere, because I can feel that my blood pressure is getting worse every minute I am with Rusty Charley.

We climb two nights of stairs, and then Charley opens a door and we step into a room where there is a pretty little red-headed doll about knee high to a flivver, who looks as if she may just get out of the hay, because her red hair is flying around every which way on her head, and her eyes seem still gummed up with sleep. At first I think she is a very cute sight indeed, and then I see something in her eyes that tells me this doll, whoever she is, is feeling very hostile to one and all.

"Hello, tootsie," Rusty Charley says. "How about some ham and eggs for me and my pal here? We are all tired out going around and about."

Well, the little red-headed doll just looks at him without

saying a word. She is standing in the middle of the floor with one hand behind her, and all of a sudden she brings this hand around, and what does she have in it but a young baseball bat, such as kids play ball with, and which cost maybe two bits; and the next thing I know I hear something go ker-bap, and I can see she smacks Rusty Charley on the side of the noggin with the bat.

Naturally I am greatly horrified at this business, and figure Rusty Charley will kill her at once, and then I will be in a jam for witnessing the murder and will be held in jail several years like all witnesses to anything in this man's town; but Rusty Charley only falls into a big rocking-chair in a corner of the room and sits there with one hand to his head, saying, "Now hold on, tootsie," and "Wait a minute there, honey." I recollect hearing him say, "We have company for breakfast," and then the little red-headed doll turns on me and gives me a look such as I will always remember, although I smile at her very pleasant and mention it is a nice morning.

Finally she says to me like this:

"So you are the trambo who keeps my husband out all night, are you, you trambo?" she says, and with this she starts for me, and I start for the door; and by this time my blood pressure is all out of whack, because I can see that Mrs. Rusty Charley is excited more than somewhat. I get my hand on the knob and just then something hits me alongside the noggin, which I afterward figure must be the baseball bat, although I remember having a sneaking idea the roof caves in on me.

How I get the door open I do not know, because I am very dizzy in the head and my legs are wobbling, but when I think back over the situation I remember going down a lot of steps very fast, and by and by the fresh air strikes me, and I figure I am in the clear. But all of a sudden I feel another strange sensation back of my head and something goes plop against my noggin, and I figure at first that maybe my blood pressure runs up so high that it squirts out the top of my bean. Then I peek around over my shoulder just once to see that Mrs. Rusty Charley is standing beside the wop peddler's cart snatching fruit and vegetables of one kind and another off the cart and chucking them at me.

But what she hits me with back of the head is not an apple, or a peach, or a rutabaga, or a cabbage, or even a casaba melon, but a brickbat that the wop has on his cart to weight down the paper sacks in which he sells his goods. It is this brickbat which makes a lump on the back of my head so big that Doc Brennan thinks it is a tumour when I go to him the next day about my stomach, and I never tell him any different.

"But," Doc Brennan says, when he takes my blood pressure again, "your pressure is down below normal now, and as far

125

as it is concerned you are in no danger whatever. It only goes to show what just a little bit of quiet living will do for a guy," Doc Brennan says. "Ten bucks, please," he says.

6

THE BLOODHOUNDS OF BROADWAY

One morning along about four bells, I am standing in front of Mindy's restaurant on Broadway with a guy by the name of Regret, who has this name because it seems he wins a very large bet the year the Whitney filly, Regret, grabs the Kentucky Derby, and can never forget it, which is maybe because it is the only very large bet he ever wins in his life.

What this guy's real name is I never hear, and anyway names make no difference to me, especially on Broadway, because the chances are that no matter what name a guy has, it is not his square name. So, as far as I am concerned, Regret is as good a name as any other for this guy I am talking about, who is a fat guy, and very gabby, though generally he is talking about nothing but horses, and how he gets beat three dirty noses the day before at Belmont, or wherever the horses are running.

In all the years I know Regret he must get beat ten thousand noses, and always they are dirty noses, to hear him tell it. In fact, I never once hear him say he is beat a clean nose, but of course this is only the way horse-racing guys talk. What Regret does for a living besides betting on horses I do not know, but he seems to do pretty well at it, because he is always around and about, and generally well dressed, and with a lot of big cigars sticking up out of his vest pocket.

It is generally pretty quiet on Broadway along about four bells in the morning, because at such an hour the citizens are mostly in speakeasies, and night clubs, and on this morning I am talking about it is very quiet, indeed, except for a guy by the name of Marvin Clay hollering at a young doll because she will not get into a taxicab with him to go to his apartment. But of course Regret and I do not pay much attention to such a scene, except that Regret remarks that the young doll seems to have more sense than you will expect to see in a doll loose on Broadway at four bells in the morning, because it is well known to one and all that any doll who goes to Marvin Clay's apartment, either has no brains whatever, or wishes to go there.

This Marvin Clay is a very prominent society guy, who is a great hand for hanging out in night clubs, and he has plenty of scratch which comes down to him from his old man, who makes it out of railroads and one thing and another. But Marvin Clay is a most obnoxious character, being loud and ungentlemanly at all times, on account of having all this scratch, and being always very rough and abusive with young dolls such as work in night clubs, and who have to stand for such treatment from Marvin Clay because he is a very good customer.

He is generally in evening clothes, as he is seldom around and about except in the evening, and he is maybe fifty years old, and has a very ugly mugg, which is covered with blotches, and pimples, but of course a guy who has so much scratch as Marvin Clay does not have to be so very handsome, at that, and he is very welcome indeed wherever he goes on Broadway. Personally, I wish no part of such a guy as Marvin Clay, although I suppose in my time on Broadway I must see a thousand guys like him, and there will always be guys like Marvin Clay on Broadway as long as they have old men to make plenty of scratch out of railroads to keep them going.

Well, by and by Marvin Clay gets the doll in the taxicab, and away they go, and it is all quiet again on Broadway, and Regret and I stand there speaking of this and that, and one thing and another, when along comes a very strange-looking guy leading two very strange-looking dogs. The guy is so thin I figure he must be about two pounds lighter than a stack of wheats. He has a long nose, and a sad face, and he is wearing a floppy old black felt hat, and he has on a flannel shirt, and baggy corduroy pants, and a see-more coat, which is a coat that lets you see more hip pockets than coat.

Personally, I never see a stranger-looking guy on Broadway,

and I wish to say I see some very strange-looking guys on Broadway in my day. But if the guy is strange-looking, the dogs are even stranger-looking, because they have big heads, and jowls that hang down like an old-time faro bank dealer's, and long ears the size of bed sheets. Furthermore, they have wrinkled faces, and big, round eyes that seem so sad I half expect to see them bust out crying.

The dogs are a sort of black and yellow in colour, and have long tails, and they are so thin you can see their ribs sticking out of their hides. I can see at once that the dogs and the guy leading them can use a few Hamburgers very nicely, but then so can a lot of other guys on Broadway at this time, leaving out the dogs.

Well, Regret is much interested in the dogs right away, because he is a guy who is very fond of animals of all kinds, and nothing will do but he must stop the guy and start asking questions about what sort of dogs they are, and in fact I am also anxious to hear myself, because while I see many a pooch in my time I never see anything like these.

"They is bloodhounds," the sad-looking guy says in a very sad voice, and with one of these accents such as Southern guys always have. "They is man-tracking bloodhounds from Georgia."

Now of course both Regret and me know what bloodhounds are because we see such animals chasing Eliza across the ice in Uncle Tom's Cabin when we are young squirts, but this is the first time either of us meet up with any bloodhounds personally, especially on Broadway. So we get to talking quite a bit to the guy, and his story is as sad as his face, and makes us both feel very sorry for him.

In fact, the first thing we know we have him and the bloodhounds in Mindy's and are feeding one and all big steaks, although Mindy puts up an awful squawk about us bringing the dogs in, and asks us what we think he is running, anyway. When Regret starts to tell him, Mindy says never mind, but not to bring any more Shetland ponies into his joint again as long as we live.

Well, it seems that the sad-looking guy's name is John Wangle, and he comes from a town down in Georgia where his uncle is the high sheriff, and one of the bloodhounds' name is Nip, and the other Tuck, and they are both trained from infancy to track down guys such as lags who escape from the county pokey, and bad niggers, and one thing and another, and after John Wangle gets the kinks out of his belly on Mindy's steaks, and starts talking good, you must either figure him a high-class liar, or the hounds the greatest man-trackers the world ever sees.

Now, looking at the dogs after they swallow six big sirloins apiece, and a lot of matzoths, which Mindy has left over from the Jewish holidays, and a job lot of goulash from the dinner bill, and some other odds and ends, the best I can figure them is hearty eaters, because they are now lying down on the floor with their faces hidden behind their ears, and are snoring so loud you can scarcely hear yourself think.

How John Wangle comes to be in New York with these bloodhounds is quite a story, indeed. It seems that a New York guy drifts into John's old home town in Georgia when the bloodhounds are tracking down a bad nigger, and this guy figures it will be a wonderful idea to take John Wangle and the dogs to New York and hire them out to the movies to track down the villains in the pictures. But when they get to New York, it seems the movies have other arrangements for tracking down their villains, and the guy runs out of scratch and blows away, leaving John Wangle and the bloodhounds stranded.

So here John Wangle is with Nip and Tuck in New York, and they are all living together in one room in a tenement house over in West Forty-ninth Street, and things are pretty tough with them, because John does not know how to get back to Georgia unless he walks, and he hears the walking is no good south of Roanoke, When I ask him why he does not write to his uncle, the high sheriff down there in Georgia, John Wangle says there are two reasons, one being that he cannot write, and the other that his uncle cannot read.

Then I ask him why he does not sell the bloodhounds, and

he says it is because the market for bloodhounds is very quiet in New York, and furthermore if he goes back to Georgia without the bloodhounds his uncle is apt to knock his ears down. Anyway, John Wangle says he personally loves Nip and Tuck very dearly, and in fact he says it is only his great love for them that keeps him from eating one or the other, and maybe both, the past week, when his hunger is very great indeed.

Well, I never before see Regret so much interested in any situation as he is in John Wangle and the bloodhounds, but personally I am getting very tired of them, because the one that is called Nip finally wakes up and starts chewing on my leg, thinking it is maybe more steak, and when I kick him in the snoot, John Wangle scowls at me, and Regret says only very mean guys are unkind to dumb animals.

But to show you that John Wangle and his bloodhounds are not so dumb, they come moseying along past Mindy's every morning after this at about the same time, and Regret is always there ready to feed them, although he now has to take the grub out on the sidewalk, as Mindy will not allow the hounds in the joint again. Naturally Nip and Tuck become very fond of Regret, but they are by no means as fond of him as John Wangle, because John is commencing to fat up very nicely, and the bloodhounds are also taking on weight.

Now what happens but Regret does not show up in front of Mindy's for several mornings hand running, because it seems that Regret makes a very nice score for himself one day against the horses, and buys himself a brand-new Tuxedo, and starts stepping out around the night clubs, and especially around Miss Missouri Martin's Three Hundred Club, where there are many beautiful young dolls who dance around with no more clothes on them than will make a pad for a crutch, and it is well known that Regret dearly loves such scenes.

Furthermore, I hear reports around and about of Regret becoming very fond of a doll by the name of Miss Lovey Lou, who works in Miss Missouri Martin's Three Hundred Club, and of him getting in some kind of a jam with Marvin Clay over this doll, and smacking Marvin Clay in the kisser, so I figure Regret is getting a little simple, as guys who hang around Broadway long enough are bound to do. Now, when John Wangle and Nip and Tuck come around looking for a hand-out, there is nothing much doing for them, as nobody else around Mindy's feels any great interest in bloodhounds, especially such interest as will cause them to buy steaks, and soon Nip and Tuck are commencing to look very sad again, and John Wangle is downcast more than somewhat.

It is early morning again, and warm, and a number of citizens are out in front of Mindy's as usual, breathing the fresh air, when along comes a police inspector by the name of

McNamara, who is a friend of mine, with a bunch of plain-clothes coppers with him, and Inspector McNamara tells me he is on his way to investigate a situation in an apartment house over in West Fifty-fourth Street, about three blocks away, where it seems a guy is shot; and not having anything else to do, I go with them, although as a rule I do not care to associate with coppers, because it arouses criticism from other citizens.

Well, who is the guy who is shot but Marvin Clay, and he is stretched out on the floor in the living-room of his apartment in evening clothes, with his shirt front covered with blood, and after Inspector McNamara takes a close peek at him, he sees that Marvin Clay is plugged smack dab in the chest, and that he seems to be fairly dead. Furthermore, there seems to be no clue whatever to who does the shooting, and Inspector McNamara says it is undoubtedly a very great mystery, and will be duck soup for the newspapers, especially as they do not have a good shooting mystery for several days.

Well, of course all this is none of my business, but all of a sudden I happen to think of John Wangle and his bloodhounds, and it seems to me it will be a great opportunity for them, so I say to the Inspector as follows:

"Listen, Mac," I say, "there is a guy here with a pair of man-tracking bloodhounds from Georgia who are very expert in tracking down matters such as this, and," I say, "maybe they can track down the rascal who shoots Marvin Clay, because the trail must be hotter than mustard right now."

Well, afterwards I hear there is much indignation over my suggestion, because many citizens feel that the party who shoots Marvin Clay is entitled to more consideration than being tracked with bloodhounds. In fact, some think the party is entitled to a medal, but this discussion does not come up until later.

Anyway, at first the Inspector does not think much of my idea, and the other coppers are very sceptical, and claim that the best way to do under the circumstances is to arrest everybody in sight and hold them as material witnesses for a month or so, but the trouble is there is nobody in sight to arrest at this time, except maybe me, and the Inspector is a broad-minded guy, and finally he says all right, bring on the bloodhounds.

So I hasten back to Mindy's, and sure enough John Wangle and Nip and Tuck are out on the sidewalk peering at every passing face in the hope that maybe one of these faces will belong to Regret. It is a very pathetic sight, indeed, but John Wangle cheers up when I explain about Marvin Clay to him, and hurries back to the apartment house with me so fast that he stretches Nip's neck a foot, and is pulling Tuck along on his stomach half the time.

Well, when we get back to the apartment, John Wangle

leads Nip and Tuck up to Marvin Clay, and they snuffle him all over, because it seems bloodhounds are quite accustomed to dead guys. Then John Wangle unhooks their leashes, and yells something at them, and the hounds begin snuffling all around and about the joint, with Inspector McNamara and the other coppers watching with great interest. All of a sudden Nip and Tuck go busting out of the apartment and into the street, with John Wangle after them, and all the rest of us after John Wangle. They head across Fifty-fourth Street back to Broadway, and the next thing anybody knows they are doing plenty of snuffling around in front of Mindy's.

By and by they take off up Broadway with their snozzles to the sidewalk, and we follow them very excited, because even the coppers now admit that it seems to be a sure thing they are red hot on the trail of the party who shoots Marvin Clay. At first Nip and Tuck are walking, but pretty soon they break into a lope, and there we are loping after them, John Wangle, the Inspector, and me, and the coppers.

Naturally, such a sight as this attracts quite some attention as we go along from any citizens stirring at this hour, and by and by milkmen are climbing down off their wagons, and scavenger guys are leaving their trucks standing where they are, and newsboys are dropping everything, and one and all joining in the chase, so by the time we hit Broadway and Fifty-sixth there is quite a delegation following the hounds with John Wangle in front, just behind Nip and Tuck, and yelling at them now and then as follows:

"Hold to it, boys!"

At Fifty-sixth the hounds turn east off Broadway and stop at the door of what seems to be an old garage, this door being closed very tight, and Nip and Tuck seem to wish to get through this door, so the Inspector and the coppers kick the door open, and who is in the garage having a big crap game but many prominent citizens of Broadway. Naturally, these citizens are greatly astonished at seeing the bloodhounds, and the rest of us, especially the coppers, and they start running every which way trying to get out of the joint, because crap shooting is quite illegal in these parts.

But the Inspector only says Ah-ha, and starts jotting down names in a note-book as if it is something he will refer to later, and Nip and Tuck are out of the joint almost as soon as they get in and are snuffling on down Fifty-sixth. They stop at four more doors in Fifty-sixth Street along, and when the coppers kick open these doors they find they are nothing but speakeasies, although one is a hop joint, and the citizens in these places are greatly put out by the excitement, especially as Inspector McNamara keeps jotting down things in his note-book.

Finally the Inspector starts glaring very fiercely at the coppers with us, and anybody can see that he is much displeased to find so much illegality going on in this district, and the coppers are starting in to hate Nip and Tuck quite freely, and one copper says to me like this:

"Why," he says, "these mutts are nothing but stool pigeons."

Well, naturally, the noise of John Wangle's yelling, and the gabble of the mob following the hounds makes quite a disturbance, and arouses many of the neighbours in the apartment houses and hotels in the side streets, especially as this is summer, and most everybody has their windows open.

In fact, we see many tousled heads poked out of windows, and hear guys and dolls inquiring as follows:

"What is going on?"

It seems that when word gets about that bloodhounds are tracking down a wrongdoer it causes great uneasiness all through the Fifties, and in fact I afterwards hear that three guys are taken to the Polyclinic suffering with broken ankles and severe bruises from hopping out of windows in the hotels we pass in the chase, or from falling off of fire-escapes.

Well, all of a sudden Nip and Tuck swing back into Seventh Avenue, and pop into the entrance of a small apartment house, and go tearing up the stairs to the first floor, and when we get there these bloodhounds are scratching vigorously at the door of Apartment B-2, and going woofle-woofle, and we are all greatly excited, indeed, but the door opens, and who is standing there but a doll by the name of Maud Milligan, who is well known to one and all as the ever-loving doll of Big Nig, the crap shooter, who is down in Hot Springs at this time taking the waters, or whatever it is guys take in Hot Springs.

Now, Maud Milligan is not such a doll as I will care to have any part of, being red-headed, and very stern, and I am glad Nip and Tuck do not waste any more time in her apartment than it takes for them to run through her living-room and across her bed, because Maud is commencing to put the old eye on such of us present as she happens to know. But Nip and Tuck are in and out of the joint before you can say scat, because it is only a two-room apartment, at that, and we are on our way down the stairs and back into Seventh Avenue again while Inspector McNamara is still jotting down something in his note-book.

Finally, where do these hounds wind up, with about four hundred citizens behind them, and everybody perspiring quite freely indeed from the exercise, but at the door of Miss Missouri Martin's Three Hundred Club, and the doorman, who is a guy by the name of Soldier Sweeney, tries to shoo them away, but Nip runs between the Soldier's legs and upsets him, and Tuck steps in the Soldier's eye in trotting over him, and most of the crowd behind the hounds tread on him in passing, so the old Soldier is pretty well flattened out at the finish.

Nip and Tuck are now more excited than somewhat, and are going zoople-zoople in loud voices as they bust into the Three Hundred Club with John Wangle and the law, and all these citizens behind them. There is a very large crowd present and Miss Missouri Martin is squatted on the back of a chair in the middle of the dance floor when we enter, and is about to start her show when she sees the mob surge in, and at first she is greatly pleased because she thinks new business arrives, and if there is anything Miss Missouri Martin dearly loves, it is new business.

But before she can say hello, sucker, or anything else whatever, Nip runs under her chair, thinking maybe he is a dachshund, and dumps Miss Missouri Martin on the dance floor, and she lays there squawking no little, while the next thing anybody knows, Nip and Tuck are over in one corner of the joint, and are eagerly crawling up and down a fat guy who is sitting there with a doll alongside of him, and who is the fat guy but Regret!

Well, as Nip and Tuck rush at Regret he naturally gets up to defend himself, but they both hit him at the same time, and over he goes on top of the doll who is with him, and who seems to be nobody but Miss Lovey Lou. She is getting quite a squashing with Regret's heft spread out over her, and she is screaming quite some, especially when Nip lets out a foot of tongue and washes her make-up off her face, reaching for Regret. In fact, Miss Lovey Lou seems to be more afraid of the bloodhounds than she does of being squashed to death, for when John Wangle and I hasten to her rescue and pull her out from under Regret she is moaning as follows:

"Oh, do not let them devour me—I will confess."

Well, as nobody but me and John Wangle seem to hear this crack, because everybody else is busy trying to split out Regret and the bloodhounds, and as John Wangle does not seem to understand what Miss Lovey Lou is mumbling about, I shove her off into the crowd, and on back into the kitchen, which is now quite deserted, what with all the help being out watching the muss in the corner, and I say to her like this:

"What is it you confess?" I say. "Is it about Marvin Clay?"

"Yes," she says. "It is about him. He is a pig," she says. "I shoot him, and I am glad of it. He is not satisfied with what he does to me two years ago, but he tries his deviltry on my baby sister. He has her in his apartment and when I find it out and go to get her, he says he will not let her go. So I shoot him. With my brother's pistol," she says, "and I take my baby sister home with me, and I hope he is dead, and gone where he belongs."

"Well, now," I say, "I am not going to give you any argument as to where Marvin Clay belongs, but," I say, "you skip out of here and go on home, and wait until we can do something about this situation, while I go back and help Regret, who seems to be in a tough spot."

"Oh, do not let these terrible dogs eat him up," she says, and with this she takes the breeze and I return to the other room to find there is much confusion indeed, because it seems that Regret is now very indignant at Nip and Tuck, especially when he discovers that one of them plants his big old paw right on the front of Regret's shirt bosom, leaving a dirty mark. So when he struggles to his feet, Regret starts letting go with both hands, and he is by no means a bad puncher for a guy who does not do much punching as a rule. In fact, he flattens Nip with a right-hand to the jaw, and knocks Tuck plumb across the room with a left hook.

Well, poor Tuck slides over the slick dance floor into Miss Missouri Martin just as she is getting to her feet again, and bowls her over once more, but Miss Missouri Martin is also indignant by this time, and she gets up and kicks Tuck in a most unladylike manner. Of course, Tuck does not know so much about Miss Martin, but he is pretty sure his old friend Regret is only playing with him, so back he goes to Regret with his tongue out, and his tail wagging, and there is no telling how long this may go on if John Wangle does not

143

step in and grab both hounds, while Inspector McNamara puts the arm on Regret and tells him he is under arrest for shooting Marvin Clay.

Well, of course everybody can see at once that Regret must be the guilty party all right, especially when it is remembered that he once had trouble with Marvin Clay, and one and all present are looking at Regret in great disgust, and saying you can see by his face that he is nothing but a degenerate type.

Furthermore, Inspector McNamara makes a speech to Miss Missouri Martin's customers in which he congratulates John Wangle and Nip and Tuck on their wonderful work in tracking down this terrible criminal and at the same time putting in a few boosts for the police department, while Regret stands there paying very little attention to what the Inspector is saying, but trying to edge himself over close enough to Nip and Tuck to give them the old foot.

Well, the customers applaud what Inspector McNamara says, and Miss Missouri Martin gets up a collection of over two C's for John Wangle and his hounds, not counting what she holds out for herself. Also the chef comes forward and takes John Wangle and Nip and Tuck back into the kitchen, and stuffs them full of food, although personally I will just as soon not have any of the food they serve in the Three Hundred Club.

They take Regret to the jail-house, and he does not seem

to understand why he is under arrest, but he knows it has something to do with Nip and Tuck and he tries to bribe one of the coppers to put the bloodhounds in the same cell with him for awhile, though naturally the copper will not consider such a proposition. While Regret is being booked at the jail-house, word comes around that Marvin Clay is not only not dead, but the chances are he will get well, which he finally does, at that.

Moreover, he finally bails Regret out, and not only refuses to prosecute him but skips the country as soon as he is able to move, although Regret lays in the sneezer for several weeks, at that, never letting on after he learns the real situation that he is not the party who plugs Marvin Clay. Naturally, Miss Lovey Lou is very grateful to Regret for his wonderful sacrifice, and will no doubt become his ever-loving wife in a minute, if Regret thinks to ask her, but it seems Regret finds himself brooding so much over the idea of an ever-loving wife who is so handy with a Roscoe that he never really asks.

In the meantime, John Wangle and Nip and Tuck go back to Georgia on the dough collected by Miss Missouri Martin, and with a big reputation as man-trackers. So this is all there is to the story, except that one night I run into Regret with a suit-case in his hand, and he is perspiring very freely, although it is not so hot, at that, and when I ask him if he is going away, he says this is indeed his general idea. Moreover, he says he is going very far away. Naturally, I ask him why this is, and Regret says to me as follows:

"Well," he says, "ever since Big Nig, the crap shooter, comes back from Hot Springs, and hears how the bloodhounds track the shooter of Marvin Clay, he is walking up and down looking at me out of the corner of his eye. In fact," Regret says, "I can see that Big Nig is studying something over in his mind, and while Big Nig is a guy who is not such a fast thinker as others, I am afraid he may finally think himself to a bad conclusion.

"I am afraid," Regret says, "that Big Nig will think himself to the conclusion that Nip and Tuck are tracking me instead of the shooter, as many evil-minded guys are already whispering around and about, and that he may get the wrong idea about the trail leading to Maud Milligan's door."

"Do you mean to tell this court," Judge Rascover says, "that this half-portion here is the desperate Twelve-Gun Tweeney?"

TOBIAS THE TERRIBLE

One night I am sitting in Mindy's restaurant on Broadway partaking heartily of some Hungarian goulash which comes very nice in Mindy's, what with the chef being personally somewhat Hungarian himself, when in pops a guy who is a stranger to me and sits down at my table.

I do not pay any attention to the guy at first as I am busy looking over the entries for the next day at Laurel, but I hear him tell the waiter to bring him some goulash, too. By and by I hear the guy making a strange noise and I look at him over my paper and see that he is crying. In fact, large tears are rolling down his face into his goulash and going plop-plop as they fall.

Now it is by no means usual to see guys crying in Mindy's restaurant, though thousands of guys come in there who often feel like crying, especially after a tough day at the track, so I commence weighing the guy up with great interest. I can see he is a very little guy, maybe a shade over five feet high and weighing maybe as much as a dime's worth of liver, and he has a moustache like a mosquito's whiskers across his upper lip, and pale blond hair and a very sad look in his eyes.

Furthermore, he is a young guy and he is wearing a suit of clothes the colour of French mustard, with slanting pockets, and I notice when he comes in that he has a brown hat sitting jack-deuce on his noggin. Anybody can see that this guy does not belong in these parts, with such a sad look and especially with such a hat.

Naturally, I figure his crying is some kind of a dodge. In fact, I figure that maybe the guy is trying to cry me out of the price of his Hungarian goulash, although if he takes the trouble to ask anybody before he comes in, he will learn that he may just as well try to cry Al Smith out of the Empire State Building.

But the guy does not say anything whatever to me but just goes on shedding tears into his goulash, and finally I get very curious about this proposition, and I speak to him as follows:

"Listen, pally," I say, "if you are crying about the goulash, you better dry your tears before the chef sees you, because," I say, "the chef is very sensitive about his goulash, and may take your tears as criticism."

"The goulash seems all right," the guy says in a voice that is just about his size. "Anyway, I am not crying about the goulash. I am crying about my sad life. Friend," the guy says, "are you ever in love?"

Well, of course, at this crack I know what is eating the guy. If I have all the tears that are shed on Broadway by guys in love, I will have enough salt water to start an opposition ocean to the Atlantic and Pacific, with enough left over to run the Great Salt Lake out of business. But I wish to say I never shed any of these tears personally, because I am never in love, and furthermore, barring a bad break, I never expect to be in love, for the way I look at it love is strictly the old phedinkus, and I tell the little guy as much.

"Well," he says, "you will not speak so harshly of love if you are acquainted, with Miss Deborah Weems."

With this he starts crying more than somewhat, and his grief is such that it touches my heart and I have half a notion to start crying with him as I am now convinced that the guy is levelling with his tears.

Finally the guy slacks up a little in his crying, and begins eating his goulash, and by and by he seems more cheerful, but then it is well known to one and all that a fair dose of Mindy's goulash will cheer up anybody no matter how sad they feel. Pretty soon the guy starts talking to me, and I make out that his name is Tobias Tweeney, and that he comes from a spot over in Bucks County, Pennsylvania, by the name of Erasmus, or some such.

Furthermore, I judge that this Erasmus is not such a large

city, but very pleasant, and that Tobias Tweeney is born and raised there and is never much of any place else in his life, although he is now rising twenty-five.

Well, it seems that Tobias Tweeney has a fine position in a shoe store selling shoes and is going along all right when he happens to fall in love with a doll by the name of Miss Deborah Weems, whose papa owns a gas station in Erasmus and is a very prominent citizen. I judge from what Tobias tells me that this Miss Deborah Weems tosses him around quite some, which proves to me that dolls in small towns are just the same as they are on Broadway.

"She is beautiful," Tobias Tweeney says, speaking of Miss Deborah Weems. "I do not think I can live without her. But," he says, "Miss Deborah Weems will have no part of me because she is daffy over desperate characters of the underworld such as she sees in the movies at the Model Theatre in Erasmus.

"She wishes to know," Tobias Tweeney says, "why I cannot be a big gunman and go around plugging people here and there and talking up to politicians and policemen, and maybe looking picturesque and romantic like Edward G. Robinson or James Cagney or even Georgie Raft. But, of course," Tobias says, "I am not the type for such a character. Anyway," he says, "Constable Wendell will never permit me to be such a character in Erasmus.

"So Miss Deborah Weems says I have no more nerve than a catfish," Tobias says, "and she goes around with a guy by the name of Joe Trivett, who runs the Smoke Shop, and bootlegs ginger extract to the boys in his back room and claims Al Capone once says 'Hello 'to him, although," Tobias says, "personally, I think Joe Trivett is nothing but a great big liar."

At this, Tobias Tweeney starts crying again, and I feel very sorry for him indeed, because I can see he is a friendly, harmless little fellow, and by no means accustomed to being tossed around by a doll, and a guy who is not accustomed to being tossed around by a doll always finds it most painful the first time.

"Why," I say, very indignant, "this Miss Deborah Weems talks great foolishness, because big gunmen always wind up nowadays with the score nine to nought against them, even in the movies. In fact," I say, "if they do not wind up this way in the movies, the censors will not permit the movies to be displayed. Why do you not hit this guy Trivett a punch in the snoot," I say, "and tell him to go on about his business?"

"Well," Tobias says, "the reason I do not hit him a punch in the snoot is because he has the idea of punching snoots first, and whose snoot does he punch but mine. Furthermore," Tobias says, "he makes my snoot bleed with the punch, and he says he will do it again if I keep hanging around Miss

Deborah Weems. And," Tobias says, "it is mainly because I do not return the punch, being too busy stopping my snoot from bleeding, that Miss Deborah Weems renounces me for ever.

"She says she can never stand for a guy who has no more nerve than me," Tobias says, "but," he says, "I ask you if I am to blame if my mother is frightened by a rabbit a few weeks before I am born, and marks me for life?

"So I leave town," Tobias says. "I take my savings of two hundred dollars out of the Erasmus bank, and I come here, figuring maybe I will meet up with some big gunmen and other desperate characters of the underworld, and get to know them, and then I can go back to Erasmus and make Joe Trivett look sick. By the way," he says, "do you know any desperate characters of the underworld?"

Well, of course I do not know any such characters, and if I do know them I am not going to speak about it, because the best a guy can get in this town if he goes around speaking of these matters is a nice kick in the pants. So I say no to Tobias Tweeney, and tell him I am more or less of a stranger myself, and then he wishes to know if I can show him a tough joint, such as he sees in the movies.

Naturally, I do not know of such a joint, but then I get to thinking about Good Time Charley's little Gingham Shoppe over in Forty-seventh Street, and how Charley is not going so good the last time I am in there, and here is maybe a chance for me to steer a little trade his way, because, after all, guys with two yards in their pocket are by no means common nowadays.

So I take Tobias Tweeney around to Good Time Charley's, but the moment we get in there I am sorry we go, because who is present but a dozen parties from different parts of the city, and none of these parties are any bargain at any time. Some of these parties, such as Harry the Horse and Angie the Ox, are from Brooklyn, and three are from Harlem, including Little Mitzi and Germany Schwartz, and several are from the Bronx, because I recognize Joey Uptown, and Joey never goes around without a few intimate friends from his own neighbourhood with him.

Afterwards I learn that these parties are to a meeting on business matters at a spot near Good Time Charley's, and when they get through with their business they drop in to give Charley a little complimentary play, for Charley stands very good with one and all in this town. Anyway, they are sitting around a table when Tobias Tweeney and I arrive, and I give them all a big hello, and they hello me back, and ask me and my friend to sit down as it seems they are in a most hospitable frame of mind.

Naturally I sit down because it is never good policy to decline an invitation from parties such as these, and I motion

Tobias to sit down, too, and I introduce Tobias all around, and we all have a couple of drinks, and then I explain to those present just who Tobias is, and how his ever-loving doll tosses him around, and how Joe Trivett punches him in the snoot.

Well, Tobias begins crying again, because no inexperienced guy can take a couple of drinks of Good Time Charley's liquor and not bust out crying, even if it is Charley's company liquor, and one and all are at once very sympathetic with Tobias, especially Little Mitzi, who is just tossed around himself more than somewhat by a doll. In fact, Little Mitzi starts crying with him.

"Why," Joey Uptown says, "I never hear of a greater outrage in my life, although," he says, "I can see there is some puppy in you at that, when you do not return this Trivett's punch. But even so," Joey says, "if I have time I will go back to this town you speak of with you and make the guy hard to catch. Furthermore," he says, "I will give this Miss Deborah Weems a piece of my mind."

Then I tell them how Tobias Tweeney comes to New York figuring he may meet up with some desperate characters of the underworld, and they hear this with great interest, and Angie the Ox speaks as follows:

"I wonder," Angie says, "if we can get in touch with anybody who knows such characters and arrange to have

Mr. Tweeney meet them, although personally," Angie says, "I loathe and despise characters of this nature."

Well, while Angie is wondering this there comes a large knock at the front door, and it is such a knock as only the gendarmes can knock, and everybody at the table jumps up. Good Time Charley goes to the door and takes a quiet gander through his peephole and we hear a loud, coarse voice speaking as follows:

"Open up, Charley," the voice says. "We wish to look over your guests. Furthermore," the voice says, "tell them not to try the back door, because we are there, too."

"It is Lieutenant Harrigan and his squad," Charley says as he comes back to the table where we are all standing. "Someone must tip him off you are here. Well," Charley says, "those who have rods to shed will shed them now."

At this, Joey Uptown steps up to Tobias Tweeney and hands him a large Betsy and says to Tobias like this:

"Put this away on you somewhere," Joey says, "and then sit down and be quiet. These coppers are not apt to bother with you," Joey says, "if you sit still and mind your own business, but," Joey says, "it will be very tough on any of us they find with a rod, especially any of us who owe the state any time, and," Joey says, "I seem to remember I owe some."

Now of course what Joey says is very true, because he is only walking around and about on parole, and some of the others present are walking around the same way, and it is a very serious matter for a guy who is walking around on parole to be caught with a John Roscoe in his pocket. So it is a very ticklish situation, and somewhat embarrassing.

Well, Tobias Tweeney is somewhat dazed by his couple of drinks of Good Time Charley's liquor and the chances are he does not realize what is coming off, so he takes Joey's rod and puts it in his hip kick. Then all of a sudden Harry the Horse and Angie the Ox and Little Mitzi and all the others step up to him and hand him their Roscoes, and Tobias Tweeney somehow manages to stow the guns away on himself and sit down before Good Time Charley opens the door and in come the gendarmes.

By this time Joey Uptown and all the others are scattered at different tables around the room, with no more than three at any one table, leaving Tobias Tweeney and me alone at the table where we are first sitting. Furthermore, everybody is looking very innocent indeed, and all hands seem somewhat surprised at the intrusion of the gendarmes, who are all young guys belonging to Harrigan's Broadway squad, and very rude.

I know Harrigan by sight, and I know most of his men, and they know there is no more harm in me than there is in a two-year-old baby, so they pay no attention to me whatever, or to Tobias Tweeney, either, but go around making Joey

Uptown, and Angie the Ox, and all the others stand up while the gendarmes fan them to see if they have any rods on them, because these gendarmes are always laying for parties such as these hoping to catch them rodded up.

Naturally the gendarmes do not find any rods on anybody, because the rods are all on Tobias Tweeney, and no gendarme is going to fan Tobias Tweeney looking for a rod after one gander at Tobias, especially at this particular moment, as Tobias is now half-asleep from Good Time Charley's liquor, and has no interest whatever in anything that is going on. In fact, Tobias is nodding in his chair.

Of course the gendarmes are greatly disgusted at not finding any rods, and Angie the Ox and Joey Uptown are telling them that they are going to see their aldermen and find out if law-abiding citizens can be stood up and fanned for rods, and put in a very undignified position like this, but the gendarmes do not seem disturbed by these threats, and Lieutenant Harrigan states as follows:

"Well," he says, "I guess maybe I get a bum steer, but," he says, "for two cents I will give all you wrong gees a good going-over just for luck."

Of course this is no way to speak to parties such as these, as they are all very prominent in their different parts of the city, but Lieutenant Harrigan is a guy who seldom cares how he talks to anybody. In fact, Lieutenant Harrigan is a very tough copper.

But he is just about to take his gendarmes out of the joint when Tobias Tweeney nods a little too far forward in his chair, and then all of sudden topples over on the floor, and five large rods pop out of his pockets and go sliding every which way around the floor, and the next thing anybody knows there is Tobias Tweeney under arrest with all the gendarmes holding on to some part of him.

Well, the next day the newspapers are plumb full of the capture of a guy they call Twelve-Gun Tweeney, and the papers say the police state that this is undoubtedly the toughest guy the world ever sees, because while they hear of two-gun guys, and even three-gun guys, they never before hear of a guy going around rodded up with twelve guns.

The gendarmes say they can tell by the way he acts that Twelve-Gun Tweeney is a mighty bloodthirsty guy, because he says nothing whatever but only glares at them with a steely glint in his eyes, although of course the reason Tobias stares at them is because he is still too dumfounded to think of anything to say.

Naturally, I figure that when Tobias comes up for air he is a sure thing to spill the whole business, and all the parties who are in Good Time Charley's when he is arrested figure the same way, and go into retirement for a time. But it seems that when Tobias finally realizes what time it is, he is getting so much attention that it swells him all up and he decides to keep on being Twelve-Gun Tweeney as long as he can, which is a decision that is a very nice break for all parties concerned.

I sneak down to Judge Rascover's court the day Tobias is arraigned on a charge of violation of the Sullivan law, which is a law against carrying rods, and the courtroom is packed with citizens eager to see a character desperate enough to lug twelve rods, and among these citizens are many dolls, pulling and hauling for position, and some of these dolls are by no means crows. Many photographers are hanging around to take pictures of Twelve-Gun Tweeney as he is led in handcuffed to gendarmes on either side of him, and with other gendarmes in front and behind him.

But one and all are greatly surprised and somewhat disappointed when they see what a little squirt Tobias is, and Judge Rascover looks down at him once, and then puts on his specs and takes another gander as if he does not believe what he sees in the first place. After looking at Tobias awhile through his specs, and shaking his head as if he is greatly puzzled, Judge Rascover speaks to Lieutenant Harrigan as follows:

"Do you mean to tell this court," Judge Rascover says, "that this half-portion here is the desperate Twelve-Gun Tweeney?"

Well, Lieutenant Harrigan says there is no doubt whatever about it, and Judge Rascover wishes to know how Tobias carries all these rods, and whereabouts, so Lieutenant Harrigan collects twelve rods from the gendarmes around the courtroom, unloads these rods, and starts in putting the guns here and there on Tobias as near as he can remember where they are found on him in the first place, with Tobias giving him a little friendly assistance.

Lieutenant Harrigan puts two guns in each of the side pockets of Tobias's coat, one in each hip pocket, one in the waistband of Tobias's pants, one in each side pocket of the pants, one up each of Tobias's sleeves, and one in the inside pocket of Tobias's coat. Then Lieutenant Harrigan states to the court that he is all finished, and that Tobias is rodded up in every respect as when they put the arm on him in Good Time Charley's joint, and Judge Rascover speaks to Tobias as follows:

"Step closer to the bench," Judge Rascover says. "I wish to see for myself just what kind of a villain you are."

Well, Tobias takes a step forward, and over he goes on his snoot, so I see right away what it is makes him keel over in Good Time Charley's joint, not figuring in Charley's liquor. The little guy is just naturally top-heavy from the rods.

Now there is much confusion as he falls and a young doll who seems to be fatter than somewhat comes shoving through the crowd in the courtroom yelling and crying, and though the gendarmes try to stop her she gets to Tobias and kneels at his side, and speaks as follows:

"Toby, darling," she says, "it is nobody but Deborah, who loves you dearly, and who always knows you will turn out to be the greatest gunman of them all. Look at me, Toby," she says, "and tell me you love me, too. We never realize what a hero you are until we get the New York papers in Erasmus last night, and I hurry to you as quickly as possible. Kiss me, Toby," the fat young doll says, and Tobias raises up on one elbow and does same, and it makes a very pleasing scene, indeed, although the gendarmes try to pull them apart, having no patience whatever with such matters.

Now Judge Rascover is watching all this business through his specs, and Judge Rascover is no sucker, but a pretty slick old codger for a judge, and he can see that there is something wrong somewhere about Tobias Tweeney being a character as desperate as the gendarmes make him out, especially when he sees that Tobias cannot pack all these rods on a bet.

So when the gendarmes pick the fat young doll off of Tobias and take a few pounds of rods off of Tobias, too, so he is finally able to get back on his pins and stand there, Judge Rascover adjourns court, and takes Tobias into his private room and has a talk with him, and the chances are Tobias tells him the truth, for the next thing anybody knows Tobias is walking away as free as the little birdies in the trees, except that he has the fat young doll clinging to him like a porous plaster, so maybe Tobias is not so free, at that.

Well, this is about all there is to the story, except that there is afterwards plenty of heat between the parties who are present in Good Time Charley's joint when Tobias is collared, because it seems that the meeting they all attend before going to Charley's is supposed to be a peace meeting of some kind and nobody is supposed to carry any rods to this meeting just to prove their confidence in each other, so everybody is very indignant when it comes out that nobody has any confidence in anybody else at the meeting.

I never hear of Tobias Tweeney but once after all this, and it is some months afterwards when Joey Uptown and Little Mitzi are over in Pennsylvania inspecting a brewery proposition, and finding themselves near the town that is called Erasmus, they decide it will be a nice thing to drop in on Tobias Tweeney and see how he is getting along.

Well, it seems Tobias is all married up to Miss Deborah Weems, and is getting along first class, as it seems the town elects him constable, because it feels that a guy with such a desperate reputation as Tobias Tweeney's is bound to make wrongdoers keep away from Erasmus if he is an officer of the law, and Tobias's first official act is to chase Joe Trivett out of town.

But along Broadway Tobias Tweeney will always be considered nothing but an ingrate for heaving Joey Uptown and Little Mitzi into the town sneezer and getting them fined fifty bobs apiece for carrying concealed weapons.

Many parties are very ticklish on the bottom of the feet, especially if the matches are lit.

8

THE SNATCHING OF BOOKIE BOB

Now it comes on the spring of 1931, after a long hard winter, and times are very tough indeed, what with the stock market going all to pieces, and banks busting right and left, and the law getting very nasty about this and that, and one thing and another, and many citizens of this town are compelled to do the best they can.

There is very little scratch anywhere and along Broadway many citizens are wearing their last year's clothes and have practically nothing to bet on the races or anything else, and it is a condition that will touch anybody's heart.

So I am not surprised to hear rumours that the snatching of certain parties is going on in spots, because while snatching is by no means a high-class business, and is even considered somewhat illegal, it is something to tide over the hard times.

Furthermore, I am not surprised to hear that this snatching is being done by a character by the name of Harry the Horse, who comes from Brooklyn, and who is a character who does not care much what sort of business he is in, and who is mobbed up with other characters from Brooklyn such as Spanish John and Little Isadore, who do not care what sort of business they are in, either.

In fact, Harry the Horse and Spanish John and Little Isadore are very hard characters in every respect, and there is considerable indignation expressed around and about when they move over from Brooklyn into Manhattan and start snatching, because the citizens of Manhattan feel that if there is any snatching done in their territory, they are entitled to do it themselves.

But Harry the Horse and Spanish John and Little Isadore pay no attention whatever to local sentiment and go on the snatch on a pretty fair scale, and by and by I am hearing rumours of some very nice scores. These scores are not extra large scores, to be sure, but they are enough to keep the wolf from the door, and in fact from three different doors, and before long Harry the Horse and Spanish John and Little Isadore are around the race-tracks betting on the horses, because if there is one thing they are all very fond of, it is betting on the horses.

Now many citizens have the wrong idea entirely of the snatching business. Many citizens think that all there is to snatching is to round up the party who is to be snatched and then just snatch him, putting him away somewhere until his family or friends dig up enough scratch to pay whatever price the snatchers are asking. Very few citizens understand that the snatching business must be well organized and very systematic.

In the first place, if you are going to do any snatching, you cannot snatch just anybody. You must know who you are snatching, because naturally it is no good snatching somebody who does not have any scratch to settle with. And you cannot tell by the way a party looks or how he lives in this town if he has any scratch, because many a party who is around in automobiles, and wearing good clothes, and chucking quite a swell is nothing but the phonus bolonus and does not have any real scratch whatever.

So of course such a party is no good for snatching, and of course guys who are on the snatch cannot go around inquiring into bank accounts, or asking how much this and that party has in a safe-deposit vault, because such questions are apt to make citizens wonder why, and it is very dangerous to get citizens to wondering why about anything. So the only way guys who are on the snatch can find out about parties worth snatching is to make a connection with some guy who can put the finger on the right party.

The finger guy must know the party he fingers has plenty of ready scratch to begin with, and he must also know that this party is such a party as is not apt to make too much

167

disturbance about being snatched, such as telling the gendarmes. The party may be a legitimate party, such as a business guy, but he will have reasons why he does not wish it to get out that he is snatched, and the finger must know these reasons. Maybe the party is not leading the right sort of life, such as running around with blondes when he has an ever-loving wife and seven children in Mamaroneck, but does not care to have his habits known, as is apt to happen if he is snatched, especially if he is snatched when he is with a blonde.

And sometimes the party is such a party as does not care to have matches run up and down the bottom of his feet, which often happens to parties who are snatched and who do not seem to wish to settle their bill promptly, because many parties are very ticklish on the bottom of the feet, especially if the matches are lit. On the other hand, maybe the party is not a legitimate guy, such as a party who is running a crap game or a swell speakeasy, or who has some other dodge he does not care to have come out, and who also does not care about having his feet tickled.

Such a party is very good indeed for the snatching business, because he is pretty apt to settle without any argument. And after a party settles one snatching, it will be considered very unethical for anybody else to snatch him again very soon, so he is not likely to make any fuss about the matter. The finger guy gets a commission of twenty-five per cent of the settlement, and one and all are satisfied and much fresh scratch comes into circulation, which is very good for the merchants. And while the party who is snatched may know who snatches him, one thing he never knows is who puts the finger on him, this being considered a trade secret.

I am talking to Waldo Winchester, the newspaper scribe, one night and something about the snatching business comes up, and Waldo Winchester is trying to tell me that it is one of the oldest dodges in the world, only Waldo calls it kidnapping, which is a title that will be very repulsive to guys who are on the snatch nowadays. Waldo Winchester claims that hundreds of years ago guys are around snatching parties, male and female, and holding them for ransom, and furthermore Waldo Winchester says they even snatch very little children and Waldo states that it is all a very, very wicked proposition.

Well, I can see where Waldo is right about it being wicked to snatch dolls and little children, but of course no guys who are on the snatch nowadays will ever think of such a thing, because who is going to settle for a doll in these times when you can scarcely even give them away? As for little children, they are apt to be a great nuisance, because their mammas are sure to go running around hollering bloody murder about them, and furthermore little children are very dangerous, indeed, what with being apt to break out with measles and mumps and one thing and another any minute and give it to everybody in the neighbourhood.

Well, anyway, knowing that Harry the Horse and Spanish John and Little Isadore are now on the snatch, I am by no means pleased to see them come along one Tuesday evening when I am standing at the corner of Fiftieth and Broadway, although of course I give them a very jolly hello, and say I hope and trust they are feeling nicely.

They stand there talking to me a few minutes, and I am very glad indeed that Johnny Brannigan, the strong-arm cop, does not happen along and see us, because it will give Johnny a very bad impression of me to see me in such company, even though I am not responsible for the company. But naturally I cannot haul off and walk away from this company at once, because Harry the Horse and Spanish John and Little Isadore may get the idea that I am playing the chill for them, and will feel hurt.

"Well," I say to Harry the Horse, "how are things going, Harry?"

"They are going no good," Harry says. "We do not beat a race in four days. In fact," he says, "we go overboard to-day. We are washed out. We owe every bookmaker at the track that will trust us, and now we are out trying to raise some scratch to pay off. A guy must pay his bookmaker no matter what."

Well, of course this is very true, indeed, because if a guy does not pay his bookmaker it will lower his business standing quite some, as the bookmaker is sure to go around putting the blast on him, so I am pleased to hear Harry the Horse mention such honourable principles.

"By the way," Harry says, "do you know a guy by the name of Bookie Bob?"

Now I do not know Bookie Bob personally, but of course I know who Bookie Bob is, and so does everybody else in this town that ever goes to a race-track, because Bookie Bob is the biggest bookmaker around and about, and has plenty of scratch. Furthermore, it is the opinion of one and all that Bookie Bob will die with this scratch, because he is considered a very close guy with his scratch. In fact, Bookie Bob is considered closer than a dead heat.

He is a short fat guy with a bald head, and his head is always shaking a little from side to side, which some say is a touch of palsy, but which most citizens believe comes of Bookie Bob shaking his head "No" to guys asking for credit in betting on the races. He has an ever-loving wife, who is a very quiet little old doll with grey hair and a very sad look in her eyes, but nobody can blame her for this when they figure that she lives with Bookie Bob for many years.

I often see Bookie Bob and his ever-loving wife eating

in different joints along in the Forties, because they seem to have no home except an hotel, and many a time I hear Bookie Bob giving her a going-over about something or other, and generally it is about the price of something she orders to eat, so I judge Bookie Bob is as tough with his ever-loving wife about scratch as he is with everybody else. In fact, I hear him bawling her out one night because she has on a new hat which she says costs her six bucks, and Bookie Bob wishes to know if she is trying to ruin him with her extravagances.

But of course I am not criticizing Bookie Bob for squawking about the hat, because for all I know six bucks may be too much for a doll to pay for a hat, at that. And furthermore, maybe Bookie Bob has the right idea about keeping down his ever-loving wife's appetite, because I know many a guy in this town who is practically ruined by dolls eating too much on him.

"Well," I say to Harry the Horse, "if Bookie Bob is one of the bookmakers you owe, I am greatly surprised to see that you seem to have both eyes in your head, because I never before hear of Bookie Bob letting anybody owe him without giving him at least one of their eyes for security. In fact," I say, "Bookie Bob is such a guy as will not give you the right time if he has two watches."

"No," Harry the Horse says, "we do not owe Bookie Bob.

But," he says, "he will be owing us before long. We are going to put the snatch on Bookie Bob."

Well, this is most disquieting news to me, not because I care if they snatch Bookie Bob or not, but because somebody may see me talking to them who will remember about it when Bookie Bob is snatched. But of course it will not be good policy for me to show Harry the Horse and Spanish John and Little Isadore that I am nervous, so I only speak as follows:

"Harry," I say, "every man knows his own business best, and I judge you know what you are doing. But," I say, "you are snatching a hard guy when you snatch Bookie Bob. A very hard guy, indeed. In fact," I say, "I hear the softest thing about him is his front teeth, so it may be very difficult for you to get him to settle after you snatch him."

"No," Harry the Horse says, "we will have no trouble about it. Our finger gives us Bookie Bob's hole card, and it is a most surprising thing, indeed. But," Harry the Horse says, "you come upon many surprising things in human nature when you are on the snatch. Bookie Bob's hole card is his ever-loving wife's opinion of him.

"You see," Harry the Horse says, "Bookie Bob has been putting himself away with his ever-loving wife for years as a very important guy in this town, with much power and influence, although of course Bookie Bob knows very well he stands about as good as a broken leg. In fact," Harry the Horse says, "Bookie Bob figures that his ever-loving wife is the only one in the world who looks on him as a big guy, and he will sacrifice even his scratch, or anyway some of it, rather than let her know that guys have such little respect for him as to put the snatch on him. It is what you call psychology," Harry the Horse says.

Well, this does not make good sense to me, and I am thinking to myself that the psychology that Harry the Horse really figures to work out nice on Bookie Bob is tickling his feet with matches, but I am not anxious to stand there arguing about it, and pretty soon I bid them all good evening, very polite, and take the wind, and I do not see Harry the Horse or Spanish John or Little Isadore again for a month.

In the meantime, I hear gossip here and there that Bookie Bob is missing for several days, and when he finally shows up again he gives it out that he is very sick during his absence, but I can put two and two together as well as anybody in this town and I figure that Bookie Bob is snatched by Harry the Horse and Spanish John and Little Isadore, and the chances are it costs him plenty.

So I am looking for Harry the Horse and Spanish John and Little Isadore to be around the race-track with plenty of scratch and betting them higher than a cat's back, but they never show up, and what is more I hear they leave Manhattan and are back in Brooklyn working every day handling beer. Naturally this is very surprising to me, because the way things are running beer is a tough dodge just now, and there is very little profit in same, and I figure that with the scratch they must make off Bookie Bob, Harry the Horse and Spanish John and Little Isadore have a right to be taking things easy.

Now one night I am in Good Time Charley Bernstein's little speak in Forty-eighth Street, talking of this and that with Charley, when in comes Harry the Horse, looking very weary and by no means prosperous. Naturally I gave him a large hello, and by and by we get to gabbing together and I ask him whatever becomes of the Bookie Bob matter, and Harry the Horse tells me as follows:

Yes [Harry the Horse says], we snatch Bookie Bob all right. In fact, we snatch him the very next night after we are talking to you, or on a Wednesday night. Our finger tells us Bookie Bob is going to a wake over in his old neighbourhood on Tenth Avenue, near Thirty-eighth Street, and this is where we pick him up.

He is leaving the place in his car along about midnight, and of course Bookie Bob is alone as he seldom lets anybody ride with him because of the wear and tear on his car cushions, and Little Isadore swings our flivver in front of him and makes him stop. Naturally Bookie Bob is greatly surprised when I poke my head into his car and tell him I wish the pleasure of his company for a short time, and at first he is inclined to argue the matter, saying I must make a mistake, but I put the old convincer on him by letting him peek down the snozzle of my John Roscoe.

We lock his car and throw the keys away, and then we take Bookie Bob in our car and go to a certain spot on Eighth Avenue where we have a nice little apartment all ready. When we get there I tell Bookie Bob that he can call up anybody he wishes and state that the snatch is on him and that it will require twenty-five G's, cash money, to take it off, but of course I also tell Bookie Bob that he is not to mention where he is or something may happen to him.

Well, I will say one thing for Bookie Bob, although everybody is always weighing in the sacks on him and saying he is no good—he takes it like a gentleman, and very calm and businesslike.

Furthermore, he does not seem alarmed, as many citizens are when they find themselves in such a situation. He recognizes the justice of our claim at once, saying as follows:

"I will telephone my partner, Sam Salt," he says. "He is the only one I can think of who is apt to have have such a sum as twenty-five G's cash money. But," he says, "if you gentlemen will pardon the question, because this is a new experience to me, how do I know everything will be okay for me after you get the scratch?"

"Why," I say to Bookie Bob, somewhat indignant, "it is well known to one and all in this town that my word is my bond. There are two things I am bound to do," I say, "and one is to keep my word in such a situation as this, and the other is to pay anything I owe a bookmaker, no matter what, for these are obligations of honour with me."

"Well," Bookie Bob says, "of course I do not know you gentlemen, and, in fact, I do not remember ever seeing any of you, although your face is somewhat familiar, but if you pay your bookmaker you are an honest guy, and one in a million. In fact," Bookie Bob says, "if I have all the scratch that is owing to me around this town, I will not be telephoning anybody for such a sum as twenty-five G's. I will have such a sum in my pants pocket for change."

Now Bookie Bob calls a certain number and talks to somebody there but he does not get Sam Salt, and he seems much disappointed when he hangs up the receiver again.

"This is a very tough break for me," he says. "Sam Salt goes to Atlantic City an hour ago on very important business and will not be back until to-morrow evening, and they do not know where he is to stay in Atlantic City. And," Bookie Bob says, "I cannot think of anybody else to call up to get this scratch, especially anybody I will care to have know I am in this situation."

"Why not call your ever-loving wife?" I say. "Maybe she can dig up this kind of scratch."

"Say," Bookie Bob says, "you do not suppose I am chump enough to give my ever-loving wife twenty-five G's, or even let her know where she can get her dukes on twenty-five G's belonging to me, do you? I give my ever-loving wife ten bucks per week for spending money," Bookie Bob says, "and this is enough scratch for any doll, especially when you figure I pay for her meals."

Well, there seems to be nothing we can do except wait until Sam Salt gets back, but we let Bookie Bob call his ever-loving wife, as Bookie Bob says he does not wish to have her worrying about his absence, and tells her a big lie about having to go to Jersey City to sit up with a sick Brother Elk.

Well, it is now nearly four o'clock in the morning, so we put Bookie Bob in a room with Little Isadore to sleep, although, personally, I consider making a guy sleep with Little Isadore very cruel treatment, and Spanish John and I take turns keeping awake and watching out that Bookie Bob does not take the air on us before paying us off. To tell the truth, Little Isadore and Spanish John are somewhat disappointed that Bookie Bob agrees to settle so promptly, because they are looking forward to tickling his feet with great relish.

Now Bookie Bob turns out to be very good company when he wakes up the next morning, because he knows a lot of race-track stories and plenty of scandal, and he keeps us much interested at breakfast. He talks along with us as if he knows us all his life, and he seems very nonchalant indeed, but the chances are he will not be so nonchalant if I tell him about Spanish John's thought.

Well, about noon Spanish John goes out of the apartment and comes back with a racing sheet, because he knows Little Isadore and I will be wishing to know what is running in different spots although we do not have anything to bet on these races, or any way of betting on them, because we are overboard with every bookmaker we know.

Now Bookie Bob is also much interested in the matter of what is running, especially at Belmont, and he is bending over the table with me and Spanish John and Little Isadore, looking at the sheet, when Spanish John speaks as follows:

"My goodness," Spanish John says, "a spot such as this fifth race with Questionnaire at four to five is like finding money in the street. I only wish I have a few bobs to bet on him at such a price," Spanish John says.

"Why," Bookie Bob says, very polite, "if you gentlemen wish to bet on these races I will gladly book to you. It is a good way to pass away the time while we are waiting for Sam

Salt, unless you will rather play pinochle;"

"But," I say, "we have no scratch to play the races, at least not much."

"Well," Bookie Bob says, "I will take your markers, because I hear what you say about always paying your bookmaker, and you put yourself away with me as an honest guy, and these other gentlemen also impress me as honest guys."

Now what happens but we begin betting Bookie Bob on the different races, not only at Belmont, but at all the other tracks in the country, for Little Isadore and Spanish John and I are guys who like plenty of action when we start betting on the horses. We write out markers for whatever we wish to bet and hand them to Bookie Bob, and Bookie Bob sticks these markers in an inside pocket, and along in the late afternoon it looks as if he has a tumour on his chest.

We get the race results by 'phone off a poolroom downtown as fast as they come off, and also the prices, and it is a lot of fun, and Little Isadore and Spanish John and Bookie Bob and I are all little pals together until all the races are over and Bookie Bob takes out the markers and starts counting himself up.

It comes out then that I owe Bookie Bob ten G's, and Spanish John owes him six G's, and Little Isadore owes him four G's, as Little Isadore beats him a couple of races out west.

Well, about this time, Bookie Bob manages to get Sam Salt on the 'phone, and explains to Sam that he is to go to a certain safe-deposit box and get out twenty-five G's, and then wait until midnight and hire himself a taxicab and start riding around the block between Fifty-first and Fifty-second, from Eighth to Ninth avenues, and to keep riding until somebody flags the cab and takes the scratch off him.

Naturally Sam Salt understands right away that the snatch is on Bookie Bob, and he agrees to do as he is told, but he says he cannot do it until the following night because he knows there is not twenty-five G's in the box and he will have to get the difference at the track the next day. So there we are with another day in the apartment and Spanish John and Little Isadore and I are just as well pleased because Bookie Bob has us hooked and we naturally wish to wiggle off.

But the next day is worse than ever. In all the years I am playing the horses I never have such a tough day, and Spanish John and Little Isadore are just as bad. In fact, we are all going so bad that Bookie Bob seems to feel sorry for us and often lays us a couple of points above the track prices, but it does no good. At the end of the day, I am in a total of twenty G's, while Spanish John owes fifteen, and Little Isadore fifteen, a total of fifty G's among the three of us. But we are never any hands to hold post-mortems on bad days, so Little Isadore goes out to a delicatessen store and lugs in a lot of nice things to eat, and we have a fine dinner, and then we sit around with Bookie Bob telling stories, and even singing a few songs together until time to meet Sam Salt.

When it comes on midnight Spanish John goes out and lays for Sam, and gets a little valise off of Sam Salt. Then Spanish John comes back to the apartment and we open the valise and the twenty-five G's are there okay, and we cut this scratch three ways.

Then I tell Bookie Bob he is free to go on about his business, and good luck to him, at that, but Bookie Bob looks at me as if he is very much surprised, and hurt, and says to me like this:

"Well, gentlemen, thank you for your courtesy, but what about the scratch you owe me? What about these markers? Surely, gentlemen, you will pay your bookmaker?"

Well, of course we owe Bookie Bob these markers, all right, and of course a man must pay his bookmaker, no matter what, so I hand over my bit and Bookie Bob puts down something in a little note-book that he takes out of his kick.

Then Spanish John and Little Isadore hand over their dough, too, and Bookie Bob puts down something more in the little note-book.

"Now," Bookie Bob says, "I credit each of your accounts with these payments, but you gentlemen still owe me a matter of twenty-five G's over and above the twenty-five I credit you with, and I hope and trust you will make arrangements to settle this at once because," he says, "I do not care to extend such accommodations over any considerable period."

"But," I say, "we do not have any more scratch after paying you the twenty-five G's on account."

"Listen," Bookie Bob says, dropping his voice down to a whisper, "what about putting the snatch on my partner, Sam Salt, and I will wait over a couple of days with you and keep booking to you, and maybe you can pull yourselves out. But of course," Bookie Bob whispers, "I will be entitled to twenty-five per cent of the snatch for putting the finger on Sam for you."

But Spanish John and Little Isadore are sick and tired of Bookie Bob and will not listen to staying in the apartment any longer, because they say he is a jinx to them and they cannot beat him in any manner, shape or form. Furthermore, I am personally anxious to get away because something Bookie Bob says reminds me of something.

It reminds me that besides the scratch we owe him, we forget to take out six G's two-fifty for the party who puts the finger on Bookie Bob for us, and this is a very serious matter indeed, because anybody will tell you that failing to pay a finger is considered a very dirty trick. Furthermore, if it gets around that you fail to pay a finger, nobody else will ever finger for you.

So [Harry the Horse says] we quit the snatching business because there is no use continuing while this obligation is outstanding against us, and we go back to Brooklyn to earn enough scratch to pay our just debts.

We are paying off Bookie Bob's IOU a little at a time, because we do not wish to ever have anybody say we welsh on a bookmaker, and furthermore we are paying off the six G's two-fifty commission we owe our finger.

And while it is tough going, I am glad to say our honest effort is doing somebody a little good, because I see Bookie Bob's ever-loving wife the other night all dressed up in new clothes and looking very happy, indeed.

And while a guy is telling me she is looking so happy because she gets a large legacy from an uncle who dies in Switzerland, and is now independent of Bookie Bob, I only hope and trust [Harry the Horse says] that it never gets out that our finger in this case is nobody but Bookie Bob's ever-loving wife.

9

THE LILY OF ST. PIERRE

There are four of us sitting in Good Time Charley Bernstein's little joint in Forty-eighth Street one Tuesday morning about four o'clock, doing a bit of quartet singing, very low, so as not to disturb the copper on the beat outside, a very good guy by the name of Carrigan, who likes to get his rest at such an hour.

Good Time Charley's little joint is called the Crystal Room, although of course there is no crystal whatever in the room, but only twelve tables, and twelve hostesses, because Good Time Charley believes in his customers having plenty of social life.

So he has one hostess to a table, and if there are twelve different customers, which is very seldom, each customer has a hostess to talk with. And if there is only one customer, he has all twelve hostesses to gab with and buy drinks for, and no customer can ever go away claiming he is lonesome in Good Time Charley's.

Personally, I will not give you a nickel to talk with Good

185

Time Charley's hostesses, one at a time or all together, because none of them are anything much to look at, and I figure they must all be pretty dumb or they will not be working as hostesses in Good Time Charley's little joint. I happen to speak of this to Good Time Charley, and he admits that I may be right, but he says it is very difficult to get any Peggy Joyces for twenty-five bobs per week.

Of course I never buy any drinks in Good Time Charley's for hostesses, or anybody else, and especially for myself, because I am a personal friend of Good Time Charley's, and he will not sell me any drinks even if I wish to buy any, which is unlikely, as Good Time Charley figures that anybody who buys drinks in his place is apt to drink these drinks, and Charley does not care to see any of his personal friends drinking drinks in his place. If one of his personal friends wishes to buy a drink, Charley always sends him to Jack Fogarty's little speak down the street, and in fact Charley will generally go with him.

So I only go to Good Time Charley's to talk with him, and to sing in quartet with him. There are very seldom any customers in Good Time Charley's until along about five o'clock in the morning after all the other places are closed, and then it is sometimes a very hot spot indeed, and it is no place to sing in quartet at such hours, because everybody around always wishes to join in, and it ruins the harmony.

But just before five o'clock it is okay, as only the hostesses are there, and of course none of them dast to join in our singing, or Good Time Charley will run them plumb out of the joint.

If there is one thing I love to do more than anything else, it is to sing in quartet. I sing baritone, and I wish to say I sing a very fine baritone, at that. And what we are singing—this morning I am talking about—is a lot of songs such as "Little White Lies," and "The Old Oaken Bucket," and "My Dad's Dinner Pail," and "Chloe," and "Melancholy Baby," and I do not know what else, including "Home, Sweet Home," although we do not go so good on this because nobody remembers all the words, and half the time we are all just going ho-hum-hum-ho-hum-hum, like guys nearly always do when they are singing "Home, Sweet Home."

Also we sing "I Can't Give You Anything but Love, Baby," which is a very fine song for quartet singing, especially when you have a guy singing a nice bass, such as Good Time Charley, who can come in on every line with a big bum-bum, like this:

I can't give you anything but luh-huh-vuh,
Bay-hay-bee!
BUM-BUM!

I am the one who holds these last words, such as love, and baby, and you can hear my fine baritone very far indeed, especially when I give a little extra roll like bay-hay-ay-ay-BEE! Then when Good Time Charley comes in with his old bum-bum, it is worth going a long way to hear.

Well, naturally, we finally get around to torch songs, as guys who are singing in quartet are bound to do, especially at four o'clock in the morning, a torch song being a song which guys sing when they have the big burnt-up feeling inside themselves over a battle with their dolls.

When a guy has a battle with his doll, such as his sweetheart, or even his ever-loving wife, he certainly feels burnt up inside himself, and can scarcely think of anything much. In fact, I know guys who are carrying the torch to walk ten miles and never know they go an inch. It is surprising how much ground a guy can cover just walking around and about, wondering if his doll is out with some other guy, and everybody knows that at four o'clock in the morning the torch is hotter than at any other time of the day.

Good Time Charley, who is carrying a torch longer than anybody else on Broadway, which is nearly a year, or ever since his doll, Big Marge, gives him the wind for a rich Cuban, starts up a torch song by Tommy Lyman, which goes as follows, very, very slow, and sad:

Gee, but it's tough
When the gang's gone home.
Out on the comer
You stand alone.

Of course there is no spot in this song for Good Time Charley's bum-bum, but it gives me a great chance with my fine baritone, especially when I come to the line that says Gee, I wish I had my old gal back again.

I do not say I can make people bust out crying and give me money with this song like I see Tommy Lyman do in night clubs, but then Tommy is a professional singer, besides writing this song for himself, so naturally he figures to do a little better with it than me. But I wish to say it is nothing for me to make five or six of the hostesses in Good Time Charley's cry all over the joint when I hit this line about Gee, I wish I had my old gal back again, and making five or six hostesses out of twelve cry is a fair average anywhere, and especially Good Time Charley's hostesses.

Well, all of a sudden who comes popping into Good Time Charley's by way of the front door, looking here and there, and around and about, but Jack O'Hearts, and he no sooner pokes his snozzle into the joint than a guy by the name of Louie the Lug, who is singing a very fair tenor with us, jumps up and heads for the back door.

But just as he gets to the door, Jack O'Hearts outs with the old equalizer and goes whangity-whang-whang at Louie the Lug. As a general proposition, Jack O'Hearts is a fair kind of a shot, but all he does to Louie the Lug is to knock his right ear off. Then Louie gets the back door open and takes it on the lam through an areaway, but not before Jack O'Hearts gets one more crack at him, and it is this last crack which brings Louie down half an hour later on Broadway, where a copper finds him and sends him to the Polyclinic.

Personally, I do not see Louie's ear knocked off, because by the second shot I am out the front door, and on my way down Forty-eighth Street, but they tell me about it afterwards.

I never know Jack O'Hearts is even mad at Louie, and I am wondering why he takes these shots at him, but I do not ask any questions, because when a guy goes around asking questions in this town people may get the idea he is such a guy as wishes to find things out.

Then the next night I run into Jack O'Hearts in Bobby's chophouse, putting on the hot meat, and he asks me to sit down and eat with him, so I sit down and order a hamburger steak, with plenty of onions, and while I am sitting there waiting for my hamburger, Jack O'Hearts says to me like this:

"I suppose," he says, "I owe you guys an apology for busting up your quartet when I toss those slugs at Louie the

Lug?"

"Well," I say, "some considers it a dirty trick at that, Jack, but I figure you have a good reason, although I am wondering what it is."

"Louie the Lug is no good," Jack says.

Well, of course I know this much already, and so does everybody else in town for that matter, but I cannot figure what it has to do with Jack shooting off ears in this town for such a reason, or by and by there will be very few people left with ears.

"Let me tell you about Louie the Lug," Jack O'Hearts says. "You will see at once that my only mistake is I do not get my shots an inch to the left. I do not know what is the matter with me lately."

"Maybe you are letting go too quick," I say, very sympathetic, because I know how it annoys him to blow easy shots.

"Maybe," he says. "Anyway, the light in Charley's dump is no good. It is only an accident I get Louie with the last shot, and it is very sloppy work all around. But now I will tell you about Louie the Lug."

It is back in 1924 [Jack O'Hearts says] that I go to St. Pierre for the first time to look after some business matters for John the Boss, rest his soul, who is at this time one of the largest operators in high-grade merchandise in the United States, especially when it comes to Scotch. Maybe you remember John the Boss, and the heat which develops around and about when he is scragged in Detroit? John the Boss is a very fine character, and it is a terrible blow to many citizens when he is scragged.

Now if you are never in St. Pierre, I wish to say you miss nothing much, because what is it but a little squirt of a burg sort of huddled up alongside some big rocks off Newfoundland, and very hard to get to, any way you go. Mostly you go there from Halifax by boat, though personally I go there in 1924 in John the Boss's schooner by the name of the *Maude,* in which we load a thousand cases of very nice merchandise for the Christmas trade.

The first time I see St. Pierre I will not give you eight cents for the whole layout, although of course it is very useful to parties in our line of business. It does not look like much, and it belongs to France, and nearly all the citizens speak French, because most of them are French, and it seems it is the custom of the French people to speak French no matter where they are, even away off up yonder among the fish.

Well, anyway, it is on this trip to St. Pierre in 1924 that I meet an old guy by the name of Doctor Armand Dorval, for what happens to me but I catch pneumonia, and it looks as if maybe I am a gone gosling, especially as there is no place in St. Pierre where a guy can have pneumonia with any comfort. But this Doctor Armand Dorval is a friend of John the Boss, and he takes me into his house and lets me be as sick there as I please, while he does his best to doctor me up.

Now this Doctor Armand Dorval is an old Frenchman with whiskers, and he has a little granddaughter by the name of Lily, who is maybe twelve years old at the time I am talking about, with her hair hanging down her back in two braids. It seems her papa, who is Doctor Armand's son, goes out one day looking for cod on the Grand Banks when Lily is nothing but a baby, and never comes back, and then her mamma dies, so old Doc raises up Lily and is very fond of her indeed.

They live alone in the house where I am sick with this pneumonia, and it is a nice, quiet little house and very old-fashioned, with a good view of the fishing boats, if you care for fishing boats. In fact, it is the quietest place I am ever in in my life, and the only place I ever know any real peace. A big fat old doll who does not talk English comes in every day to look after things for Doctor Armand and Lily, because it seems Lily is not old enough to keep house as yet, although she makes quite a nurse for me.

Lily talks English very good, and she is always bringing me things, and sitting by my bed and chewing the rag with me about this and that, and sometimes she reads to me out of a book which is called *Alice in Wonderland,* and which is nothing but a pack of lies, but very interesting in spots. Furthermore, Lily has a big, blond, dumb-looking doll by the name of Yvonne, which she makes me hold while she is reading to me, and I am very glad indeed that the *Maude* goes on back to the United States and there is no danger of any of the guys walking in on me while I am holding this doll, or they will think I blow my topper.

Finally, when I am able to sit up around the house of an evening I play checkers with Lily, while old Doctor Armand Dorval sits back in a rocking-chair, smoking a pipe and watching us, and sometimes I sing for her. I wish to say I sing a first-class tenor, and when I am in the war business in France with the Seventy-seventh Division I am always in great demand for singing a quartet. So I sing such songs to Lily as "There's a Long, Long Trail," and "Mademoiselle from Armentières," although of course when it comes to certain spots in this song I just go dum-dum-dee-dum and do not say the words right out.

By and by Lily gets to singing with me, and we sound very good together, especially when we sing the "Long, Long Trail," which Lily likes very much, and even old Doctor Armand joins in now and then, although his voice is very terrible. Anyway, Lily and me and Doctor Armand become very good pals indeed, and what is more I meet up with other citizens of St. Pierre and become friends with them, and they are by no means bad people to know, and it is certainly a nice thing to be able to walk up and down without being afraid every other guy you meet is going to chuck a slug at you, or a copper put the old sleeve on you and say that they wish to see you at headquarters.

Finally I get rid of this pneumonia and take the boat to Halifax, and I am greatly surprised to find that Doctor Armand and Lily are very sorry to see me go, because never before in my life do I leave a place where anybody is sorry to see me go.

But Doctor Armand seems very sad and shakes me by the hand over and over again, and what does Lily do but bust out crying, and the first thing I know I am feeling sad myself and wishing that I am not going. So I promise Doctor Armand I will come back some day to see him, and then Lily hauls off and gives me a big kiss right in the smush and this astonishes me so much that it is half an hour afterwards before I think to wipe it off.

Well, for the next few months I find myself pretty busy back in New York, what with one thing and another, and I do not have time to think much of Doctor Armand Dorval and Lily, and St. Pierre, but it comes along the summer of 1925, and I am all tired out from getting a slug in my chest in the run-in with Jerk Donovan's mob in Jersey, for I am now in beer and have no more truck with the boats.

But I get to thinking of St. Pierre and the quiet little house of Doctor Armand Dorval again, and how peaceful it is up there, and nothing will do but what I must pop off to Halifax, and pretty soon I am in St. Pierre once more. I take a raft of things for Lily with me, such as dolls, and handkerchiefs, and perfume, and a phonograph, and also a set of razors for Doctor Armand, although afterwards I am sorry I take these razors because I remember the old Doc does not shave and may take them as a hint I do not care for his whiskers. But as it turns out the Doc finds them very useful in operations, so the razors are a nice gift after all.

Well, I spend two peaceful weeks there again, walking up and down in the daytime and playing checkers and singing with Lily in the evening, and it is tough tearing myself away, especially as Doctor Armand Dorval looks very sad again and Lily bursts out crying, louder than before. So nearly every year after this I can hardly wait until I can get to St. Pierre for a vacation, and Doctor Armand Dorval's house is like my home, only more peaceful.

Now in the summer of 1928 I am in Halifax on my way to St. Pierre, when I run across Louie the Lug, and it seems Louie is a lammister out of Detroit on account of some job or other, and is broke, and does not know which way to turn. Personally, I always figure Louie a petty-larceny kind of guy, with no more moxie than a canary bird, but he always dresses well, and always has a fair line of guff, and some guys stand for him. Anyway, here he is in trouble, so what happens but I take him with me to St. Pierre, figuring he can lay dead there until things blow over.

Well, Lily and old Doctor Armand Dorval are certainly glad to see me, and I am just as glad to see them, especially Lily, for she is now maybe sixteen years old and as pretty a doll as ever steps in shoe leather, what with her long black hair, and her big black eyes, and a million dollars' worth of personality. Furthermore, by this time she swings a very mean skillet, indeed, and gets me up some very tasty fodder out of fish and one thing and another.

But somehow things are not like they used to be at St. Pierre with this guy Louie the Lug around, because he does not care for the place whatever, and goes roaming about very restless, and making cracks about the citizens, and especially the dolls, until one night I am compelled to tell him to keep his trap closed, although at that the dolls in St. Pierre, outside of Lily, are no such lookers as will get Ziegfeld heated up.

But even in the time when St. Pierre is headquarters for many citizens of the United States who are in the business of handling merchandise out of there, it is always sort of underhand that such citizens will never have any truck with the dolls at St. Pierre. This is partly because the dolls at St. Pierre never give the citizens of the United States a tumble, but more because we do not wish to get in any trouble around there, and if there is anything apt to cause trouble it is dolls.

Now I suppose if I have any brains I will see that Louie is playing the warm for Lily, but I never think of Lily as anything but a little doll with her hair in braids, and certainly not a doll such as a guy will start pitching to, especially a guy who calls himself one of the mob.

I notice Louie is always talking to Lily when he gets a chance, and sometimes he goes walking up and down with her, but I see nothing in this, because after all any guy is apt to get lonesome at St. Pierre and go walking up and down with anybody, even a little young doll. In fact, I never see Louie do anything that strikes me as out of line, except he tries to cut in on the singing between Lily and me, until I tell him one tenor at a time is enough in any singing combination. Personally, I consider Louie the Lug's tenor very flat, indeed.

Well, it comes time for me to go away, and I take Louie with me, because I do not wish him hanging around St. Pierre alone, especially as old Doctor Armand Dorval does not seem to care for him whatever, and while Lily seems as sad as ever to see me go I notice that for the first time she does not kiss me good-bye. But I figure this is fair enough, as she is now quite a young lady, and the chances are a little particular about who she kisses.

I leave Louie in Halifax and give him enough dough to go on to Denver, which is where he says he wishes to go, and I never see him again until the other night in Good Time Charley's. But almost a year later, when I happen to be in Montreal, I hear of him. I am standing in the lobby of the Mount Royal Hotel thinking of not much, when a guy by the name of Bob the Bookie, who is a hustler around the race tracks, gets to talking to me and mentions Louie's name. It brings back to me a memory of my last trip to St. Pierre, and I get to thinking that this is the longest stretch I ever go in several years without a visit there and of the different things that keep me from going.

I am not paying much attention to what Bob says, because he is putting the blast on Louie for running away from an ever-loving wife and a couple of kids in Cleveland several years before, which is something I do not know about Louie, at that. Then I hear Bob saying like this:

"He is an awful rat any way you take him. Why, when he hops out of here two weeks ago, he leaves a little doll he brings with him from St. Pierre dying in a hospital without a nickel to her name. It is a sin and a shame."

"Wait a minute, Bob," I say, waking up all of a sudden.

"Do you say a doll from St. Pierre? What-for looking kind of a doll, Bob?" I say.

"Why," Bob says, "she is black-haired, and very young, and he calls her Lily, or some such. He is knocking around Canada with her for quite a spell. She strikes me as a t. b., but Louie's dolls always look this way after he has them a while. I judge," Bob says, "that Louie does not feed them any too good."

Well, it is Lily Dorval, all right, but never do I see such a change in anybody as there is in the poor little doll I find lying on a bed in a charity ward in a Montreal hospital. She does not look to weigh more than fifty pounds, and her black eyes are sunk away back in her head, and she is in tough shape generally. But she knows me right off the bat and tries to smile at me.

I am in the money very good at this time, and I have Lily moved into a private room, and get her all the nurses the law allows, and the best croakers in Montreal, and flowers, and one thing and another, but one of the medicos tells me it is even money she will not last three weeks, and 7 to 5 she does not go a month. Finally Lily tells me what happens, which is the same thing that happens to a million dolls before and will happen to a million dolls again. Louie never leaves Halifax, but cons her into coming over there to him, and she goes because she loves him, for this is the way dolls are, and personally I will never have them any other way.

"But," Lily whispers to me, "the bad, bad thing I do is to tell poor old Grandfather I am going to meet you, Jack O'Hearts, and marry you, because I know he does not like Louie and will never allow me to go to him. But he loves you, Jack O'Hearts, and he is so pleased in thinking you are to be his son. It is wrong to tell Grandfather this story, and wrong to use your name, and to keep writing him all this time making him think I am your wife, and with you, but I love Louie, and I wish Grandfather to be happy because he is very, very old. Do you understand, Jack O'Hearts?"

Now of course all this is very surprising news to me, indeed, and in fact I am quite flabbergasted, and as for understanding it, all I understand is she got a rotten deal from Louie the Lug and that old Doctor Armand Dorval is going to be all busted up if he hears what really happens. And thinking about this nice old man, and thinking of how the only place I ever know peace and quiet is now ruined, I am very angry with Louie the Lug.

But this is something to be taken up later, so I dismiss him from my mind, and go out and get me a marriage licence and a priest, and have this priest marry me to Lily Dorval just two days before she looks up at me for the last time, and smiles a little smile, and then closes her eyes for good and all. I wish to say, however, that up to this time I have no more idea of getting myself a wife than I have of jumping out the window, which is practically no idea at all.

I take her body back to St. Pierre myself in person, and we bury her in a little cemetery there, with a big fog around and about, and the siren moaning away very sad, and old Doctor Armand Dorval whispers to me like this:

"You will please to sing the song about the long trail, Jack O'Hearts."

So I stand there in the fog, the chances are looking like a big sap, and I sing as follows:

"There's a long, long trail a-winding
Into the land of my dreams,
Where the nightingale is singing,
And the white moon beams."

But I can get no farther than this, for something comes up in my throat, and I sit down by the grave of Mrs. Jack O'Hearts, who was Lily Dorval, and for the first time I remember I bust out crying.

So [he says] this is why I say Louie the Lug is no good.

Well, I am sitting there thinking that Jack O'Hearts is right about Louie, at that, when in comes Jack's chauffeur, a guy by the name of Fingers, and he steps up to Jack and says, very low:

"Louie dies half an hour ago at the Polyclinic."

"What does he say before he goes?" Jack asks.

"Not a peep," Fingers says.

"Well," Jack O'Hearts says, "it is sloppy work, at that. I ought to get him the first crack. But maybe he has a chance to think a little of Lily Dorval."

Then he turns to me and says like this:

"You guys need not feel bad about losing your tenor, because," he says, "I will be glad to fill in for him at all times."

Personally I do not think Jack's tenor is as good as Louie the Lug's, especially when it comes to hitting the very high notes in such songs as Sweet Adeline, because he does not hold them long enough to let Good Time Charley in with his bum-bum.

But of course this does not go if Jack O'Hearts hears it, as I am never sure he does not clip Louie the Lug just to get a place in our quartet, at that.

10

HOLD 'EM, YALE!

What Iam doing in New Haven on the day of a very large football game between the Harvards and the Yales is something which calls for quite a little explanation, because I am not such a guy as you will expect to find in New Haven at any time, and especially on the day of a large football game.

But there I am, and the reason I am there goes back to a Friday night when I am sitting in Mindy's restaurant on Broadway thinking of very little except how I can get hold of a few potatoes to take care of the old overhead. And while I am sitting there, who comes in but Sam the Gonoph, who is a ticket speculator by trade, and who seems to be looking all around and about.

Well, Sam the Gonoph gets to talking to me, and it turns out that he is looking for a guy by the name of Gigolo Georgie, who is called Gigolo Georgie because he is always hanging around night clubs wearing a little moustache and white spats, and dancing with old dolls. In fact, Gigolo

Georgie is nothing but a gentleman bum, and I am surprised that Sam the Gonoph is looking for him.

The next thing anybody knows she shins up one of the posts faster than you can say scat.

But it seems that the reason Sam the Gonoph wishes to find Gigolo Georgie is to give him a good punch in the snoot, because it seems that Gigolo Georgie promotes Sam for several duckets to the large football game between the Harvards and the Yales to sell on commission, and never kicks back anything whatever to Sam. Naturally Sam considers Gigolo Georgie nothing but a rascal for doing such a thing to him, and Sam says he will find Gigolo Georgie and give him a going-over if it is the last act of his life.

Well, then, Sam explains to me that he has quite a few nice duckets for the large football game between the Harvards and the Yales and that he is taking a crew of guys with him to New Haven the next day to hustle these duckets, and what about me going along and helping to hustle these duckets and making a few bobs for myself, which is an invitation that sounds very pleasant to me, indeed.

Now of course it is very difficult for anybody to get nice duckets to a large football game between the Harvards and the Yales unless they are personally college guys, and Sam the Gonoph is by no means a college guy. In fact, the nearest Sam ever comes to a college is once when he is passing through the yard belonging to the Princetons, but Sam is on the fly at the time as a gendarme is after him, so he does not really see much of the college.

But every college guy is entitled to duckets to a large

football game with which his college is connected, and it is really surprising how many college guys do not care to see large football games even after they get their duckets, especially if a ticket spec such as Sam the Gonoph comes along offering them a few bobs more than the duckets are worth. I suppose this is because a college guy figures he can see a large football game when he is old, while many things are taking place around and about that it is necessary for him to see while he is young enough to really enjoy them, such as the Follies.

Anyway, many college guys are always willing to listen to reason when Sam the Gonoph comes around offering to buy their duckets, and then Sam takes these duckets and sells them to customers for maybe ten times the price the duckets call for, and in this way Sam does very good for himself.

I know Sam the Gonoph for maybe twenty years, and always he is speculating in duckets of one kind and another. Sometimes it is duckets for the world's series, and sometimes for big fights, and sometimes it is duckets for nothing but lawn-tennis games, although why anybody wishes to see such a thing as lawn tennis is always a very great mystery to Sam the Gonoph and everybody else.

But in all those years I see Sam dodging around under the feet of the crowds at these large events, or running through the special trains offering to buy or sell duckets, I never hear of Sam personally attending any of these events except maybe a baseball game, or a fight, for Sam has practically no interest in anything but a little profit on his duckets.

He is a short, chunky, black-looking guy with a big beezer, and he is always sweating even on a cold day, and he comes from down around Essex Street, on the lower East Side. Moreover, Sam the Gonoph's crew generally comes from the lower East Side, too, for as Sam goes along he makes plenty of potatoes for himself and branches out quite some, and has a lot of assistants hustling duckets around these different events.

When Sam is younger the cops consider him hard to get along with, and in fact his monicker, the Gonoph, comes from his young days down on the lower East Side, and I hear it is Yiddish for thief, but of course as Sam gets older and starts gathering plenty of potatoes, he will not think of stealing anything. At least not much, and especially if it is anything that is nailed down.

Well, anyway, I meet Sam the Gonoph and his crew at the information desk in Grand Central the next morning, and this is how I come to be in New Haven on the day of the large football game between the Harvards and the Yales.

For such a game as this, Sam has all his best hustlers, including such as Jew Louie, Nubbsy Taylor, Benny South Street and old Liverlips, and to look at these parties you will never suspect that they are top-notch ducket hustlers. The best you will figure them is a lot of guys who are not to be met up with in a dark alley, but then ducket-hustling is a rough-and-tumble dodge and it will scarcely be good policy to hire female impersonators.

Now while we are hustling these duckets out around the main gates of the Yale Bowl I notice a very beautiful little doll of maybe sixteen or seventeen standing around watching the crowd, and I can see she is waiting for somebody, as many dolls often do at football games. But I can also see that this little doll is very much worried as the crowd keeps going in, and it is getting on toward game time. In fact, by and by I can see this little doll has tears in her eyes and if there is anything I hate to see it is tears in a doll's eyes.

So finally I go over to her, and I say as follows: "What is eating you, little Miss?"

"Oh," she says, "I am waiting for Elliot. He is to come up from New York and meet me here to take me to the game, but he is not here yet, and I am afraid something happens to him. Furthermore," she says, the tears in her eyes getting very large, indeed, "I am afraid I will miss the game because he has my ticket."

"Why," I say, "this is a very simple proposition. I will sell you a choice ducket for only a sawbuck, which is ten dollars in your language, and you are getting such a bargain only because the game is about to begin, and the market is going down."

"But," she says, "I do not have ten dollars. In fact, I have only fifty cents left in my purse, and this is worrying me very much, for what will I do if Elliot does not meet me? You see," she says, "I come from Miss Peevy's school at Worcester, and I only have enough money to pay my railroad fare here, and of course I cannot ask Miss Peevy for any money as I do not wish her to know I am going away."

Well, naturally all this is commencing to sound to me like a hard-luck story such as any doll is apt to tell, so I go on about my business because I figure she will next be trying to put the lug on me for a ducket, or maybe for her railroad fare back to Worcester, although generally dolls with hard-luck stories live in San Francisco.

She keeps on standing there, and I notice she is now crying more than somewhat, and I get to thinking to myself that she is about as cute a little doll as I ever see, although too young for anybody to be bothering much about. Furthermore, I get to thinking that maybe she is on the level, at that, with her story.

Well, by this time the crowd is nearly all in the Bowl, and only a few parties such as coppers and hustlers of one kind and another are left standing outside, and there is much cheering going on inside, when Sam the Gonoph comes up looking very much disgusted, and speaks as follows:

"What do you think?" Sam says. "I am left with seven duckets on my hands, and these guys around here will not pay as much as face value for them, and they stand me better than three bucks over that. Well," Sam says, "I am certainly not going to let them go for less than they call for if I have to eat them. What do you guys say we use these duckets ourselves and go in and see the game? Personally," Sam says, "I often wish to see one of these large football games just to find out what makes suckers willing to pay so much for duckets."

Well, this seems to strike one and all, including myself, as a great idea, because none of the rest of us ever see a large football game either, so we start for the gate, and as we pass the little doll who is still crying, I say to Sam the Gonoph like this:

"Listen, Sam," I say, "you have seven duckets, and we are only six, and here is a little doll who is stood up by her guy, and has no ducket, and no potatoes to buy one with, so what about taking her with us?"

Well, this is all right with Sam the Gonoph, and none of the others object, so I step up to the little doll and invite her to go with us, and right away she stops crying and begins smiling, and saying we are very kind indeed. She gives Sam the Gonoph an extra big smile, and right away Sam is saying she is very cute, indeed, and then she gives old Liverlips an even bigger smile, and what is more she takes old Liverlips by the arm and walks with him, and old Liverlips is not only very much astonished, but very much pleased. In fact, old Liverlips begins stepping out very spry, and Liverlips is not such a guy as cares to have any part of dolls, young or old.

But while walking with old Liverlips, the little doll talks very friendly to Jew Louie and to Nubbsy Taylor and Benny South Street, and even to me, and by and by you will think to see us that we are all her uncles, although of course if this little doll really knows who she is with, the chances are she will start chucking faints one after the other.

Anybody can see that she has very little experience in this wicked old world, and in fact is somewhat rattle-headed, because she gabs away very freely about her personal business. In fact, before we are in the Bowl she lets it out that she runs away from Miss Peevy's school to elope with this Elliot, and she says the idea is they are to be married in Hartford after the game. In fact, she says Elliot wishes to go to Hartford and be married before the game.

"But," she says, "my brother John is playing substitute with the Yales to-day, and I cannot think of getting married to anybody before I see him play, although I am much in love with Elliot. He is a wonderful dancer," she says, "and very romantic. I meet him in Atlantic City last summer. Now we are eloping," she says, "because my father does not care for Elliot whatever. In fact, my father hates Elliot, although he only sees him once, and it is because he hates Elliot so that my father sends me to Miss Peevy's school in Worcester. She is an old pill. Do you not think my father is unreasonable?" she says.

Well, of course none of us have any ideas on such propositions as this, although old Liverlips tells the little doll he is with her right or wrong, and pretty soon we are inside the Bowl and sitting in seats as good as any in the joint. It seems we are on the Harvards' side of the field, although of course I will never know this if the little doll does not mention it.

She seems to know everything about this football business, and as soon as we sit down she tries to point out her brother playing substitute for the Yales, saying he is the fifth guy from the end among a bunch of guys sitting on a bench on the other side of the field all wrapped in blankets. But we cannot make much of him from where we sit, and anyway it does not look to me as if he has much of a job.

It seems we are right in the middle of all the Harvards and they are making an awful racket, what with yelling, and singing, and one thing and another, because it seems the game is going on when we get in, and that the Harvards are shoving the Yales around more than somewhat. So our little doll lets everybody know she is in favour of the Yales by yelling, "Hold 'em, Yale!"

Personally, I cannot tell which are the Harvards and which are the Yales at first, and Sam the Gonoph and the others are as dumb as I am, but she explains the Harvards are wearing the red shirts and the Yales the blue shirts, and by and by we are yelling for the Yales to hold 'em, too, although of course it is only on account of our little doll wishing the Yales to hold 'em, and not because any of us care one way or the other.

Well, it seems that the idea of a lot of guys and a little doll getting right among them and yelling for the Yales to hold 'em is very repulsive to the Harvards around us, although any of them must admit it is very good advice to the Yales, at that, and some of them start making cracks of one kind and another, especially at our little doll. The chances are they are very jealous because she is out-yelling them, because I will say one thing for our little doll, she can yell about as loud as anybody I ever hear, male or female.

A couple of Harvards sitting in front of old Liverlips are imitating our little doll's voice, and making guys around them laugh very heartily, but all of a sudden these parties leave their seats and go away in great haste, their faces very pale, indeed, and I figure maybe they are both taken sick at the same moment, but afterwards I learn that Liverlips takes a big shiv out of his pocket and opens it and tells them very confidentially that he is going to carve their ears off.

Naturally, I do not blame the Harvards for going away in great haste, for Liverlips is such a looking guy as you will figure to take great delight in carving off ears. Furthermore, Nubbsy Taylor and Benny South Street and Jew Louie and even Sam the Gonoph commence exchanging such glances with other Harvards around us who are making cracks at our little doll that presently there is almost a dead silence in our neighbourhood, except for our little doll yelling, "Hold 'em, Yale!" You see by this time we are all very fond of our little doll because she is so cute looking and has so much zing in her, and we do not wish anybody making cracks at her or at us either, and especially at us.

In fact, we are so fond of her that when she happens to mention that she is a little chilly, Jew Louie and Nubbsy Taylor slip around among the Harvards and come back with four steamer rugs, six mufflers, two pairs of gloves, and a thermos bottle full of hot coffee for her, and Jew Louie says if she wishes a mink coat to just say the word. But she already has a mink coat. Furthermore, Jew Louie brings her a big bunch of red flowers that he finds on a doll with one of the Harvards, and he is much disappointed when she says it is the wrong colour for her.

Well, finally the game is over, and I do not remember

much about it, although afterwards I hear that our little doll's brother John plays substitute for the Yales very good. But it seems that the Harvards win, and our little doll is very sad indeed about this, and is sitting there looking out over the field, which is now covered with guys dancing around as if they all suddenly go daffy, and it seems they are all Harvards, because there is really no reason for the Yales to do any dancing.

All of a sudden our little doll looks toward one end of the field, and says as follows:

"Oh, they are going to take our goal posts!"

Sure enough, a lot of the Harvards are gathering around the posts at this end of the field, and are pulling and hauling at the posts, which seem to be very stout posts, indeed. Personally, I will not give you eight cents for these posts, but afterwards one of the Yales tells me that when a football team wins a game it is considered the proper caper for this team's boosters to grab the other guy's goal posts. But he is not able to tell me what good the posts are after they get them, and this is one thing that will always be a mystery to me.

Anyway, while we are watching the goings-on around the goal posts, our little doll says come on and jumps up and runs down an aisle and out on to the field, and into the crowd around the goal posts, so naturally we follow her. Somehow she manages to wiggle through the crowd of Harvards around the posts, and the next thing anybody knows she shins up one of the posts faster than you can say scat, and pretty soon is roosting out on the cross-bar between the posts like a chipmunk.

Afterwards she explains that her idea is the Harvards will not be ungentlemanly enough to pull down the goal posts with a lady roosting on them, but it seems these Harvards are no gentlemen, and keep on pulling, and the posts commence to teeter, and our little doll is teetering with them, although of course she is in no danger if she falls because she is sure to fall on the Harvards' noggins, and the way I look at it, the noggin of anybody who will be found giving any time to pulling down goal posts is apt to be soft enough to break a very long fall.

Now Sam the Gonoph and old Liverlips and Nubbsy Taylor and Benny South Street and Jew Louie and I reach the crowd around the goal posts at about the same time, and our little doll sees us from her roost and yells to us as follows:

"Do not let them take our posts!"

Well, about this time one of the Harvards who seems to be about nine feet high reaches over six other guys and hits me on the chin and knocks me so far that when I pick myself up I am pretty well out of the way of everybody and have a chance to see what is going on.

217

Afterwards somebody tells me that the guy probably thinks I am one of the Yales coming to the rescue of the goal posts, but I wish to say I will always have a very low opinion of college guys, because I remember two other guys punch me as I am going through the air, unable to defend myself.

Now Sam the Gonoph and Nubbsy Taylor and Jew Louie and Benny South Street and old Liverlips somehow manage to ease their way through the crowd until they are under the goal posts, and our little doll is much pleased to see them, because the Harvards are now making the posts teeter more than somewhat with their pulling, and it looks as if the posts will go any minute.

Of course Sam the Gonoph does not wish any trouble with these parties, and he tries to speak nicely to the guys who are pulling at the posts, saying as follows:

"Listen," Sam says, "the little doll up there does not wish you to take these posts."

Well, maybe they do not hear Sam's words in the confusion, or if they do hear them they do not wish to pay any attention to them, for one of the Harvards mashes Sam's derby hat down over his eyes, and another smacks old Liverlips on the left ear, while Jew Louie and Nubbsy Taylor and Benny South Street are shoved around quite some.

"All right," Sam the Gonoph says, as soon as he can pull his hat off his eyes, "all right, gentlemen, if you wish to play this way. Now, boys, let them have it!"

So Sam the Gonoph and Nubbsy Taylor and Jew Louie and Benny South Street and old Liverlips begin letting them have it, and what they let them have it with is not only their dukes, but with the good old difference in their dukes, because these guys are by no means suckers when it comes to a battle, and they all carry something in their pockets to put in their dukes in case of a fight, such as a dollar's worth of nickels rolled up tight.

Furthermore, they are using the old leather, kicking guys in the stomach when they are not able to hit them on the chin, and Liverlips is also using his noodle to good advantage, grabbing guys by their coat lapels and yanking them into him so he can butt them between the eyes with his noggin, and I wish to say that old Liverlips' noggin is a very dangerous weapon at all times.

Well, the ground around them is soon covered with Harvards, and it seems that some Yales are also mixed up with them, being Yales who think Sam the Gonoph and his guys are other Yales defending the goal posts, and wishing to help out. But of course Sam the Gonoph and his guys cannot tell the Yales from the Harvards, and do not have time to ask which is which, so they are just letting everybody have it who comes along. And while all this is going on our little doll is sitting up on the cross-bar and yelling plenty of encouragement to Sam and his guys.

Now it turns out that these Harvards are by no means soft touches in a scrabble such as this, and as fast as they are flattened they get up and keep belting away, and while the old experience is running for Sam the Gonoph and Jew Louie and Nubbsy Taylor and Benny South Street and old Liverlips early in the fight, the Harvards have youth in their favour.

Pretty soon the Harvards are knocking down Sam the Gonoph, then they start knocking down Nubbsy Taylor, and by and by they are knocking down Benny South Street and Jew Louie and Liverlips, and it is so much fun that the Harvards forget all about the goal posts. Of course as fast as Sam the Gonoph and his guys are knocked down they also get up, but the Harvards are too many for them, and they are getting an awful shellacking when the nine-foot guy who flattens me, and who is knocking down Sam the Gonoph so often he is becoming a great nuisance to Sam, sings out:

"Listen," he says, "these are game guys, even if they do go to Yale. Let us cease knocking them down," he says, "and give them a cheer."

So the Harvards knock down Sam the Gonoph and Nubbsy Taylor and Jew Louie and Benny South Street and old Liverlips just once more and then all the Harvards put their heads together and say rah-rah-rah, very loud, and go away, leaving the goal posts still standing, with our little doll still roosting on the cross-bar, although afterwards I hear some Harvards who are not in the fight get the posts at the other end of the field and sneak away with them. But I always claim these posts do not count.

Well, sitting there on the ground because he is too tired to get up from the last knockdown, and holding one hand to his right eye, which is closed tight, Sam the Gonoph is by no means a well guy, and all around and about him is much suffering among his crew. But our little doll is hopping up and down chattering like a jaybird and running between old Liverlips, who is stretched out against one goal post, and Nubbsy Taylor, who is leaning up against the other, and she is trying to mop the blood off their kissers with a handkerchief the size of a postage stamp.

Benny South Street is laying across Jew Louie and both are still snoring from the last knockdown, and the Bowl is now pretty much deserted except for the newspaper scribes away up in the press box, who do not seem to realize that the Battle of the Century just comes off in front of them. It is coming on dark, when all of a sudden a guy pops up out of the dusk wearing white spats and an overcoat with a fur collar, and he rushes up to our little doll.

"Clarice," he says, "I am looking for you high and low. My train is stalled for hours behind a wreck the other side of

Bridgeport, and I get here just after the game is over. But," he says, "I figure you will be waiting somewhere for me. Let us hurry on to Hartford, darling," he says.

Well, when he hears this voice, Sam the Gonoph opens his good eye wide and takes a peek at the guy. Then all of a sudden Sam jumps up and wobbles over to the guy and hits him a smack between the eyes. Sam is wobbling because his legs are not so good from the shellacking he takes off the Harvards, and furthermore he is away off in Ins punching as the guy only goes to his knees and comes right up standing again as our little doll lets out a screech and speaks as follows:

"Oo-oo!" she says. "Do not hit Elliot! He is not after our goal posts!"

"Elliot?" Sam the Gonoph says. "This is no Elliot. This is nobody but Gigolo Georgie. I can tell him by his white spats," Sam says, "and I am now going to get even for the pasting I take from the Harvards."

Then he nails the guy again and this time he seems to have a little more on his punch, for the guy goes down and Sam the Gonoph gives him the leather very good, although our little doll is still screeching, and begging Sam not to hurt Elliot. But of course the rest of us know it is not Elliot, no matter what he may tell her, but only Gigolo Georgie.

Well, the rest of us figure we may as well take a little

something out of Georgie's hide, too, but as we start for him he gives a quick wiggle and hops to his feet and tears across the field, and the last we see of him is his white spats flying through one of the portals.

Now a couple of other guys come up out of the dusk, and one of them is a tall, fine-looking guy with a white moustache and anybody can see that he is somebody, and what happens but our little doll runs right into his arms and kisses him on the white moustache and calls him daddy and starts to cry more than somewhat, so I can see we lose our little doll then and there. And now the guy with the white moustache walks up to Sam the Gonoph and sticks out his duke and says as follows:

"Sir," he says, "permit me the honour of shaking the hand which does me the very signal service of chastising the scoundrel who just escapes from the field. And," he says, "permit me to introduce myself to you. I am J. Hildreth Van Cleve, president of the Van Cleve Trust. I am notified early to-day by Miss Peevy of my daughter's sudden departure from school, and we learn she purchases a ticket for New Haven. I at once suspect this fellow has something to do with it. Fortunately," he says, "I have these private detectives here keeping tab on him for some time, knowing my child's schoolgirl infatuation for him, so we easily trail him here. We are on the train with him, and arrive in time for your last little scene with him. Sir," he says, "again I thank you."

"I know who you are, Mr. Van Cleve," Sam the Gonoph says. "You are the Van Cleve who is down to his last forty million. But," he says, "do not thank me for putting the slug on Gigolo Georgie. He is a bum in spades, and I am only sorry he fools your nice little kid even for a minute, although," Sam says, "I figure she must be dumber than she looks to be fooled by such a guy as Gigolo Georgie."

"I hate him," the little doll says. "I hate him because he is a coward. He does not stand up and fight when he is hit like you and Liverlips and the others. I never wish to see him again."

"Do not worry," Sam the Gonoph says. "I will be too close to Gigolo Georgie as soon as I recover from my wounds for him to stay in this part of the country."

Well, I do not see Sam the Gonoph or Nubbsy Taylor or Benny South Street or Jew Louie or Liverlips for nearly a year after this, and then it comes on fall again and one day I get to thinking that here it is Friday and the next day the Harvards are playing the Yales a large football game in Boston.

I figure it is a great chance for me to join up with Sam the Gonoph again to hustle duckets for him for this game, and I know Sam will be leaving along about midnight with his crew. So I go over to the Grand Central station at such a time, and sure enough he comes along by and by, busting through the crowd in the station with Nubbsy Taylor and Benny South Street and Jew Louie and old Liverlips at his heels, and they seem very much excited.

"Well, Sam," I say, as I hurry along with them, "here I am ready to hustle duckets for you again, and I hope and trust we do a nice business."

"Duckets!" Sam the Gonoph says. "We are not hustling duckets for this game, although you can go with us, and welcome. We are going to Boston," he says, "to root for the Yales to kick hell out of the Harvards and we are going as the personal guests of Miss Clarice Van Cleve and her old man."

"Hold 'em, Yale!" old Liverlips says, as he pushes me to one side and the whole bunch goes trotting through the gate to catch their train, and I then notice they are all wearing blue feathers in their hats with a little white Y on these feathers such as college guys always wear at football games, and that moreover Sam the Gonoph is carrying a Yale pennant.

11

EARTHQUAKE

Personally, I do not care for coppers, but I believe in being courteous to them at all times, so when Johnny Brannigan comes into Mindy's restaurant one Friday evening and sits down in the same booth with me, because there are no other vacant seats in the joint, I give him a huge hello.

Furthermore, I offer him a cigarette and say how pleased I am to see how well he is looking, although as a matter of fact Johnny Brannigan looks very terrible, what with big black circles under his eyes and his face thinner than somewhat.

In fact, Johnny Brannigan looks as if he is sick, and I am secretly hoping that it is something fatal, because the way I figure it there are a great many coppers in this world, and a few less may be a good thing for one and all concerned.

But naturally I do not mention this hope to Johnny Brannigan, as Johnny Brannigan belongs to what is called the gunman squad and is known to carry a blackjack in his pants pocket and furthermore he is known to boff guys on their noggins with this jack if they get too fresh with him, and for all I know Johnny Brannigan may consider such a hope about his health very fresh indeed.

Earthquake

Now the last time I see Johnny Brannigan before this is in Good Time Charley Bernstein's little joint in Forty-eighth Street with three other coppers, and what Johnny is there for is to put the arm on a guy by the name of Earthquake, who is called Earthquake because he is so fond of shaking things up.

In fact, at the time I am speaking of, Earthquake has this whole town shaken up, what with shooting and stabbing and robbing different citizens, and otherwise misconducting himself, and the law wishes to place Earthquake in the electric chair, as he is considered a great knock to the community.

Now the only reason Brannigan does not put the arm on Earthquake at this time is because Earthquake picks up one of Good Time Charley Bernstein's tables and kisses Johnny Brannigan with same, and furthermore, Earthquake outs with the old equalizer and starts blasting away at the coppers who are with Johnny Brannigan, and he keeps them so busy dodging slugs that they do not have any leisure to put the arm on him, and the next thing anybody knows, Earthquake takes it on the lam out of there.

Well, personally, I also take it on the lam myself, as I do not wish to be around when Johnny Brannigan comes to, as I figure Johnny may be somewhat bewildered and will start boffing people over the noggin with his jack thinking they are all Earthquake, no matter who they are, and I do not see

228

Johnny again until this evening in Mindy's.

But in the meantime I hear rumours that Johnny Brannigan is out of town looking for Earthquake, because it seems that while misconducting himself Earthquake severely injures a copper by the name of Mulcahy. In fact, it seems that Earthquake injures him so severely that Mulcahy hauls off and dies, and if there is one thing that is against the law in this town it is injuring a copper in such a manner. In fact, it is apt to cause great indignation among other coppers.

It is considered very illegal to severely injure any citizen in this town in such a way as to make him haul off and die, but naturally it is not apt to cause any such indignation as injuring a copper, as this town has more citizens to spare than coppers.

Well, sitting there with Johnny Brannigan, I get to wondering if he ever meets up with Earthquake while he is looking for him, and if so how he comes out, for Earthquake is certainly not such a guy as I will care to meet up with, even if I am a copper.

Earthquake is a guy of maybe six foot three, and weighing a matter of two hundred and twenty pounds, and all these pounds are nothing but muscle. Anybody will tell you that Earthquake is one of the strongest guys in this town, because it seems he once works in a foundry and picks up much of his muscle there. In fact, Earthquake likes to show how strong he is at all times, and one of his ways of showing this is to grab a full-sized guy in either duke and hold them straight up in the air over his head.

Sometimes after he gets tired of holding these guys over his head, he will throw them plumb away, especially if they are coppers, or maybe knock their noggins together and leave them with their noggins very sore indeed. When he is in real good humour, Earthquake does not think anything of going into a night club and taking it apart and chucking the pieces out into the street, along with the owner and the waiters and maybe some of the customers, so you can see Earthquake is a very high-spirited guy, and full of fun.

Personally, I do not see why Earthquake does not get a job in a circus as a strong guy, because there is no percentage in wasting all this strength for nothing, but when I mention this idea to Earthquake one time, he says he cannot bear to think of keeping regular hours such as a circus might wish.

Well, Johnny Brannigan does not have anything to say to me at first as we sit there in Mindy's, but by and by he looks at me and speaks as follows:

"You remember Earthquake?" he says. "You remember he is very strong?"

"Strong?" I say to Johnny Brannigan. "Why, there is nobody stronger than Earthquake. Why," I say, "Earthquake is strong enough to hold up a building."

"Yes," Johnny Brannigan says, "what you say is very true. He is strong enough to hold up a building. Yes," he says, "Earthquake is very strong indeed. Now I will tell you about Earthquake."

It is maybe three months after Earthquake knocks off Mulcahy [Johnny Brannigan says] that we get a tip he is in a town by the name of New Orleans, and because I am personally acquainted with him, I am sent there to put the arm on him. But when I get to this New Orleans, I find Earthquake blows out of there and does not leave any forwarding address.

Well, I am unable to get any trace of him for some days, and it looks as if I am on a bust, when I happen to run into a guy by the name of Saul the Soldier, from Greenwich Village. Saul the Soldier winds up in New Orleans following the horse races, and he is very glad indeed to meet a friend from his old home town, and I am also glad to meet Saul, because I am getting very lonesome in New Orleans. Well, Saul knows New Orleans pretty well, and he takes me around and about, and finally I ask him if he can tell me where Earthquake is, and Saul speaks as follows:

"Why," Saul says, "Earthquake sails away on a ship for Central America not long ago with a lot of guys that are going to join a revolution there. I think," Saul says, "they are going to a place by the name of Nicaragua."

Well, I wire my headquarters and they tell me to go after Earthquake no matter where he is, because it seems the bladders back home are asking what kind of a police force do we have, anyway, and why is somebody not arrested for something.

I sail on a fruit steamer, and finally I get to this Nicaragua, and to a town that is called Managua.

Well, for a week or so I knock around here and there looking for Earthquake, but I cannot find hide or hair of him, and I am commencing to think that Saul the Soldier gives me a bum steer.

It is pretty hot in this town of Managua, and of an afternoon when I get tired of looking for Earthquake I go to a little park in the centre of the town where there are many shade trees. It is a pretty park, although down there they call it a plaza, and across from this plaza there is a big old two-story stone building that seems to be a convent, because I see many nuns and small female kids popping in and out of a door on one side of the building, which seems to be the main entrance.

One afternoon I am sitting in the little plaza when a big guy in sloppy white clothes comes up and sits down on another bench near me, and I am greatly surprised to see that this guy is nobody but Earthquake.

He does not see me at first, and in fact he does not know

I am present until I step over to him and out with my jack and knock him bow-legged; because, knowing Earthquake, I know there is no use starting out with him by shaking hands. I do not boff him so very hard, at that, but just hard enough to make him slightly insensible for a minute, while I put the handcuffs on him.

Well, when he opens his eyes, Earthquake looks up at the trees, as if he thinks maybe a coconut drops down and beans him, and it is several minutes before he sees me, and then he leaps up and roars, and acts as if he is greatly displeased. But then he discovers that he is handcuffed, and he sits down again and speaks as follows:

"Hello, copper," Earthquake says. "When do you get in?"

I tell him how long I am there, and how much inconvenience he causes me by not being more prominent, and Earthquake says the fact of the matter is he is out in the jungles with a lot of guys trying to rig up a revolution, but they are so slow getting started they finally exasperate him, and he comes into town.

Well, finally we get to chatting along very pleasant about this and that, and although he is away only a few months, Earthquake is much interested in what is going on in New York and asks me many questions, and I tell him that the liquor around town is getting better.

"Furthermore, Earthquake," I say, "they are holding a nice warm seat for you up at Ossining."

"Well, copper," Earthquake says, "I am sorry I scrag Mulcahy, at that. In fact," he says, "it really is an accident. I do not mean to scrag him. I am aiming at another guy, copper," he says. "In fact," he says, "I am aiming at you."

Now about this time the bench seems to move from under me, and I find myself sitting on the ground, and the ground also seems to be trying to get from under me, and I hear loud crashing noises here and there, and a great roaring, and at first I think maybe Earthquake takes to shaking things up, when I see him laid out on the ground about fifty feet from me.

I get to my pins, but the ground is still wobbling somewhat and I can scarcely walk over to Earthquake, who is now sitting up very indignant, and when he sees me he says to me like this:

"Personally," he says, "I consider it a very dirty trick for you to boff me again when I am not looking."

Well, I explain to Earthquake that I do not boff him again, and that as near as I can figure out what happens is that we are overtaken by what he is named for, which is an earthquake, and looking around and about, anybody can see that this is very true, as great clouds of dust are rising from piles of stone and timber where fair-sized buildings stand a

234

few minutes before, and guys and dolls are running every which way.

Now I happens to look across at the convent, and I can see that it is something of a wreck and is very likely to be more so any minute, as the walls are teetering this way and that, and mostly they are teetering inward. Furthermore, I can hear much screeching from inside the old building.

Then I notice the door in the side of the building that seems to be the main entrance to the convent is gone, leaving the doorway open, and now I must explain to you about this doorway, as it figures quite some in what later comes off. It is a fairly wide doorway in the beginning with a frame of heavy timber set in the side of the stone building, with a timber arch at the top, and the wall around this doorway seems to be caving in from the top and sides, so that the doorway is now shaped like the letter V upside down, with the timber framework bending, instead of breaking.

As near as I can make out, this doorway is the only entrance to the convent that is not closed up by falling stone and timber, and it is a sure thing that pretty soon this opening will be plugged up, too, so I speak to Earthquake as follows:

"Earthquake," I say, "there are a lot of nuns and kids in this joint over here, and I judge from the screeching going on inside that some of them are very much alive. But," I say, "they will not be alive in a few minutes, because the walls are going to tip over and make jelly of them."

"Why, yes," Earthquake says, taking a peek at the convent, "what you say seems reasonable. Well, copper," he says, "what is to be done in this situation?"

"Well," I say, "I see a chance to snatch a few of them out of there if you will help me. Earthquake," I say, "I understand you are a very strong guy?"

"Strong?" Earthquake says. "Why," he says, "you know I am maybe the strongest guy in the world."

"Earthquake," I say, "you see the doorway yonder? Well, Earthquake, if you are strong enough to hold this doorway apart and keep it from caving in, I will slip in through it and pass out any nuns and kids that may be alive."

"Why," Earthquake says, "this is as bright an idea as I ever hear from a copper. Why," he says, "I will hold this doorway apart until next Pancake Tuesday."

Then Earthquake holds out his dukes and I unlock the cuffs. Then he runs over to the doorway of the convent, and I run after him.

This doorway is now closing in very fast indeed, from the weight of tons of stones pressing against the timber frame, and by the time we get there the letter V upside down is so very narrow from top to bottom that Earthquake has a tough time wedging himself into what little opening is left.

But old Earthquake gets in, facing inward, and once in, he begins pushing against the door-frame on either side of him, and I can see at once how he gets his reputation as a strong guy. The doorway commences to widen, and as it widens Earthquake keeps spraddling his legs apart, so that pretty soon there is quite a space between his legs. His head is bent forward so far his chin is resting on his wishbone, as there is plenty of weight on Earthquake's neck and shoulders, and in fact he reminds me of pictures I see of a guy by the name of Atlas holding up the world.

It is through the opening between his spraddled-out legs that I pop, looking for the nuns and the kids. Most of them are in a big room on the ground floor of the building, and they are all huddled up close together screeching in chorus.

I motion them to follow me, and I lead them back over the wreckage, and along the hall to the spot where Earthquake is holding the doorway apart, and I wish to state at this time he is doing a very nice job of same.

But the weight on Earthquake's shoulders must be getting very hefty indeed, because his shoulders are commencing to stoop under it, and his chin is now almost down to his stomach, and his face is purple.

Now through Earthquake's spraddled-out legs, and into the street outside the convent wall, I push five nuns and fifteen female kids. One old nun refuses to be pushed through

Earthquake's legs, and I finally make out from the way she is waving her hands around and about that there are other kids in the convent, and she wishes me to get them, too.

Well, I can see that any more delay is going to be something of a strain on Earthquake, and maybe a little irritating to him, so I speak to him as follows:

"Earthquake," I say, "you are looking somewhat peaked to me, and plumb tired out. Now then," I say, "if you will step aside, I will hold the doorway apart awhile, and you can go with this old nun and find the rest of the kids."

"Copper," Earthquake says, speaking from off his chest because he cannot get his head up very high, "I can hold this doorway apart with my little fingers if one of them is not sprained, so go ahead and round up the rest."

So I let the old nun lead me back to another part of the building, where I judge she knows there are more kids, and in fact the old nun is right, but it only takes one look to show me there is no use taking these kids out of the place.

Then we go back to Earthquake, and he hears us coming across the rubbish and half-raises his head from off his chest and looks at me, and I can see the sweat is dribbling down his kisser and his eyes are bugging out, and anybody can see that he is quite upset. As I get close to him he speaks to me as follows:

"Get her out quick," he says. "Get the old doll out."

So I push the old nun through Earthquake's spraddled-out legs into the open, and I notice there is not as much space between these legs as formerly, so I judge the old mumblety-pegs are giving out. Then I say to Earthquake like this:

"Well, Earthquake," I say, "it is now time for you and me to be going. I will go outside first," I say, "and then you can ease yourself out, and we will look around for a means of getting back to New York, as headquarters will be getting worried."

"Listen, copper," Earthquake says, "I am never going to get out of this spot. If I move an inch forward or an inch backward, down comes this whole shebang. But, copper," he says, "I see before I get in here that it is a hundred to one against me getting out again, so do not think I am trapped without knowing it. The way I look at it," Earthquake says, "it is better than the chair, at that. I can last a few minutes longer," he says, "and you better get outside."

Well, I pop out between Earthquake's spraddled-out legs, because I figure I am better off outside than in, no matter what, and when I am outside I stand there looking at Earthquake and wondering what I can do about him. But I can see that he is right when he tells me that if he moves one way or another the cave-in will come, so there seems to be nothing much I can do.

Then I hear Earthquake calling me, and I step up close

enough to hear him speak as follows:

"Copper," he says, "tell Mulcahy's people I am sorry. And do not forget that you owe old Earthquake whatever you figure your life is worth. I do not know yet why I do not carry out my idea of letting go all holds the minute you push the old nun out of here, and taking you with me wherever I am going. Maybe," he says, "I am getting soft-hearted. Well, good-bye, copper," he says.

"Good-bye, Earthquake," I say, and I walk away.

So, [Johnny Brannigan says], now you know about Earthquake.

"Well," I say, "this is indeed a harrowing story, Johnny. But," I say, "if you leave Earthquake holding up anything maybe he is still holding it up, because Earthquake is certainly a very strong guy."

"Yes," Johnny Brannigan says, "he is very strong indeed. But," he says, "as I am walking away another shock hits, and when I get off the ground again and look at the convent, I can see that not even Earthquake is strong enough to stand off this one."

12

"GENTLEMEN, THE KING!"

On Tuesday evenings I always go to Bobby's Chop House to get myself a beef stew, the beef stews in Bobby's being very nourishing, indeed, and quite reasonable. In fact, the beef stews in Bobby's are considered a most fashionable dish by one and all on Broadway on Tuesday evenings.

So on this Tuesday evening I am talking about, I am in Bobby's wrapping myself around a beef stew and reading the race results in the *Journal,* when who comes into the joint but two old friends of mine from Philly, and a third guy I never see before in my life, but who seems to be an old sort of guy, and very fierce looking.

One of these old friends of mine from Philly is a guy by the name of Izzy Cheesecake, who is called Izzy Cheesecake because he is all the time eating cheesecake around delicatessen joints, although of course this is nothing against him, as cheesecake is very popular in some circles, and goes very good with java. Anyway, this Izzy Cheesecake has another name, which is Morris something, and he is slightly Jewish, and has a large beezer, and is considered a handy man in many respects.

The other old friend of mine from Philly is a guy by the name of Kitty Quick, who is maybe thirty-two or three years old, and who is a lively guy in every way. He is a great hand for wearing good clothes, and he is mobbed up with some very good people in Philly in his day, and at one time has plenty of dough, although I hear that lately things are not going so good for Kitty Quick, or for anybody else in Philly, as far as that is concerned.

Now of course I do not rap to these old friends of mine from Philly at once, and in fact I put the *Journal* up in front of my face, because it is never good policy to rap to visitors in this town, especially visitors from Philly, until you know why they are visiting. But it seems that Kitty Quick spies me before I can get the *Journal* up high enough, and he comes over to my table at once, bringing Izzy Cheesecake and the other guy with him, so naturally I give them a big hello, very cordial, and ask them to sit down and have a few beef stews with me, and as they pull up chairs, Kitty Quick says to me like this:

"Do you know Jo-jo from Chicago?" he says, pointing his thumb at the third guy.

Well, of course I know Jo-jo by his reputation, which is very alarming, but I never meet up with him before, and if it is left to me, I will never meet up with him at all, because Jo-jo is considered a very uncouth character, even in Chicago.

He is an Italian, and a short wide guy, very heavy set, and slow moving, and with jowls you can cut steaks off of, and sleepy eyes, and he somehow reminds me of an old lion I once see in a cage in Ringling's circus. He has a black moustache, and he is an old-timer out in Chicago, and is pointed out to visitors to the city as a very remarkable guy because he lives as long as he does, which is maybe forty years.

His right name is Antonio something, and why he is called Jo-jo I never hear, but I suppose it is because Jo-jo is handier than Antonio. He shakes hands with me, and says he is pleased to meet me, and then he sits down and begins taking on beef stew very rapidly while Kitty Quick says to me as follows:

"Listen," he says, "do you know anybody in Europe?"

Well, this is a most unexpected question, and naturally I am not going to reply to unexpected questions by guys from Philly without thinking them over very carefully, so to gain time while I think, I say to Kitty Quick:

"Which Europe do you mean?"

"Why," Kitty says, greatly surprised, "is there more than one Europe? I mean the big Europe on the Atlantic Ocean. This is the Europe where we are going, and if you know anybody there we will be glad to go around and say hello to them for you. We are going to Europe on the biggest proposition anybody ever hears of," he says. "In fact," he says, "it is a proposition which will make us all rich. We are sailing to-night."

Well, offhand I cannot think of anybody I know in Europe, and if I do know anybody there I will certainly not wish such parties as Kitty Quick, and Izzy Cheesecake, and Jo-jo going around saying hello to them, but of course I do not mention such a thought out loud. I only say I hope and trust that they have a very good *bon voyage* and do not suffer too much from seasickness. Naturally I do not ask what their proposition is, because if I ask such a question they may think I wish to find out, and will consider me a very nosey guy, but I figure the chances are they are going to look after some commercial matter, such as Scotch, or maybe cordials.

Anyway, Kitty Quick and Izzy Cheesecake and Jo-jo eat up quite a few beef stews, and leave me to pay the check, and this is the last I see or hear of any of them for several months. Then one day I am in Philly to see a prizefight, and I run into Kitty Quick on Broad Street, looking pretty much the same as usual, and I ask him how he comes out in Europe.

"It is no good," Kitty says. "The trip is something of a bust, although we see many interesting sights, and have quite a few experiences. Maybe," Kitty says, "you will like to hear why we go to Europe? It is a very unusual story, indeed, and is by no means a lie, and I will be pleased to tell it to someone I think will believe it."

So we go into Walter's restaurant, and sit down in a corner, and order up a little java, and Kitty Quick tells me the story as follows:

It all begins [Kitty says] with a certain big lawyer coming to me here in Philly, and wishing to know if I care to take up a proposition which will make me rich, and naturally I say I can think of nothing that will please me more, because at this time things are very bad indeed in Philly, what with investigations going on here and there, and plenty of heat around and about, and I do not have more than a few bobs in my pants pocket, and can think of no way to get any more.

So this lawyer takes me to the Ritz-Carlton hotel, and there he introduces me to a guy by the name of Count Saro, and the lawyer says he will okay anything Saro has to say to me 100 per cent, and then he immediately takes the wind as if he does not care to hear what Saro has to say. But I know this mouthpiece is not putting any proposition away as okay unless he knows it is pretty much okay, because he is a smart guy at his own dodge, and everything else, and has plenty of coco-nuts.

Now this Count Saro is a little guy with an eyebrow moustache, and he wears striped pants, and white spats, and a cutaway coat, and a monocle in one eye, and he seems to be a foreign nobleman, although he talks English first rate. I do not care much for Count Saro's looks, but I will say one thing for him he is very businesslike, and gets down to cases at once.

He tells me that he is the representative of a political party in his home country in Europe which has a King, and this country wishes to get rid of the King, because Count Saro says Kings are out of style in Europe, and that no country can get anywhere with a King these days. His proposition is for me to take any assistants I figure I may need and go over and get rid of this King, and Count Saro says he will pay two hundred G's for the job in good old American scratch, and will lay twenty-five G's on the line at once, leaving the balance with the lawyer to be paid to me when everything is finished.

Well, this is a most astonishing proposition, indeed, because while I often hear of propositions to get rid of other guys, I never before hear of a proposition to get rid of a King. Furthermore, it does not sound reasonable to me, as getting rid of a King is apt to attract plenty of attention, and criticism, but Count Saro explains to me that his country is a small, out-of-the-way country, and that his political party will take control of the telegraph wires and everything else as soon as I get rid of the King, so nobody will give the news much of a tumble outside the country.

"Everything will be done very quietly, and in good order," Count Saro says, "and there will be no danger to you whatever."

Well, naturally I wish to know from Count Saro why he does not get somebody in his own country to do such a job, especially if he can pay so well for it, and he says to me like this:

"Well," he says, "in the first place there is no one in our country with enough experience in such matters to be trusted, and in the second place we do not wish anyone in our country to seem to be tangled up with getting rid of the King. It will cause internal complications," he says. "An outsider is more logical," he says, "because it is quite well known that in the palace of the King there are many valuable jewels, and it will seem a natural play for outsiders, especially Americans, to break into the palace to get these jewels, and if they happen to get rid of the King while getting the jewels, no one will think it is anything more than an accident, such as often occurs in your country."

Furthermore, Count Saro tells me that everything will be laid out for me in advance by his people, so I will have no great bother getting into the palace to get rid of the King, but he says of course I must not really take the valuable jewels, because his political party wishes to keep them for itself.

Well, I do not care much for the general idea at all, but Count Saro whips out a bundle of scratch, and weeds off twenty-five large coarse notes of a G apiece, and there it is in front of me, and looking at all this dough, and thinking how tough times are, what with banks busting here and there, I am very much tempted indeed, especially as I am commencing to think this Count Saro is some kind of a nut, and is only speaking through his hat about getting rid of a King.

"Listen," I say to Count Saro, as he sits there watching me, "how do you know I will not take this dough off of you and then never do anything whatever for it?"

"Why," he says, much surprised, "you are recommended to me as an honest man, and I accept your references. Anyway," he says, "if you do not carry out your agreement with me, you will only hurt yourself, because you will lose a hundred and seventy-five G's more and the lawyer will make you very hard to catch."

Well, the upshot of it is I shake hands with Count Saro, and then go out to find Izzy Cheesecake, although I am still thinking Count Saro is a little daffy, and while I am looking for Izzy, who do I see but Jo-jo, and Jo-jo tells me that he is on a vacation from Chicago for awhile, because it seems somebody out there claims he is a public enemy, which Jo-jo says is nothing but a big he, as he is really very fond of the public at all times.

Naturally I am glad to come across a guy such as Jo-jo, because he is most trustworthy, and naturally Jo-jo is very glad to hear of a proposition that will turn him an honest dollar while he is on his vacation. So Jo-jo and Izzy and I have a meeting, and we agree that I am to have a hundred G's for finding the plant, while Izzy and Jo-jo are to get fifty G's apiece, and this is how we come to go to Europe.

Well, we land at a certain spot in Europe, and who is there to meet us but another guy with a monocle, who states that his name is Baron von Terp, or some such, and who says he is representing Count Saro, and I am commencing to wonder if Count Saro's country is filled with one-eyed guys. Anyway, this Baron von Terp takes us travelling by trains and automobiles for several days, until finally after an extra long hop in an automobile we come to the outskirts of a nice-looking little burg, which seems to be the place we are headed for.

Now Baron von Terp drops us in a little hotel on the outskirts of the town, and says he must leave us because he cannot afford to be seen with us, although he explains he does not mean this as a knock to us. In fact, Baron von Terp says he finds us very nice travelling companions, indeed, except for Jo-jo wishing to engage in target practice along the route with his automatic Roscoe, and using such animals as stray dogs and chickens for his targets. He says he does not even mind Izzy Cheesecake's singing, although personally I will always consider this one of the big drawbacks to the journey.

Before he goes, Baron von Terp draws me a rough diagram of the inside of the palace where we are to get rid of the King, giving me a layout of all the rooms and doors. He says usually there are guards in and about this palace, but that his people arrange it so these guards will not be present around nine o'clock this night, except one guy who may be on guard at the door of the King's bedroom, and Baron von Terp says if we guzzle this guy it will be all right with him, because he does not like the guy, anyway.

But the general idea, he says, is for us to work fast and quietly, so as to be in and out of there inside of an hour or so, leaving no trail behind us, and I say this will suit me and Izzy Cheesecake and Jo-jo very well, indeed, as we are getting tired of travelling, and wish to go somewhere and take a long rest.

Well, after explaining all this, Baron von Terp takes the wind, leaving us a big fast car with an ugly-looking guy driving it who does not talk much English, but is supposed to know all the routes, and it is in this car that we leave the little hotel just before nine o'clock as per instructions, and head for the palace, which turns out to be nothing but a large square old building in the middle of a sort of park, with the town around and about, but some distance off.

Ugly-face drives right into this park and up to what seems to be the front door of the building, and the three of us get out of the car, and Ugly-face pulls the car off into the shadow of some trees to wait for us.

Personally, I am looking for plenty of heat when we start to go into the palace, and I have the old equalizer where I can get at it without too much trouble, while Jo-jo and Izzy Cheesecake also have their rods handy. But just as Baron von Terp tells us, there are no guards around, and in fact there is not a soul in sight as we walk into the palace door, and find ourselves in a big hall with paintings, and armour, and old swords, and one thing and another hanging around and about, and I can see that this is a perfect plant, indeed.

I out with my diagram and see where the King's bedroom is located on the second floor, and when we get there, walking very easy, and ready to start blasting away if necessary, who is at the door but a big tall guy in a uniform, who is very much surprised at seeing us, and who starts to holler something or other, but what it is nobody will ever know, because just as he opens his mouth, Izzy Cheesecake taps him on the noggin with the butt of a forty-five, and knocks him cock-eyed.

Then Jo-jo grabs some cord off a heavy silk curtain which is hanging across the door, and ties the guy up good and tight, and wads a handkerchief into his kisser in case the guy comes to, and wishes to start hollering again, and when all this is done, I quietly turn the knob of the door to the King's bedroom, and we step into a room that looks more like a young convention hall than it does a bedroom, except that it is hung around and about with silk drapes, and there is much gilt furniture here and there.

Well, who is in this room but a nice-looking doll, and a little kid of maybe eight or nine years old, and the kid is in a big bed with a canopy over it like the entrance to a night club, only silk, and the doll is sitting alongside the bed reading to the kid out of a book. It is a very homelike scene, indeed, and causes us to stop and look around in great surprise, for we are certainly not expecting such a scene at all.

As we stand there in the middle of the room somewhat confused the doll turns and looks at us, and the little kid sits up in bed. He is a fat little guy with a chubby face, and a lot of curly hair, and eyes as big as pancakes, and maybe bigger. The doll turns very pale when she sees us, and shakes so the book she is reading falls to the floor, but the kid does not seem scared, and he says to us in very good English like this:

"Who are you?" he says.

Well, this is a fair question, at that, but naturally we do not wish to state who we are at this time, so I say:

"Never mind who we are, where is the King?"

"The King?" the kid says, sitting up straight in the bed, "why, I am the King."

Now of course this seems a very nonsensical crack to us, because we have brains enough to know that Kings do not come as small as this little squirt, and anyway we are in no mood to dicker with him, so I say to the doll as follows:

"Listen," I say, "we do not care for any kidding at this time, because we are in a great hurry. Where is the King?"

"Why," she says, her voice trembling quite some, "this is indeed the King, and I am his governess. Who are you, and what do you want? How do you get in here?" she says. "Where are the guards;"

"Lady," I say, and I am greatly surprised at myself for being so patient with her, "this kid may be a King, but we want the big King. We want the head King himself," I say.

"There is no other," she says, and the little kid chips in like this:

"My father dies two years ago, and I am the King in his place," he says. "Are you English like Miss Peabody here?" he says. "Who is the funny looking old man back there?"

Well, of course Jo-jo is funny looking, at that, but no

one ever before is impolite enough to speak of it to his face, and Jo-jo begins growling quite some, while Izzy Cheesecake speaks as follows:

"Why," Izzy says, "this is a very great outrage. We are sent to get rid of a King, and here the King is nothing but a little punk. Personally," Izzy says, "I am not in favour of getting rid of punks, male or female."

"Well," Jo-jo says, "I am against it myself as a rule, but this is a pretty fresh punk."

"Now," I say, "there seems to be some mistake around here, at that. Let us sit down and talk things over quietly, and see if we cannot get this matter straightened out. It looks to me," I say, "as if this Count Saro is nothing but a swindler."

"Count Saro," the doll says, getting up and coming over to me, and looking very much alarmed. "Count Saro, do you say? Oh, sir, Count Saro is a very bad man. He is the tool of the Grand Duke Gino of this country, who is this little boy's uncle. The Grand Duke will be king himself if it is not for this boy, and we suspect many plots against the little chap's safety. Oh, gentlemen," she says, "you surely do not mean any harm to this poor orphan child?"

Well, this is about the first time in their lives that Jo-jo and Izzy Cheesecake are ever mentioned by anybody as gentlemen, and I can see that it softens them up quite some, especially as the little kid is grinning at them very cheerful, although of course he will not be so cheerful if he knows who he is grinning at.

"Why," Jo-jo says, "the Grand Duke is nothing but a rascal for wishing harm to such a little guy as this, although of course," Jo-jo says, "if he is a grownup King it will be a different matter."

"Who are you?" the little kid says again.

"We are Americans," I say, very proud to mention my home country. "We are from Philly and Chicago, two very good towns, at that."

Well, the little kid's eyes get bigger than ever, and he climbs right out of bed and walks over to us looking very cute in his blue silk pyjamas, and his bare feet.

"Chicago?" he says. "Do you know Mr. Capone?"

"Al?" says Jo-jo. "Do I know Al? Why, Al and me are just like this," he says, although personally I do not believe Al Capone will know Jo-jo if he meets him in broad daylight. "Where do you know Al from?" he asks.

"Oh, I do not know him," the kid says. "But I read about him in the magazines, and about the machine guns, and the pineapples. Do you know about the pineapples;" he says.

"Do I know about the pineapples?" Jo-jo says, as if his feelings are hurt by the question. "He asks me do I know about the pineapples. Why," he says, "look here."

And what does Jo-jo do but out with a little round gadget

which I recognize at once as a bomb such as these Guineas like to chuck at people they do not like, especially Guineas from Chicago. Of course I never know Jo-jo is packing this article around and about with him, and Jo-jo can see I am much astonished, and by no means pleased, because he says to me like this:

"I bring this along in case of a bear fight," he says. "They are very handy in a bear fight."

Well, the next thing anybody knows we are all talking about this and that very pleasant, especially the little kid and Jo-jo, who is telling lies faster than a horse can trot, about Chicago and Mr. Capone, and I hope and trust that Al never hears some of the lies Jo-jo tells, or he may hold it against me for being with Jo-jo when these lies come off.

I am talking to the doll, whose name seems to be Miss Peabody, and who is not so hard to take, at that, and at the same time I am keeping an eye on Izzy Cheesecake, who is wandering around the room looking things over. The chances are Izzy is trying to find a few of the valuable jewels such as I mention to him when telling him about the proposition of getting rid of the King, and in fact I am taking a stray peek here and there myself, but I do not see anything worth while.

This Miss Peabody is explaining to me about the politics of the country, and it seems the reason the Grand Duke wishes to get rid of the little kid King and be King himself is because he has a business deal on with a big nation near by which wishes to control the kid King's country. I judge from what Miss Peabody tells me that this country is no bigger than Delaware county, Pa., and it seems to me a lot of bother about no more country than this, but Miss Peabody says it is a very nice little country, at that.

She says it will be very lovely indeed if it is not for the Grand Duke Gino, because the little kid King stands okay with the people, but it seems the old Grand Duke is pretty much boss of everything, and Miss Peabody says she is personally long afraid that he will finally try to do something very drastic indeed to get rid of the kid King on account of the kid seeming so healthy. Well, naturally I do not state to her that our middle name is drastic, because I do not wish Miss Peabody to have a bad opinion of us.

Now nothing will do but Jo-jo must show the kid his automatic, which is as long as your arm, and maybe longer, and the kid is greatly delighted, and takes the rod and starts pointing it here and there and saying boom-boom, as kids will do. But what happens but he pulls the trigger, and it seems that Jo-jo does not have the safety on, so the Roscoe really goes boom-boom twice before the kid can take his finger off the trigger.

Well, the first shot smashes a big jar over in one corner

of the room, which Miss Peabody afterwards tells me is worth fifteen G's if it is worth a dime, and the second slug knocks off Izzy Cheesecake's derby hat, which serves Izzy right, at that, as he is keeping his hat on in the presence of a lady. Naturally these shots are very disturbing to me at the moment, but afterwards I learn they are a very good thing indeed, because it seems a lot of guys who are hanging around outside, including Baron von Terp, and several prominent politicians of the country, watching and listening to see what comes off, hurry right home to bed, figuring the King is got rid of as per contract, and wishing to be found in bed if anybody comes around asking questions.

Well, Jo-jo is finally out of lies about Chicago and Mr. Capone, when the little kid seems to get a new idea and goes rummaging around the room looking for something, and just as I am hoping he is about to donate the valuable jewels to us he comes up with a box, and what is in this box but a baseball bat, and a catcher's mitt, and a baseball, and it is very strange indeed to find such homelike articles so far away from home, especially as Babe Ruth's name is on the bat.

"Do you know about these things?" the little kid asks Jo-jo. "They are from America, and they are sent to me by one of our people when he is visiting there, but nobody here seems to know what they are for."

"Do I know about them?" Jo-jo says, fondling them very tenderly, indeed. "He asks me do I know about them. Why," he says, "in my time I am the greatest hitter on the West Side Blues back in dear old Chi."

Well, now nothing will do the kid but we must show him how these baseball articles work, so Izzy Cheesecake, who claims he is once a star back-stopper with the Vine Streets back in Philly, puts on a pad and mask, and Jo-jo takes the bat and lays a small sofa pillow down on the floor for a home plate, and insists that I pitch to him. Now it is years since I handle a baseball, although I wish to say that in my day I am as good an amateur pitcher as there is around Gray's Ferry in Philly, and the chances are I will be with the A's if I do not have other things to do.

So I take off my coat, and get down to the far end of the room, while Jo-jo squares away at the plate, with Izzy Cheesecake behind it. I can see by the way he stands that Jo-jo is bound to be a sucker for a curve, so I take a good windup, and cut loose with the old fadeaway, but of course my arm is not what it used to be, and the ball does not break as I expect, so what happens but Jo-jo belts the old apple right through a high window in what will be right field if the room is laid off like Shibe Park.

Well Jo-jo starts running as if he is going to first, but of course there is no place in particular for him to run, and he almost knocks his brains out against a wall, and the ball is lost, and the game winds up right there, but the little kid is tickled silly over this business, and even Miss Peabody laughs, and she does not look to me like a doll who gets many laughs out of life, at that.

It is now nearly ten o'clock, and Miss Peabody says if she can find anybody around she will get us something to eat, and this sounds very reasonable, indeed, so I step outside the door and bring in the guy we tie up there, who seems to be wide awake by now, and very much surprised, and quite indignant, and Miss Peabody says something to him in a language which I do not understand. When I come to think it all over afterwards, I am greatly astonished at the way I trust Miss Peabody, because there is no reason why she shall not tell the guy to get the law, but I suppose I trust her because she seems to have an honest face.

Anyway, the guy in the uniform goes away rubbing his noggin, and pretty soon in comes another guy who seems to be a butler, or some such, and who is also greatly surprised at seeing us, and Miss Peabody rattles off something to him and he starts hustling in tables, and dishes, and sandwiches, and coffee, and one thing and another in no time at all.

Well, there we are, the five of us sitting around the table eating and drinking, because what does the butler do but bring in a couple of bottles of good old pre-war champagne, which is very pleasant to the taste, although Izzy Cheesecake embarrasses me no little by telling Miss Peabody that if she can dig up any considerable quantity of this stuff he will make her plenty of bobs by peddling it in our country, and will also cut the King in.

When the butler fills the wine-glasses the first time, Miss Peabody picks hers up, and looks at us, and naturally we have sense enough to pick ours up, too, and then she stands up on her feet and raises her glass high above her head, and says like this:

"Gentlemen, The King!"

Well, I stand up at this, and Jo-jo and Izzy Cheesecake stand up with me, and we say, all together:

"The King!"

And then we swig our champagne, and sit down again and the little kid laughs all over and claps his hands and seems to think it is plenty of fun, which it is, at that, although Miss Peabody does not let him have any wine, and is somewhat indignant when she catches Jo-jo trying to slip him a snort under the table.

Well, finally the kid does not wish us to leave him at all, especially Jo-jo, but Miss Peabody says he must get some sleep, so we tell him we will be back some day, and we take our hats and say good-bye, and leave him standing in the bedroom door with Miss Peabody at his side, and the little kid's arm is around her waist, and I find myself wishing it is my arm, at that.

Of course we never go back again, and in fact we get out of the country this very night, and take the first boat out of the first seaport we hit and return to the United States of America, and the gladdest guy in all the world to see us go is Ugly-face, because he has to drive us about a thousand miles with the muzzle of a rod digging into his ribs.

So [Kitty Quick says] now you know why we go to Europe.

Well, naturally, I am greatly interested in his story, and especially in what Kitty says about the pre-war champagne, because I can see that there may be great business opportunities in such a place if a guy can get in with the right people, but one thing Kitty will never tell me is where the country is located, except that it is located in Europe.

"You see," Kitty says, "we are all strong Republicans here in Philly, and I will not get the Republican administration of this country tangled up in any international squabble for the world. You see," he says, "when we land back home I find a little item of cable news in a paper which says the Grand Duke Gino dies as a result of injuries received in an accident in his home some weeks before.

"And," Kitty says, "I am never sure but what these injuries may be caused by Jo-jo insisting on Ugly-face driving us around to the Grand Duke's house the night we leave and popping his pineapple into the Grand Duke's bedroom window."

"How is it going with you, Sam?"

13

A NICE PRICE

One hot morning in June, I am standing in front of the Mohican Hotel in the city of New London, Conn., and the reason I am in such a surprising spot is something that makes a long story quite a bit longer.

It goes back to a couple of nights before, when I am walking along Broadway and I run into Sam the Gonoph, the ticket speculator, who seems to have a very sour expression on his puss, although, even when Sam the Gonoph is looking good-natured his puss is nothing much to see.

Now Sam the Gonoph is an old friend of mine, and in fact I sometimes join up with him and his crew to hustle duckets to one thing and another when he is short-handed, so I give him a big hello, and he stops and the following conversation ensues:

"How is it going with you, Sam?" I say to Sam the Gonoph, although of course I do not really care two pins how it is going with him. "You look as if you are all sored up at somebody."

"No," Sam says, "I am not sored up at anybody. I am never sored up at anybody in my life, except maybe Society Max, and of course everybody knows I have a perfect right to be sored up at Society Max, because look at what he does to me."

Well, what Sam the Gonoph says is very true, because what Society Max does to Sam is to steal Sam's fiancée off of him a couple of years before this, and marry her before Sam has time to think. This fiancée is a doll by the name of Sonia, who resides up in the Bronx, and Sam the Gonoph is engaged to her since the year of the Dempsey-Firpo fight, and is contemplating marrying her almost any time, when Society Max bobs up.

Many citizens afterwards claim that Max does Sam the Gonoph a rare favour, because Sonia is commencing to fat up in spots, but it breaks Sam's heart just the same, especially when he learns that Sonia's papa gives the happy young couple twenty big G's in old-fashioned folding money that nobody ever knows the papa has, and Sam figures that Max must get an inside tip on this dough and that he takes an unfair advantage of the situation.

"But," Sam the Gonoph says, "I am not looking sored up at this time because of Society Max, although of course it is well known to one and all that I am under oath to knock his ears down the first time I catch up with him. As a matter of fact, I do not as much as think of Society Max for a year or more, although I hear he deserts poor Sonia out in Cincinnati after spending her dough and leading her a dog's life, including a few off-hand pastings—not that I am claiming Sonia may not need a pasting now and then.

"What I am looking sored up about," Sam says, "is because I must get up into Connecticut to-morrow to a spot that is called New London to dispose of a line of merchandise."

"Why, Sam," I say, "what can be doing in such a place?"

"Oh," Sam says, "a large boat race is coming up between the Harvards and the Yales. It comes up at New London every year, and is quite an interesting event from what I read in the papers about it, but the reason I am sored up about going to-morrow is because I wish to spend the week-end on my farm in New Jersey to see how my onions are doing. Since I buy this farm in New Jersey, I can scarcely wait to get over there on week-ends to watch my onions grow.

"But," Sam the Gonoph says, "this is an extra large boat race this year, and I am in possession of many choice duckets, and am sure to make plenty of black ink for myself, and business before pleasure is what I always say. By the way," Sam says, "do you ever see a boat race?"

Well, I say that the only boat races I ever see are those that come off around the race tracks, such a race being a race that is all fixed up in advance, and some of them are pretty raw, if you ask me, and I am by no means in favour of things of this kind unless I am in, but Sam the Gonoph says these races are by no manner of means the same thing as the boat races he is talking about.

"I never personally witness one myself," Sam says, "but the way I understand it is a number of the Harvards and the Yales, without any clothes on, get in row boats and row, and row, and row until their tongues hang out, and they are all half-dead. Why they tucker themselves out in this fashion I do not know and," Sam says, "I am too old to start trying to find out why these college guys do a lot of things to themselves.

"But," Sam says, "boat racing is a wonderful sport, and I always have a nice trade at New London, Conn., and if you wish to accompany me and Benny South Street and Liverlips and maybe collect a few bobs for yourself, you are as welcome as the flowers in May."

So there I am in front of the Mohican Hotel in New London, Conn., with Sam the Gonoph and Benny South Street and old Liverlips, who are Sam the Gonoph's best hustlers, and all around and about is a very interesting sight, to be sure, as large numbers of the Harvards and the Yales are passing in and out of the hotel and walking up and down and back and forth, and making very merry, one way and another.

Well, after we are hustling our duckets for a couple of hours and it is coming on noon, Benny South Street goes into the hotel lobby to buy some cigarettes, and by and by he comes out looking somewhat excited, and states as follows:

"Say," Benny says, "there's a guy inside with his hands full of money offering to lay three to one that the Yales win the boat race. He says he has fifteen G's cash with him to wager at the price stated."

"Are there any takers?" Sam the Gonoph asks.

"No, not many," Benny says. "From all I hear, the Yales figure. In fact, all the handicappers I speak with have them on top, so the Harvards do not care for any part of the guy's play. But," Benny says, "there he is, offering three to one."

"Three to one?" Sam the Gonoph says, as if he is mentioning these terms to himself. "Three to one, eh? It is a nice price."

"It is a lovely price," old Liverlips puts in.

Well, Sam the Gonoph stands there as if he is thinking, and Benny South Street seems to be thinking, too, and even old Liverlips seems to be thinking, and by and by I even find myself thinking, and finally Sam the Gonoph says like this:

"I do not know anything about boat races," Sam says, "and the Yales may figure as you say, but nothing between human beings is one to three. In fact," Sam the Gonoph says, "I long ago come to the conclusion that all life is six to five against. And anyway," he says, "how can anybody let such odds as these get away from them? I think I will take a small nibble at this proposition. What about you, Benny?"

"I will also nibble," Benny South Street says. "I will never forgive myself in this world if I let this inviting offer go and it turns out the Harvards win."

Well, we all go into the hotel lobby, and there is a big, grey-haired guy in a white cap and white pants standing in the centre of a bunch of other guys, and he has money in both hands. I hear somebody say he is one of the real old-time Yales, and he is speaking in a loud voice as follows:

"Why," he says, "what is the matter, Harvards, are you cowards, or are you just broke? If you are broke, I will take your markers and let you pay me on the instalment plan. But," he says, "bet me. That is all, just bet me."

Personally, I have a notion to let on I am one of the Harvards and slip the guy a nice marker, but I am afraid he may request some identification and I do not have anything on me to prove I am a college guy, so I stand back and watch Sam the Gonoph shove his way through the crowd with a couple of C notes in his hand, and Benny South Street is right behind him.

"I will take a small portion of the Harvards at the market," Sam the Gonoph says, as he offers the grey-haired guy his dough.

"Thank you, my friend," the guy says, "but I do not think

we are acquainted," he says. "Who do you wish to hold the stakes?"

"You hold them yourself, Mr. Campbell," Sam the Gonoph says. "I know you, although you do not know me, and I will gladly trust you with my dough. Furthermore, my friend here, who also wishes a portion of the Harvards, will trust you."

So the grey-haired guy says that both Sam the Gonoph and Benny South Street are on at 3 to 1, and thanks again to them, at that, and when we get outside, Sam explains that he recognizes the guy as nobody but Mr. Hammond Campbell, who is a very important party in every respect and who has more dough than Uncle Sam has bad debts. In fact, Sam the Gonoph seems to feel that he is greatly honoured in getting to bet with Mr. Hammond Campbell, although from the way Mr. Campbell takes their dough, I figure he thinks that the pleasure is all his.

Well, we go on hustling our duckets but neither Sam the Gonoph nor Benny South Street seem to have much heart in their work, and every now and then I see one or the other slip into the hotel lobby, and it comes out that they are still nibbling at the 3 to 1, and finally I slip in myself and take a little teensy nibble for twenty bobs myself, because the way I look at it, anything that is good enough for Sam the Gonoph is good enough for me.

Now Sam the Gonoph always carries quite a little ready money on his body, and nobody will deny that Sam will send it along if he likes a proposition, and by and by he is down for a G on the Harvards, and Benny South Street has four C's going for him, and there is my double saw, and even old Liverlips weakens and goes for a pound note, and ordinarily Liverlips will not bet a pound that he is alive.

Furthermore, Mr. Hammond Campbell says we are about the only guys in town that do bet him and that we ought to get degrees off the Harvards for our loyalty to them, but of course what we are really loyal to is the 3 to 1. Finally, Mr. Campbell says he has to go to lunch, but that if we feel like betting him any more we can find him on board his yacht, the *Hibiscus,* out in the river, and maybe he will boost the price up to $3\frac{1}{2}$ to 1.

So I go into the hotel and get a little lunch myself, and when I am coming out a nice-looking young doll who is walking along in front of me accidentally drops her poke from under her arm, and keeps right on walking. Naturally, I pick it up, but several parties who are standing around in the lobby see me do it, so I call to the young doll and when she turns around I hand her the poke, and she is very grateful to me, to be sure. In fact, she thanks me several times, though once will do, and then all of a sudden she says to me like this:

"Pardon me," the young doll says, "but are you not one of the gentlemen I see wagering with my papa that the Harvards will win the boat race?"

"Yes," I say, "and what is more, we may keep on wagering him. In fact," I say, "a friend of mine by the name of Sam the Gonoph is just now contemplating wiring home for another G to accept your papa's generous offer of three-and-a-half to one."

"Oh," the young doll says, "do not do it. You are only throwing your money away. The Harvards have no chance whatever of winning the boat race. My papa is never wrong on boat races. I only wish he is to-day."

And with this she sits down in a chair in the lobby and begins crying boo-hoo until her mascara is running down her cheeks, and naturally I am greatly embarrassed by this situation, as I am afraid somebody may come along and think maybe she is my step-child and that I am just after chastising her.

"You see," the young doll says, "a boy I like a very, very great deal belongs to the Harvards' crew and when I tell him a couple of weeks ago that my papa says the Yales are bound to win, he grows very angry and says what does my papa know about it, and who is my papa but an old money-bags, anyway, and to the dickens with my papa. Then when I tell him my papa always knows about these things, Quentin grows still angrier, and we quarrel and he says all right, if the Harvards lose he will never, never, never see me again as long as he lives. And Quentin is a very obstinate and unreasonable boy, and life is very sad for me."

Well, who comes along about now but Sam the Gonoph and naturally he is somewhat surprised by the scene that is presented to his eyes, so I explain to him, and Sam is greatly touched and very sympathetic, for one thing about Sam is he is very tender-hearted when it comes to dolls who are in trouble.

"Well," Sam says, "I will certainly be greatly pleased to see the Harvards win the boat race myself, and in fact," he says, "I am just making a few cautious inquiries around here and there to see if there is any chance of stiffening a couple of the Yales, so we can have a little help in the race.

"But," Sam says, "one great trouble with these college propositions is they are always levelling, though I cannot see why it is necessary. Anyway," he says, "it looks as if we cannot hope to do any business with the Yales, but you dry your eyes, little miss, and maybe old Sam can think up something."

At this the young doll stops her bawling and I am very glad of it, as there is nothing I loathe and despise so much as a doll bawling, and she looks up at Sam with a wet smile and says to him like this:

"Oh, do you really think you can help the Harvards win the boat race?"

Well, naturally Sam the Gonoph is not in a position to make any promises on this point, but he is such a guy as will tell a doll in distress anything whatever if he thinks it will give her a little pleasure for a minute, so he replies as follows:

"Why, who knows?" Sam says. "Who knows, to be sure? But anyway do not bawl any more, and old Sam will give this matter further consideration."

And with this Sam pats the young doll on the back so hard he pats all the breath out of her and she cannot bawl any more even if she wishes to, and she gets up and goes away looking very happy, but before she goes she says:

"Well, I hear somebody say that from the way you gentlemen are betting on the Harvards you must know something and," she says, "I am very glad I have the courage to talk to you. It will be a wonderful favour to Quentin and me if you help the Harvards win, even though it costs my papa money. Love is more than gold," she says.

Personally, I consider it very wrong for Sam the Gonoph to be holding out hope to a young doll that he is unable to guarantee, but Sam says he does not really promise anything and that he always figures if he can bring a little joy into any life, no matter how, he is doing a wonderful deed, and that anyway we will never see the young doll again, and furthermore, what of it?

Well, I cannot think what of it just off-hand, and anyway I am glad to be rid of the young doll, so we go back to disposing of the duckets we have left.

Now the large boat race between the Harvards and the Yales takes place in the early evening, and when it comes on time for the race one and all seem to be headed in the direction of the river, including all the young guys with the stir haircuts, and many beautiful young dolls wearing blue and red flowers, and old guys in sports pants and flat straw hats, and old dolls who walk as if their feet hurt them, and the chances are they do, at that.

Well, nothing will do Sam the Gonoph but we must see the boat race, too, so we go down to the railroad station to take the very train for which we are hustling duckets all day, but by the time we get there the race train is pulling out, so Benny South Street says the next best thing for us to do is to go down to the dock and hire a boat to take us out on the river.

But when we get to the dock, it seems that all the boats around are hired and are already out on the river, but there is an old pappy guy with a chin whisker sitting in a rickety-looking little motor-boat at the dock, and this old guy says he will take us out where we can get a good peek at the race for a buck apiece.

Personally, I do not care for the looks of the boat, and neither does Benny South Street nor old Liverlips, but Sam the Gonoph is so anxious to see the race that finally we all get into the boat and the old guy heads her out into the river, which seems to be filled with all kinds of boats decorated with flags and one thing and another, and with guys and dolls walking back and forth on these boats.

Anybody must admit that it is quite a sight, and I am commencing to be glad I am present, especially when Benny South Street tells me that these guys and dolls on the boats are very fine people and worth plenty of money. Furthermore, Benny South Street points out many big white boats that he says are private yachts, and he tells me that what it costs to keep up these private yachts is a sin and a shame when you start to figure out the number of people in the world who are looking for breakfast money. But then Benny South Street is always talking of things of this kind, and sometimes I think maybe he is a dynamiter at heart.

We go putt-putting along under a big bridge and into a sort of lane of boats, and Benny South Street says we are now at the finish line of the large boat race and that the Harvards and the Yales row down this lane from away up the river, and that it is here that they have their tongues hanging out and are nearly all half-dead.

Well, it seems that we are in the way, because guys start yelling at us from different boats and shaking their fists at us, and it is a good thing for some of them that they are not close enough for us to get a pop at them, but the old pappy guy keeps the motor-boat putt-putting and sliding in and out among the boats until we come to a spot that he says is about a hundred yards above the finish and a great spot to see the best part of the race.

We are slipping alongside of a big white boat that Benny South Street says is a private yacht and that has a little set of stair steps running down one side almost into the water, when all of a sudden Sam the Gonoph notices his feet are wet, and he looks down and sees that the motor-boat is half-full of water and furthermore that the boat is commencing to sink.

Now this is quite a predicament, and naturally Sam the Gonoph lets out a slight beef and wishes to know what kind of accommodations we are paying for, anyway, and then the old pappy guy notices the water and the sinking, and he seems somewhat put out about the matter, especially as the water is getting up around his chin whiskers.

So he steers the boat up against the stair steps on the yacht and all of us, including the old pappy guy, climb out on to the stairs just as the motor-boat gives a last snort and sinks from sight. The last I see of the motor-boat is the hind end sticking up in the air a second before it disappears, and I remember the name that is painted on the hind end. The name is *Baby Mine.*

Well, Sam the Gonoph leads the way up the stairs to the deck of the yacht, and who meets us at the head of the stairs but Mr. Hammond Campbell in person, and who is right behind him but the young doll I am talking with in the hotel lobby, and at first Mr. Campbell thinks that we come out to his yacht to pick up a little of his $3\frac{1}{2}$ to 1, and he is greatly disappointed when he learns that such is by no means our purpose and that we are merely the victims of disaster.

As for the young doll, whose name turns out to be Clarice, she gazes at Sam the Gonoph and me with her eyes full of questions, but we do not get a chance to talk to her as things begin occurring at once.

There are quite a number of guys and dolls on the yacht, and it is a very gay scene to be sure, as they walk around laughing and chatting, when all of a sudden I see Sam the Gonoph staring at a guy and doll who are leaning over the rail talking very earnestly and paying no attention to what is going on around and about them.

The guy is a tall, dark-complected young guy with a little moustache, and he is wearing white flannel pants and a blue coat with brass buttons, and white shoes, and he is a very foreign-looking guy, to be sure. The doll is not such a young doll, being maybe around middle age, giving her a few points the best of it, but she is a fine-looking doll, at that, especially if you like dolls with grey hair, which personally I am not so much in favour of.

I am close enough to Sam the Gonoph to hear him breathing heavily as he stares at this guy and doll, and finally the dark-complected young guy looks up and sees Sam and at the same instant Sam starts for him, and as Sam starts the young guy turns and takes to running in the other direction from Sam along the deck, but before he takes to running I can see that it is nobody but Society Max.

Naturally, I am somewhat surprised at seeing Society Max at a boat race between the Harvards and the Yales, because I never figure him such a guy as will be interested in matters of this kind, although I remember that Society Max is once a life guard at Coney Island, and in fact it is at Coney Island that Sonia gets her first peek at his shape and is lost for ever to Sam the Gonoph, so I get to thinking that maybe Society Max is fond of all aquatic events.

Now of course the spectacle of Sam the Gonoph pursuing Society Max along the deck is quite surprising to one and all, except Benny South Street and old Liverlips and myself, who are aware of the reason, and Mr. Hammond Campbell wishes to know what kind of game they are playing, especially after they round the deck twice, with Society Max showing much foot, but none of us feel called on to explain. Finally the other guys and dolls on the yacht enter into the spirit of the chase, even though they do not know what it is all about, and they shout encouragement to both Sam the Gonoph and Society Max, although Max is really the favourite.

There is no doubt but what Society Max is easily best in a sprint, especially as Sam the Gonoph's pants legs are wet from the sinking motor-boat and he is carrying extra weight, but Sam is a wonderful doer over a route, and on the third trip around the deck, anybody can see that he is cutting down Max's lead,

Well, every time they pass the grey-haired doll that Society Max is talking to when we come on the yacht she asks what is the matter, Max, and where are you going, Max, and other questions that seem trivial at such a time, but Max never has an opportunity to answer, as he has to save all his breath to keep ahead of Sam the Gonoph, and in fact Sam the Gonoph stops talking, too, and just keeps plugging along with a very determined expression on his puss.

Well, now all the whistles on the boats in the river around us start blowing, and it seems this is because the large boat race between the Harvards and the Yales is now approaching the finish, and one and all on our yacht rush to the side of the yacht to see it, forgetting about everything else, and the side they rush to is the same side the stair steps are on.

But I am too much interested in Sam the Gonoph's pursuit of Society Max to pay any attention to the boat race, and as they come around the deck the fifth or sixth time, I can see that Sam will have Max in the next few jumps, when all of a sudden Society Max runs right down the stairs and dives off into the river, and he does it so fast that nobody seems to notice him except Sam the Gonoph and me and the grey-haired doll, and I am the only one that notices her fall in a big faint on the deck as Max dives.

Naturally, this is not a time to be bothering with fainting dolls, so Sam the Gonoph and me run to the side of the yacht and watch the water to see where Society Max comes up, but he does not appear at once, and I remember hearing he is a wonderful diver when he is a life guard, so I figure he is going to keep under water until he is pretty sure he is too far away for Sam the Gonoph to hit him with anything, such as maybe a slug from a Betsy.

Of course Sam the Gonoph does not happen to have a Betsy on him, but Society Max can scarcely be expected to know this, because the chances are he remembers that Sam often has such an article in his pants pocket when he is around New York, so I suppose Society Max plays it as safe as possible.

Anyway, we do not see hide or hair of him, and in the meantime the excitement over the large boat race between

the Harvards and the Yales is now so terrific that I forget
Society Max and try to get a peek at it.

But all I remember is seeing the young doll, Clarice,
kissing Sam the Gonoph smack-dab on his homely puss,
and jumping up and down in considerable glee, and stating
that she knows all along that Sam will figure out some way
for the Harvards to win, although she does not know yet
how he does it, and hearing Mr. Hammond Campbell using
language even worse than Sam the Gonoph employs when
he is pursuing Society Max, and saying he never sees such a
this-and-that boat race in all his born days.

Then I get to thinking about the grey-haired doll, and I
go over and pick her up and she is still about two-thirds out
and is saying to herself, as follows:

"Max, oh, my dear, dear Max."

Well, by and by Mr. Hammond Campbell takes Sam the
Gonoph into a room on the yacht and pays him what is
coming to all of us on the race, and then he takes to asking
about Society Max, and when Sam the Gonoph explains
how Max is a terrible fink and what he does to Sonia and
all, Mr. Hammond Campbell hands Sam five large G's extra,
and states to him as follows:

"This," he says, "is for preventing my sister, Emma, from
making a fool of herself. She picks this Max up somewhere
in Europe and he puts himself away with her as a Russian

nobleman, and she is going to marry him next week, although from what you tell me it will be bigamy on his part. By the way," Mr. Hammond Campbell says, "not that it makes any difference, but I wonder whatever becomes of the guy?"

I am wondering this somewhat myself, not that I really care what becomes of Society Max, but I do not find out until later in the evening when I am at the Western Union office in New London, Conn., sending a telegram for Sam the Gonoph to the guy who runs his farm in New Jersey telling the guy to be sure and watch the onions, and I hear a newspaper scribe talking about the large boat race.

"Yes," the newspaper scribe says, "the Yales are leading by a boat length up to the last hundred yards and going easy, and they seem to be an absolute cinch to win, when No. 6 man in their boat hits something in the water and breaks his oar, throwing the rest of the crew out of kilter long enough for the Harvards to slip past and win. It is the most terrible upset of the dope in history," he says.

"Now," the scribe says, "of course a broken oar is not unheard of in a boat race, but what No. 6 says he hits is a guy's head which pops out of the water all of a sudden right alongside the Yales' boat, and which disappears again as the oar hits it.

"Personally," the scribe says, "I will say No. 6 is seeing things but for the fact that a Coast Guard boat which is laying away down the river below the finish just reports that it picks up a guy out of the river who seems to be alive and all right except he has a lump on his noggin a foot high."

I do not see Sam the Gonoph again until it comes on fall, when I run into him in Mindy's restaurant on Broadway, and Sam says to me like this:

"Say," he says, "do you remember what a hit I make with the little doll because she thinks I have something to do with the Harvards winning the large boat race? Well," Sam the Gonoph says, "I just get a note from her asking me if I can do anything about a football game that the Harvards have coming up with the Dartmouths next month."

His mamma cries all over Israel Ib's vest.

14

BROADWAY FINANCIER

Of all the scores made by dolls on Broadway the past twenty-five years, there is no doubt but what the very largest score is made by a doll who is called Silk, when she knocks off a banker by the name of Israel lb, for the size of Silk's score is three million one hundred bobs and a few odd cents.

It is admitted by one and all who know about these matters that the record up to this time is held by a doll by the name of Irma Teak, who knocks off a Russian duke back in 1911 when Russian dukes are considered very useful by dolls, although of course in these days Russian dukes are about as useful as dandruff. Anyway, Irma Teak's score off this Russian duke is up around a million, and she moves to London with her duke and chucks quite a swell around there for a time. But finally Irma Teak goes blind, which is a tough break for her as she can no longer see how jealous she is making other dolls with her diamonds and sables and one thing and another, so what good are they to her, after all?

I know Irma Teak when she is a show doll at the old

Winter Garden, and I also know the doll by the name of
Mazie Mitz, who is in a Florodora revival, and who makes a
score of maybe three hundred G's off a guy who has a string
of ten-cent stores, and three hundred G's is by no means
hay. But Mazie Mitz finally hauls off and runs away with a
saxophone player she is in love with and so winds up back
of the fifteen ball.

Furthermore, I know Clara Simmons, the model from
Rickson's, who gets a five-story town house and a country
place on Long Island off a guy in Wall Street for birthday
presents, and while I never meet this guy personally, I always
figure he must be very dumb because anybody who knows
Clara Simmons knows she will be just as well satisfied
with a bottle of perfume for a birthday present. For all I
know, Clara Simmons may still own the town house and
the country place, but she must be shoving on toward forty
now, so naturally nobody on Broadway cares what becomes
of her.

I know a hundred other dolls who run up different scores,
and some of them are very fair scores, indeed, but none of
these scores are anything much alongside Silk's score off
Israel Ib, and this score is all the more surprising because
Silk starts out being greatly prejudiced against bankers. I am
no booster for bankers myself, as I consider them very stony-
hearted guys, but I am not prejudiced against them. In fact,

I consider bankers very necessary, because if we do not have bankers many citizens will not be able to think of anybody to give a check on.

It is quite a while before she meets Israel lb that Silk explains to me why she is prejudiced against bankers. It is when she is nothing but a chorus doll in Johnny Oakley's joint on Fifty-third Street, and comes into Mindy's after she gets through work, which is generally along about four o'clock in the morning.

At such an hour many citizens are sitting around Mindy's resting from the crap games and one thing and another, and dolls from the different joints around and about, including chorus dolls and hostesses, drop in for something to eat before going home, and generally these dolls are still in their make-up and very tired.

Naturally they come to know the citizens who are sitting around, and say hello, and maybe accept the hospitality of these citizens, such as java and Danish pastry, or maybe a few scrambled eggs, and it is all very pleasant and harmless, because a citizen who is all tuckered out from shooting craps is not going to get any high blood pressure over a tired chorus doll or a hostess, and especially a hostess.

Well, one morning Silk is sitting at my table guzzling a cup of java and a piece of apple pie, when in comes The Greek looking very weary, The Greek being a high shot who is well known far and wide. He drops into a chair alongside me and orders a Bismarck herring with sliced onions to come along, which is a dish that is considered most invigorating, and then The Greek mentions that he is playing the bank for twenty-four hours hand running, so right away Silk speaks up as follows:

"I hate banks," she says. "Furthermore," she says, "I hate bankers. If it is not for a banker maybe I will not be slaving in Johnny Oakley's dirty little drum for thirty bobs per week. Maybe my mamma will still be alive, and I will be living at home with her instead of in a flea bag in Forty-seventh Street.

"My mamma once saves up three hundred bobs from scrubbing floors in an office building to send me to school," Silk says, "and a banker in one of the buildings where she does this scrubbing tells her to put her dough in his bank, and what happens but the bank busts and it is such a terrible blow to my mamma that she ups and dies. I am very small at the time," Silk says, "but I can remember standing in front of the busted bank with my mamma, and my mamma crying her eyes out."

Well, personally, I consider Silk's crack about Johnny Oakley's joint uncalled for, as it is by no means little, but I explain to her that what The Greek is talking about is a faro bank, and not a bank you put money in, as such a bank is called a jug, and not a bank at all, while faro bank is a gambling game, and the reason I explain this to Silk is because everybody always explains things to her.

The idea is everybody wishes Silk to be well smartened up, especially everybody who hangs out around Mindy's, because she is an orphan and never has a chance to go to school, and we do not wish her to grow up dumb like the average doll, as one and all are very fond of Silk from the first minute she bobs up around Mindy's.

Now at this time Silk is maybe seventeen years old and weighs maybe ninety pounds, sopping wet, and she is straight up and down like a boy. She has soft brown hair and brown eyes that seem too big for her face, and she looks right at you when she talks to you and she talks to you like one guy to another guy. In fact, I always claim there is more guy in Silk than there is doll, as she finally gets so she thinks like a guy, which is maybe because she associates more with guys than she does with other dolls and gets a guy's slant on things in general.

She loves to sit around Mindy's in the early morning gabbing with different citizens, although she does more listening than gabbing herself, and she loves to listen to gab about horse-racing and baseball and fights and crap-shooting and to guys cutting up old touches and whatever else is worth gabbing about, and she seldom sticks in her oar, except maybe to ask a question. Naturally a doll who is willing to listen instead of wishing to gab herself is bound to be popular because if there is anything most citizens hate and despise it is a gabby doll.

So then many citizens take a real interest in Silk's education, including Regret, the horse-player, who explains to her how to build up a sucker to betting on a hot horse, although personally I do not consider such knowledge of any more value to a young doll just starting out in the world than the lesson Big Nig, the crap shooter, gives her one night on how to switch in a pair of tops on a craps game.

Then there is Doc Daro, who is considered one of the highest-class operators that ever rides the tubs in his day, being a great hand for travelling back and forth across the ocean and out-playing other passengers at bridge and poker and one thing and another, but who finally gets rheumatism in his hands so bad he can no longer shuffle the cards. And of course if Doc Daro cannot shuffle the cards there is no sense whatever in him trying to play games of skill any more.

Doc Daro is always telling Silk what rascals guys are and explaining to her the different kinds of business they will try to give her, this being the same kind of business the Doc gives dolls himself in his time. The Doc has an idea that a young doll who is battling Broadway needs plenty of education along such lines, but Silk tells me privately that she is jerry to the stuff Doc is telling her when she is five years old.

The guy I figure does Silk the most good is an old pappy guy by the name of Professor D, who is always reading books when he is not busy doping the horses. In fact, Professor D is considered somewhat daffy on the subject of reading books, but it seems he gets the habit from being a teacher in a college out in Ohio before he becomes a horse-player. Anyway, Professor D takes to giving Silk books to read, and what is more she reads them and talks them over afterward with the professor, who is greatly pleased by this.

"She is a bright little doll," Professor D says to me one day. "Furthermore," the professor says, "she has soul."

"Well," I say, "Big Nig claims she can palm a pair of dice as good as anybody he ever sees."

But the professor only says heigh-ho, and goes along, and I can see he does not consider me a character worth having much truck with, even though I am as much interested in Silk's education as anybody else.

Well, what happens one night but the regular singer in Johnny Oakley's joint, a doll by the name of Myrtle Marigold, hauls off and catches the measles from her twelve-year-old son, and as Johnny has enough trouble getting customers into his joint without giving them the measles after getting them there, he gives Myrtle Marigold plenty of wind at once.

But there he is without anybody to sing "Stacker Lee" to his customers, "Stacker Lee" being a ditty with which Myrtle Marigold panics the customers, so Johnny looks his chorus over and finally asks Silk if she can sing. And Silk says she can sing all right, but that she will not sing "Stacker Lee," because she considers it a low-down lullaby, at best. She says she will sing something classical and, being desperate for singing, Johnny Oakley says go ahead. So what does Silk do but sing a very old song called "Annie Laurie," which she learns from her mamma, and she sings this song so loud that sobs are heard all over the joint.

Of course if anybody investigates they will learn that the sobbing is being done by Professor D and Big Nig and The Greek, who happen to be in the joint at the time, and what they are sobbing about is the idea of Silk singing at all, but Johnny Oakley considers her a big hit and keeps her singing "Annie Laurie" right along, and one night Harry Fitz, the booking agent, drops in and hears her singing and tells Ziegfeld he discovers a doll with a brand-new style.

Naturally Ziggie signs her up at once for the Follies, because he has great faith in Harry Fitz's judgment but after Ziggie hears Silk sing he asks her if she can do anything else, and is greatly relieved when he learns she can dance.

So Silk becomes a Ziegfeld dancer, and she is quite

a sensation with the dramatic critics on the night she opens because she dances with all her clothes on, which is considered a very great novelty indeed. The citizens around Mindy's chip in and send Silk a taxicab full of orchids, and a floral pillow, and Professor D contributes a book called *The Outline of History*, and Silk is the happiest doll in town.

A year goes by, and what a year in the Follies does for Silk is most astonishing. Personally, I never see a lot of change in her looks, except her figure fills out so it has bumps here and there where a doll is entitled to have bumps, and her face grows to fit her eyes more, but everybody else claims she becomes beautiful, and her picture is always in the papers and dozens of guys are always hanging around after her and sending her flowers and one thing and another.

One guy in particular starts sending her jewellery, which Silk always brings around to Mindy's for Jewellery Joe to look at, this Jewellery Joe being a guy who peddles jewellery along Broadway for years, and who can tell you in a second what a piece of jewellery is worth.

Jewellery Joe finds that the jewellery Silk brings around is nothing much but slum, and naturally he advises her to have no further truck with any party who cannot send in anything better than this, but one morning she shows up in Mindy's with an emerald ring the size of a cake of soap, and the minute Jewellery Joe sees the emerald he tells

Silk that whoever donates this is worthy of very careful consideration.

Now it seems that the party who sends the emerald is nobody but Israel Ib, the banker who owns the jug down on the lower East Side that is called the Bank of the Bridges, and the way Silk comes to connect with him is most unusual. It is through a young guy by the same of Simeon Slotsky, who is a teller in Israel Ib's jug, and who sees Silk dancing one night in the Follies and goes right off his ka-zip about her.

It is this Simeon Slotsky who is sending the jewellery that Silk first brings around, and the way he is buying this jewellery is by copping a little dough out of the jug now and then which does not belong to him. Naturally this is a most dishonest action, and by and by they catch up with Simeon Slotsky in the jug, and Israel Ib is going to place him in the pokey.

15

THE BRAIN GOES HOME

One night The Brain is walking me up and down Broadway in front of Mindy's Restaurant, and speaking of this and that, when along comes a red-headed raggedy doll selling apples at five cents per copy, and The Brain, being very fond of apples, grabs one out of her basket and hands her a five-dollar bill.

The red-headed raggedy doll, who is maybe thirty-odd and is nothing but a crow as far as looks are concerned, squints at the finnif, and says to The Brain like this:

"I do not have change for so much money," she says, "but I will go and get it in a minute."

"You keep the change," The Brain says, biting a big hunk out of the apple and taking my arm to start me walking again.

Well, the raggedy doll looks at The Brain again, and it seems to me that all of a sudden there are large tears in her eyes as she says:

"Oh, thank you, sir! Thank you, thank you, and God bless

you, sir!"

And then she goes on up the street in a hurry, with her hands over her eyes and her shoulders shaking, and The Brain turns around very much astonished, and watches her until she is out of sight.

"Why, my goodness!" The Brain says. "I give Doris Clare ten G's last night, and she does not make half as much fuss over it as this doll does over a pound note."

"Well," I say, "maybe the apple doll needs a pound note more than Doris needs ten G's."

"Maybe so," The Brain says. "And of course, Doris gives me much more in return than just an apple and a God bless me. Doris gives me her love. I guess," The Brain says, "that love costs me about as much dough as any guy that ever lives."

"I guess it does," I say, and the chances are we both guess right, because off-hand I figure that if The Brain gets out on three hundred G's per year for love, he is running his love business very economically indeed, because it is well known to one and all that The Brain has three different dolls, besides an ever-loving wife.

In fact, The Brain is sometimes spoken of by many citizens as the "Love King," but only behind his back, because The Brain likes to think his love affairs are a great secret to all but maybe a few, although the only guy I ever see in this town who does not know all about them is a guy who is deaf, dumb, and blind.

I once read a story about a guy by the name of King Solomon who lives a long time ago and who has a thousand dolls all at once, which is going in for dolls on a very large scale indeed, but I guarantee that all of King Solomon's dolls put together are not as expensive as any one of The Brain's dolls. The overhead on Doris Clare alone will drive an ordinary guy daffy, and Doris is practically frugal compared to Cynthia Harris and Bobby Baker.

Then there is Charlotte, who is The Brain's ever-loving wife and who has a society bug and needs plenty of coconuts at all times to keep her a going concern. I once hear The Brain tell Bobby Baker that his ever-loving wife is a bit of an invalid, but as a matter of fact there is never anything the matter with Charlotte that a few bobs will not cure, although of course this goes for nearly every doll in this world who is an invalid.

When a guy is knocking around Broadway as long as The Brain, he is bound to accumulate dolls here and there, but most guys accumulate one at a time, and when this one runs out on him, as Broadway dolls will do, he accumulates another, and so on, and so on, until he is too old to care about such matters as dolls, which is when he is maybe a hundred and four years old, although I hear of several guys who beat even this record.

But when The Brain accumulates a doll he seems to keep her accumulated, and none of them ever run out on him, and while this will be a very great nuisance to the average guy, it pleases The Brain no little because it makes him think he has a very great power over dolls.

"They are not to blame if they fall in love with me," The Brain says to me one night. "I will not cause one of them any sorrow for all the world."

Well, of course, it is most astonishing to me to hear a guy as smart as The Brain using such language, but I figure he may really believe it, because The Brain thinks very good of himself at all times. However, some guys claim that the real reason The Brain keeps all his dolls is because he is too selfish to give them away, although personally I will not take any of them if The Brain throws in a cash bonus, except maybe Bobby Baker.

Anyway, The Brain keeps his dolls accumulated, and furthermore he spends plenty of dough on them, what with buying them automobiles and furs and diamonds and swell places to live in—especially swell places to live in. One time I tell The Brain he will save himself plenty if he hires a house and bunches his dolls together in one big happy family, instead of having them scattered all over town, but The Brain says this idea is no good.

"In the first place," he says, "they do not know about each other, except Doris and Cynthia and Bobby know about Charlotte, although she does not know about them. They each think they are the only one with me. So if I corral them all together they will be jealous of each other over my love. Anyway," The Brain says, "such an arrangement will be very immoral and against the law. No," he says, "it is better to have them in different spots, because think of the many homes it gives me to go to in case I wish to go home. In fact," The Brain says, "I guess I have more homes to go to than any other guy on Broadway."

Well, this may be true, but what The Brain wants with a lot of different homes is a very great mystery on Broadway, because he seldom goes home, anyway, his idea in not going home being that something may happen in this town while he is at home that he is not in on. The Brain seldom goes anywhere in particular. He never goes out in public with any one of his dolls, except maybe once or twice a year with Charlotte, his ever-loving wife, and finally he even stops going with her because Doris Clare says it does not look good to Doris's personal friends.

The Brain marries Charlotte long before he becomes the biggest guy in gambling operations in the East, and a millionaire two or three times over, but he is never much of a hand to sit around home and chew the fat with his ever-loving wife, as husbands often do. Furthermore, when he is poor he has to live in a neighbourhood which is too far away for it to be convenient for him to go home, so finally he gets out of the habit of going there.

But Charlotte is not such a doll as cares to spend more than one or two years looking at the pictures on the wall, because it seems the pictures on her wall are nothing but pictures of cows in the meadows and houses covered with snow, so she does not go home any more than necessary, either, and has her own friends and is very happy indeed, especially after The Brain gets so he can send in right along.

I will say one thing about The Brain and his dolls: he never picks a crow. He has a very good eye for faces and shapes, and even Charlotte, his ever-loving wife, is not a crow, although she is not as young as she used to be. As for Doris Clare, she is one of the great beauties on the Ziegfeld roof in her day, and while her day is by no means yesterday, or even the day before, Doris holds on pretty well in the matter of looks. Giving her a shade the best of it, I will say that Doris is thirty-two or -three, but she has plenty of zing left in her, at that, and her hair remains very blonde, no matter what.

In fact, The Brain does not care much if his dolls are blonde or brunette, because Cynthia Harris's hair is as black as the inside of a wolf, while Bobby Baker is betwixt and between, her hair being a light brown. Cynthia Harris is more of a Johnny-come-lately than Doris, being out of Mr. Earl Carroll's "Vanities," and I hear she first comes to New York as Miss Somebody in one of these beauty contests which she will win hands down if one of the judges does not get a big wink from a Miss Somebody Else.

Of course, Cynthia is doing some winking herself at this time, but it seems that she picks a guy to wink at thinking he is one of the judges, when he is nothing but a newspaperman and has no say whatever about the decision.

Well, Mr. Earl Carroll feels sorry for Cynthia, so he puts her in the "Vanities" and lets her walk around raw, and The Brain sees her, and the next thing anybody knows she is riding in a big foreign automobile the size of a rum chaser, and is chucking a terrible swell.

Personally, I always consider Bobby Baker the smartest of all The Brain's dolls, because she is just middling as to looks and she does not have any of the advantages of life like Doris Clare and Cynthia Harris, such as jobs on the stage where they can walk around showing off their shapes to guys such as The Brain. Bobby Baker starts off as nothing but a private secretary to a guy in Wall Street, and naturally she is always wearing clothes, or anyway, as many clothes as an ordinary doll wears nowadays, which is not so many, at that.

It seems that The Brain once has some business with the

guy Bobby works for and happens to get talking to Bobby, and she tells him how she always wishes to meet him, what with hearing and reading about him, and how he is just as handsome and romantic-looking as she always pictures him to herself.

Now I wish to say I will never call any doll a liar, being at all times a gentleman, and for all I know, Bobby Baker may really think The Brain is handsome and romantic-looking, but personally I figure if she is not lying to him, she is at least a little excited when she makes such a statement to The Brain. The best you can give The Brain at this time is that he is very well dressed.

He is maybe forty years old, give or take a couple of years, and he is commencing to get a little bunchy about the middle, what with sitting down at card-tables so much and never taking any exercise outside of walking guys such as me up and down in front of Mindy's for a few hours every night. He has a clean-looking face, always very white around the gills, and he has nice teeth and a nice smile when he wishes to smile, which is never at guys who owe him dough.

And I will say for The Brain he has what is called personality. He tells a story well, although he is always the hero of any story he tells, and he knows how to make himself agreeable to dolls in many ways. He has a pretty fair sort of education, and while dolls such as Cynthia and Doris, and maybe Charlotte, too, will rather have a charge account at Carrier's than all the education in Yale and Harvard put together, it seems that Bobby Baker likes highbrow gab, so naturally she gets plenty of same from The Brain.

Well, pretty soon Bobby is riding around in a car bigger than Cynthia's, though neither is as big as Doris's car, and all the neighbours' children over in Flatbush, which is where Bobby hails from, are very jealous of her and running around spreading gossip about her, but keeping their eyes open for big cars themselves. Personally, I always figure The Brain lowers himself socially by taking up with a doll from Flatbush, especially as Bobby Baker soon goes in for literary guys, such as newspaper scribes and similar characters around Greenwich Village.

But there is no denying Bobby Baker is a very smart little doll, and in the four or five years she is one of The Brain's dolls, she gets more dough out of him than all the others put together, because she is always telling him how much she loves him, and saying she cannot do without him, while Doris Clare and Cynthia Harris sometimes forget to mention this more than once or twice a month.

Now what happens early one morning but a guy by the name of Daffy Jack hauls off and sticks a shiv in The Brain's left side. It seems that this is done at the request of a certain party by the name of Homer Swing, who owes The Brain plenty of dough in a gambling transaction, and who becomes very indignant when The Brain presses him somewhat for payment. It seems that Daffy Jack, who is considered a very good shiv artist, aims at The Brain's heart, but misses it by a couple of inches, leaving The Brain with a very bad cut in his side which calls for some stitching.

Big Nig, the crap shooter, and I are standing at Fifty-second Street and Seventh Avenue along about 2 a.m., speaking of not much, when The Brain comes stumbling out of Fifty-second Street, and falls in Big Nig's arms, practically ruining a brand-new topcoat which Big Nig pays sixty bucks for a few days back with the blood that is coming out of the cut. Naturally, Big Nig is indignant about this, but we can see that it is no time to be speaking to The Brain about such matters. We can see that The Brain is carved up quite some, and is in a bad way.

Of course, we are not greatly surprised at seeing The Brain in this condition, because for years he is practically no price around this town, what with this guy and that being anxious to do something or other to him, but we are never expecting to see him carved up like a turkey. We are expecting to see him with a few slugs in him, and both Big Nig and me are very angry to think that there are guys around who will use such instruments as a knife on anybody.

But while we are thinking it over, The Brain says to me

like this:

"Call Hymie Weissberger, and Doc Frisch," he says, "and take me home."

Naturally, a guy such as The Brain wishes his lawyer before he wishes his doctor, and Hymie Weissberger is The Brain's mouthpiece, and a very sure-footed guy, at that.

"Well," I say, "we better take you to a hospital where you can get good attention at once."

"No," The Brain says. "I wish to keep this secret. It will be a bad thing for me right now to have this get out, and if you take me to a hospital they must report it to the coppers. Take me home."

Naturally, I say which home, being somewhat confused about The Brain's homes, and he seems to study a minute as if this is a question to be well thought out.

"Park Avenue," The Brain says finally, so Big Nig stops a taxicab, and we help The Brain into the cab and tell the jockey to take us to the apartment house on Park Avenue near Sixty-fourth where The Brain's ever-loving wife Charlotte lives.

When we get there, I figure it is best for me to go up first and break the news gently to Charlotte, because I can see what a shock it is bound to be to any ever-loving wife to have her husband brought home in the early hours of the morning all shivved up.

Well, the door man and the elevator guy in the apartment house give me an argument about going up to The Brain's apartment, saying a blow out of some kind is going on there, but after I explain to them that The Brain is sick, they let me go. A big fat butler comes to the door of the apartment when I ring, and I can see there are many dolls and guys in evening clothes in the apartment, and somebody is singing very loud.

The butler tries to tell me I cannot see Charlotte, but I finally convince him it is best, so by and by she comes to the door, and a very pleasant sight she is, at that, with jewellery all over her. I stall around awhile, so as not to alarm her too much, and then I tell her The Brain meets with an accident and that we have him outside in a cab, and ask her where we shall put him.

"Why," she says, "put him in a hospital, of course. I am entertaining some very important people to-night, and I cannot have them disturbed by bringing in a hospital patient. Take him to a hospital, and tell him I will come and see him to-morrow and bring him some broth."

I try to explain to her that The Brain does not need any broth, but a nice place to lie down in, but finally she gets very testy with me and shuts the door in my face, saying as follows:

"Take him to a hospital, I tell you. This is a ridiculous

307

hour for him to be coming home, anyway. It is twenty years since he comes home so early."

Then as I am waiting for the elevator, she opens the door again just a little bit and says:

"By the way, is he hurt bad?"

I say we do not know how bad he is hurt, and she shuts the door again, and I go back to the cab again, thinking what a heartless doll she is, although I can see where it will be very inconvenient for her to bust up her party, at that.

The Brain is lying back in the corner of the cab, his eyes half-closed, and by this time it seems that Big Nig stops the blood somewhat with a handkerchief, but The Brain acts somewhat weak to me. He sort of rouses himself when I climb in the cab, and when I tell him his ever-loving wife is not home he smiles a bit and whispers:

"Take me to Doris."

Now Doris lives in a big apartment house away over on West Seventy-second Street near the Drive, and I tell the taxi jockey to go there while The Brain seems to slide off into a doze. Then Big Nig leans over to me and says to me like this:

"No use taking him there," Big Nig says. "I see Doris going out to-night all dressed up in her ermine coat with this actor guy, Jack Walen, she is struck on. It is a very great scandal around and about the way they carry on. Let us take him to Cynthia," Nig says. "She is a very large-hearted doll who will be very glad to take him in."

Now Cynthia Harris has a big suite of rooms that cost fifteen G's a year in a big hotel just off Fifth Avenue, Cynthia being a doll who likes to be downtown so if she hears of anything coming off anywhere she can get there very rapidly. When we arrive at the hotel I call her on the house 'phone and tell her I must see her about something very important, so Cynthia says for me to come up.

It is now maybe three-fifteen, and I am somewhat surprised to find Cynthia home, at that, but there she is, and looking very beautiful indeed in a négligée with her hair hanging down, and I can see that The Brain is no chump when it comes to picking them. She gives me a hello pleasant enough, but as soon as I explain what I am there for, her kisser gets very stern and she says to me like this:

"Listen," she says, "I got trouble enough around this joint, what with two guys getting in a fight over me at a little gathering I have here last night and the house copper coming in to split them out, and I do not care to have any more. Suppose it gets out that The Brain is here? What will the newspapers print about me? Think of my reputation!"

Well, in about ten minutes I can see there is no use arguing with her, because she can talk faster than I can, and mostly she talks about what a knock it will be to her reputation if she takes The Brain in, so I leave her standing at the door in her négligée, still looking very beautiful, at that.

There is now nothing for us to do but take The Brain to Bobby Baker, who lives in a duplex apartment in Sutton Place over by the East River, where the swells set up a colony of nice apartments in the heart of an old tenement-house neighbourhood, and as we are on our way there with The Brain lying back in the cab just barely breathing, I say to Big Nig like this:

"Nig," I say, "when we get to Bobby's, we will carry The Brain in without asking her first and just dump him on her so she cannot refuse to take him in, although," I say, "Bobby Baker is a nice little doll, and I am pretty sure she will do anything she can for him, especially," I say, "since he pays fifty G's for this apartment we are going to."

So when the taxicab stops in front of Bobby's house, Nig and I take The Brain out of the cab and lug him between us up to the door of Bobby's apartment, where I ring the bell. Bobby opens the door herself, and I happen to see a guy's legs zip into a room in the apartment behind her, although of course there is nothing wrong in such a sight, even though the guy's legs are in pink pyjamas.

Naturally, Bobby is greatly astonished to see us with The Brain dangling between us, but she does not invite us in as I explain to her that The Brain is stabbed and that his last words are for us to take him to his Bobby. Furthermore, she does not let me finish my story which will be very sad indeed, if she keeps on listening.

"If you do not take him away from here at once," Bobby says, before I am down to the pathetic part, "I will call the cops and you guys will be arrested on suspicion that you know something about how he gets hurt."

Then she slams the door on us, and we lug The Brain back down the stairs into the street, because all of a sudden it strikes us that Bobby is right, and if The Brain is found in our possession all stabbed up, and he happens to croak, we are in a very tough spot, because the cops just naturally love to refuse to believe guys like Big Nig and me, no matter what we say.

Furthermore, the same idea must hit the taxicab jockey after we lift The Brain out of the cab, because he is nowhere to be seen, and there we are away over by the East River in the early morning, with no other taxis in sight, and a cop liable to happen along any minute.

Well, there is nothing for us to do but get away from there, so Big Nig and I start moving, with me carrying The Brain's feet, and Big Nig Ins head. We get several blocks away from Sutton Place, going very slow and hiding in dark doorways when we hear anybody coming, and now we are in a section of tenement houses, when all of a sudden up out of the basement of one of these tenements pops a doll.

She sees us before we can get in a dark place, and she seems to have plenty of nerve for a doll, because she comes right over to us and looks at Big Nig and me, and then looks at The Brain, who loses his hat somewhere along the line, so his pale face is plain to be seen by even the dim street light.

"Why," the doll says, "it is the kind gentleman who gives me the five dollars for the apple—the money that buys the medicine that saves my Joey's life. What is the matter?"

"Well," I say to the doll, who is still raggedy and still red-headed, "there is nothing much the matter except if we do not get him somewhere soon, this guy will up and croak on us."

"Bring him into my house," she says, pointing to the joint she just comes out of. "It is not much of a place, but you can let him rest there until you get help. I am just going over here to a drug store to get some more medicine for Joey, although he is out of danger now, thanks to this gentleman."

So we lug The Brain down the basement steps with the doll leading the way, and we follow her into a room that smells like a Chinese laundry and seems to be full of kids sleeping on the floor. There is only one bed in the room, and it is not much of a bed any way you take it, and there seems to be a kid in this bed, too, but the red-headed doll rolls this kid over to one side of the bed and motions us to lay The

Brain alongside of the kid. Then she gets a wet rag and starts bathing The Brain's noggin.

He finally opens his eyes and looks at the red-headed raggedy doll, and she grins at him very pleasant. When I think things over afterwards, I figure The Brain is conscious of much of what is going on when we are packing him around, although he does not say anything, maybe because he is too weak. Anyway, he turns his head to Big Nig, and says to him like this:

"Bring Weissberger and Frisch as quick as you can," he says. "Anyway, get Weissberger. I do not know how bad I am hurt, and I must tell him some things."

Well, The Brain is hurt pretty bad, as it turns out, and in fact he never gets well, but he stays in the basement dump until he dies three days later, with the red-headed raggedy doll nursing him alongside her sick kid Joey, because the croaker, old Doc Frisch, says it is no good moving The Brain, and may only make him pop off sooner. In fact, Doc Frisch is much astonished that The Brain lives at all, considering the way we lug him around.

I am present at The Brain's funeral at Wiggins's Funeral Parlours, like everybody else on Broadway, and I wish to say I never see more flowers in all my life. They are all over the casket and knee-deep on the floor, and some of the pieces must cost plenty, the price of flowers being what they are in this town nowadays. In fact, I judge it is the size and cost of the different pieces that makes me notice a little bundle of faded red carnations not much bigger than your fist that is laying alongside a pillow of violets the size of a horse blanket.

There is a small card tied to the carnations, and it says on this card, as follows: "To a kind gentleman," and it comes to my mind that out of all the thousands of dollars' worth of flowers there, these faded carnations represent the only true sincerity. I mention this to Big Nig, and he says the chances are I am right, but that even true sincerity is not going to do The Brain any good where he is going.

Anybody will tell you that for off-hand weeping at a funeral The Brain's ever-loving wife Charlotte does herself very proud indeed, but she is not one-two-seven with Doris Clare, Cynthia Harris, and Bobby Baker. In fact, Bobby Baker weeps so loud that there is some talk of heaving her out of the funeral altogether.

However, I afterwards hear that loud as they are at the funeral, it is nothing to the weep they all put on when it comes out that The Brain has Hymie Weissberger draw up a new will while he is dying and leaves all his dough to the red-headed raggedy doll, whose name seems to be O'Halloran, and who is the widow of a bricklayer and has five kids.

Well, at first all the citizens along Broadway say it is a

wonderful thing for The Brain to do, and serves his ever-loving wife and Doris and Cynthia and Bobby just right; and from the way one and all speaks you will think they are going to build a monument to The Brain for his generosity to the red-headed raggedy doll.

But about two weeks after he is dead, I hear citizens saying the chances are the red-headed raggedy doll is nothing but one of The Brain's old-time dolls, and that maybe the kids are his and that he leaves them the dough because his conscience hurts him at the finish, for this is the way Broadway is. But personally I know it cannot be true, for if there is one thing The Brain never has it is a conscience.

CPSIA information can be obtained
at www.ICGtesting.com
Printed in the USA
LVHW112156270319
612118LV00001B/72/P